HOLMES
OF THE
RAJ

HOLMES
OF THE
RAJ

Vithal Rajan

RANDOM HOUSE INDIA

Published by Random House India in 2010
13579108642

Copyright © Vithal Rajan 2010

Random House Publishers India Private Limited
MindMill Corporate Tower, 2nd Floor, Plot No 24A
Sector 16A, Noida 201301, UP

Random House Group Limited
20 Vauxhall Bridge Road
London SW1V 2SA
United Kingdom

978 81 8400 104 4

Typeset in Adobe Caslon by Jojy Philip

Printed and bound in India by Replika Press

In memory of my grandfather, V.C. Srinivasa Acharya, educator and first manager of the Oxford University Press, Madras, who stepped into the first story and compelled me to write the rest.

Contents

Preface

These are yet unpublished stories of Sir Arthur Conan Doyle, and until recently, no one knew of their existence. Linguistic and handwriting experts are even now engaged in authenticating their authorship. Why the stories were not published in their day remains a mystery. Holmesian experts argue that the stories might have been truthful accounts of political events, the publication of which Whitehall may have discouraged in the years leading to the First World War. The manuscript, along with other personal papers of Sir Arthur Conan Doyle, had been kept in storage at the offices of a London lawyer, and remained forgotten for years. A collection of Sir Arthur Conan Doyle's papers, belonging to the estate of his daughter, the late Dame Jean Conan Doyle, came up for auction at Christie's a while ago. While the complete collection was valued at over two million pounds sterling, this manuscript itself was acquired independently by an anonymous purchaser for an undisclosed sum, and later sent to me, as a gift for my daughter on the occasion of her wedding. Perhaps the gift was made because my grandfather is mentioned in the first story, but I have no way of being certain.

The stories seem fairly accurate in their depiction of people who shaped Indian history in the late nineteenth and early twentieth centuries. In the notes to this book, I shall briefly state what historical texts say about the dramatis personae, although many of the incidents recounted here are not recorded elsewhere, and it is left to us to conjecture whether there is any truth to them or they are pure artifice, intended to be nothing more than a good story. Are Dr Watson's occasional distortions of accepted historical facts deliberate, or are they the natural outcome of a personal account written long after the events it seeks to describe? No one knows. In some cases, however, we can be sure they reveal new facts. I have done my best to edit an unusual manuscript, and make Dr Watson's account more accessible to the general public. Any irregularities are entirely due to my shortcomings as an editor.

Vithal Rajan
Hyderabad, 2010

The Case of the Murdering Saint

It was at the end of a chilly autumn morning in 1888 that a news story caught my eye at the breakfast table, as I was poring over dispatches I had received from a friend in India.

"My God, Holmes," I cried, "have you heard about the police arresting this pious humbug of a priest? Excellent detective work, I must say, and it's heartening to know that Scotland Yard has trained these colonial beggars in Madras to do a half-decent job!"

Holmes stopped chewing on an oatcake, from a somewhat burnt pile that Mrs Hudson's niece had placed on the table. Our indispensable landlady was in Brighton visiting her sister, who had taken a turn for the worse. "This girl doesn't know how to cook the simplest of breakfasts!" pronounced Holmes.

"I suppose you need to be a Scottish lass to know how to cook an oatcake," I said mildly.

"Not at all, Watson!" retorted Holmes. "All human cultures have the knowledge to make an edible pancake with the grains of the land. The Breton *gallette*, for instance—I once wrote a monograph tracing its history to the Tamil dosa. The Tamil is a very clever fellow. Soon he will be opening curry houses all over London, I assure you!" Holmes lit his meerschaum and drew on the pipe for a few thoughtful moments. "However, one should never jump to conclusions, my dear Watson, and believe that even the damnably clever Tamils are better at detective work than our own flatfooted bobbies. You are no doubt referring to the case of the Shankaracharya, or head, of the Kumbakonam Mutt.[1] A most venerable gentleman of some seventy years, although an out-and-out pagan, God forgive him! He has been most diabolically framed, and if the truth were out, Whitehall could be at war within seventy-two hours!"

"You astound me, Holmes!" I cried.

Holmes smiled grimly. "Watson, you may have noted my strange absences from home of late," he began. "I have been engaged in very strange meetings in some of the most unsavoury places you can find by the East India Docks. There is a military power that actively seeks to disturb the tranquillity of the Indian Government. And what better way than to inflame religious hatred among peoples who still bear a medieval sense of loyalty to their religion? You certainly remember how close we came to losing the Empire only a few decades ago! And if this plot is traced to the camps of the Indian Government's enemy, war would be the stern rejoinder of our Cabinet."

"Assuredly, Holmes," I said in some agitation, "that would be the alarming conclusion. But are you sure that this distant nonentity of a pagan priest is a pawn in the hands of an enemy power..."

"The Shankaracharya is a key figure within the Great

Game, as it is played out in India," said Holmes, cutting me short. "Make no mistake. Nor are you right to jump to the conclusion that he is a pawn of a foreign power. A man may be made use of without his knowledge, as indeed some of the most respected and wiliest British politicians have been in the recent past—surely you have not forgotten the activities of Miss Irene Adler, and the purloining of the Kohinoor diamond for twelve anxious hours from the very person of an august lady meeting with her Cabinet?" I knew the case well and some day might be able to place all the facts before the public. Holmes continued, "For several months past, some close friends of mine who spend most of their waking hours in the recesses of Zurich banks, have kept me informed of large flows of money whose origins and destinations are shrouded in mystery. Even when I was undecided whether it was worth my interest, I received this cursive note, which although unsigned, is written in the unmistakable hand of Herr Bleichroder—you know, the well-known Hamburg financier of Chancellor Bismark himself."

Extracting a single sheet of expensive handmade paper from a plain manila envelope, he tossed it across the table to me. A few lines were scrawled hastily sans salutations or signature of any kind. It said baldly:

Have a care, my good friend. Your enquiries are getting to be known in the Highest Circles. Leave the East to its Mysteries. I shall issue no further warning. This itself is more than I dare. Your grateful friend, who remembers the help you gave the Levantine Bank of Isaac & Sons three years ago.

"Far from discouraging me, Watson, this missive has made me even more intent on getting to the bottom of the case involving the Shankaracharya," said Holmes determinedly.

At that moment, the parlour maid entered in some haste. "I don't know what to make of it, Sir," she said, trying to regain her composure. "There is an Eastern gentleman who wishes to see you urgently. He was loitering outside the door, and gestured to me through the drawing room window. I opened the door only when I saw that he seemed to be a proper gentleman, Sir, Mrs Hudson not being here and all, Sir, and he assured me in good English, Sir, that he was uncertain whether it would be polite to knock, but craved permission to see you now!"

With a triumphant look thrown in my direction, Holmes requested her to show in our guest. "I don't know, I am sure," she said, retreating, "but he is dressed like the Mikado himself, and at this hour of the morning!"

Our guest, who appeared a few moments later, was a tall, thin, middle-aged Indian of saturnine countenance, with heavy hooded eyes, which, from under a tall white turban, quickly but politely seemed to take our measure. He laid aside a heavy black alpaca coat over a chair, and as he advanced we saw that he was neatly dressed in a long, dark brown, close-fitting jacket worn over a thin white dhoti. Long black woollen stockings and thin black shoes encased his feet. Two strings of large pearls were coiled round his throat, and emeralds glinted on his earlobes. He stretched out his hand unhesitatingly toward Sherlock Holmes. "I am sorry to incommode you at this unreasonable hour, Mr Holmes, but my business does not wait. I am Subramania Swamy Ayer, from Madras, at present carrying out research at the School of Oriental Studies, and I..."[2]

"Not the Mr Subramania Ayer," said Holmes, cutting him short, "who read an excellent paper on the Sangam poets at the Asiatic Society last Thursday? I would have been there but for another pressing engagement." "Indeed, Sir!" cried our guest. "You do me too much honour to mention a rather amateurish piece of scholarship. But I am he. I have been expressly charged by my sovereign to seek the help of the best detective in London to clear up a matter of the utmost delicacy. While time is of the essence, still it is of paramount importance to maintain secrecy..." and he looked uncertainly in my direction.

"Dr Watson is a trusted colleague of long standing," said Holmes calmly. "You may speak as frankly in his presence as you might with the Archbishop."

"Well, since I must, I must," said Mr Ayer, making up his mind after a little hesitation. "God knows, it is all over the vernacular press, thanks to the thoughtless liberalism of Lord Ripon who had the Vernacular Press Act repealed in 1878. India is not England, Sir, and well-meaning interference does not necessarily help the Queen's Indian subjects. Now, the Indian press, Sir, must be guided with a firm hand, without appearing to muzzle loyal or responsible opinion. The right to express oneself only belongs to the responsible and the learned, it cannot be vested in every Tom, Dick, and Harry..."

"Indeed, Sir, there is some truth in what you say," broke in Holmes, not unkindly, "but different men have different opinions about progress. And Lord Ripon's opinions weigh for much in this land."

"Sir, I have the highest respect for His Lordship," said Mr Ayer. "But his Christian kindliness has been taken advantage of by rogues, Sir, I can tell you. I had better start at the beginning."

"You had better," said Holmes gravely. "The matter concerning the Shankaracharya is of the highest importance, not only to the Government of India, but also to the British Cabinet."

"You amaze me!" cried Mr Ayer in astonishment. "You have already guessed at my mission! Nay, I am sure you already know more than any other Englishman about this affair on the fringes of the British Empire. I was rather disappointed when I was advised by Inspector Lestrade of Scotland Yard yesterday to come to you. I was hoping a senior policeman would be appointed, but now I see his was the sanest advice. Sir, two days ago I received a long coded telegram from my sovereign, the Ranee of Kanchee, to engage the best detective in London, and request his presence in Madras as soon as may be. Money is no object to her. The P & O liner, *The Coromandel Star*, leaves for Madras the day after tomorrow. I do not mean to presume, but may I book first-class cabins on it, on the port side of course, through my agent?"

Holmes seemed to be in two minds, whether to smile or to frown. At last, he said gently, "You must tell me all you know, and then Dr Watson and I shall decide whether we can be of any assistance. As Inspector Lestrade might have told you, I have lately been much preoccupied with a case that could have grave repercussions for the Ottoman Empire. Geologists seem to have discovered oil on the Tigris, and the Czar is at loggerheads not only with the Sultan, but with our own Queen about its possession. But pray, Sir, tell us the whole of it."

There was not much to tell that had not already been reported in the newspapers. The accountant of the Mutt, or Hindoo monastery, had been found murdered in his simple home. Eyewitnesses trusted by the local police had actually seen the head priest, or the Shankaracharya, go in and out of the place of the crime the night before the body was discovered. The high priest was known to have had open, and sometimes angry, disputes in the past with his accountant. He had been arrested by the police on the strongest possible circumstantial evidence. When questioned, the high priest had said simply that he was guilty, and then refused to say any more. Religious passions had been aroused. The people refused to believe any police statement, and held the Government of India, and those in charge in Madras, of trying to bring Hinduism into disrepute and convert people to Christianity. Officials watched the development of the tense situation with the gravest concern. The army had been put on alert, and the fact that memories of 1857 were still fresh in the minds of the generals hardly helped. The Ranee of Kanchee, in whose principality the incidents had occurred, wished the rumours to be scotched and the truth to be known, so that law and order might once again prevail. In the public interest she was willing to spare no expense. She had contacted Mr Ayer, a member of her entourage, who was in London at the time, to engage the services of the best detective he could find.

Holmes was silent for a few minutes after Mr Ayer had put all the facts he knew before us. "The case has many points of interest," he said at last, lighting up his pipe again. "Remind me, Watson, to buy a better one before we set sail. This one does not draw as well as it should."

"Then, it is settled," said Mr Ayer, springing up. "With your leave I shall depart now to put all my affairs in order, and make suitable arrangements for our travel. I assure you, Mr Holmes, you have made the right decision, and you will not find the Ranee ungrateful. She is the soul of generosity and rectitude."

After our visitor had gone, Holmes remained buried in thought for a long time, puffing on his pipe, with his legs stretched out under the table.

"Our new acquaintance has been very frank, and yet he has been secretive also. Did you mark his open regard for his Ranee, Watson?"

"I thought it was very proper, Holmes," I said. "It does credit to him, and to her."

"Twice he called her his 'sovereign', Watson, did that not strike you as strange?" Holmes asked with a wry smile. "He should have but one sovereign, and that is Her Most Gracious Majesty, Queen Victoria."

That day and the next were spent in fevered preparations for our departure. Holmes had responsibilities, some of which I knew; and arrangements had to be made for others to take care of his cases until we returned, perhaps three months later. Even Lestrade was pressed into service to hold the fort until our return. I sent an urgent telegram to Mrs Hudson to shorten her visit to her sister and return to take charge of 221B, Baker Street. My own wants were simple, and I knew the country, having served there earlier as a military doctor. I crammed everything I needed into a large Gladstone bag, and wondered for a moment before tossing in my old service revolver. I might not need it since we were on a mission involving priests, but it had a reassuringly familiar feel, having stood between me and death on our bloody retreat from Afghanistan.

The night before our departure, Mycroft Holmes, Sherlock's elder brother, called us round to his club. Mycroft wielded more power than most Cabinet ministers, but few men knew about it. We found him by a secluded table near a window from where he could watch the street. "Sherlock, I have called up some of the best Napoleon brandy in the club," he said, moving his vast bulk into a deep wing-chair. "It may help us ponder your strange mission. Whitehall places the greatest importance on your successfully helping out the Government of India. I have sent out all the necessary telegrams, and you will find people in Madras waiting to help you. A very good man there is a Colonel Pickering, an expert on obscure languages, of all things, but now serving as Commissioner of Police in Madras. He has a feel for natives, and we are very grateful to him for reading many inscrutable oriental minds like an open book. But this matter of the Shankaracharya is beyond even his great powers. There is no doubt that forces, who have no business there, have been at work. It is intolerable that they should meddle with the British Empire!"

"Well, it is a struggle for supremacy, is it not?" said Sherlock Holmes mildly. "I don't know how long we can hold the peace. Perhaps we can in Madras this time round. But what happens when there is an irredentist German population, as in South Africa? In any case, Mycroft, Armageddon, if it is to come, will come in Europe, not on the contested fringes of Empire."

"Yes, it may come to that," said Mycroft grimly. "But we have to guard democracy wherever we have planted it on the globe. It may be the worst form of government, but for all the other ones."

"Come, Mycroft, I did not think to see you indulging in epigrams like the fashionable Mr Oscar Wilde," said Holmes acidly.

Mycroft held up a deprecating hand. "Not my own, I confess," he said taking a gulp of brandy. "Randolph Churchill tells me—and he is to be trusted when not dabbling in his country's accounts—that his son, Winston, is the author of this *bon mot*.[3] Wasting his time in Harrow, I should think. Out of the mouth of babes, but true enough to fight for."

Before Holmes could reply, Mycroft caught sight of a figure entering the club and said, "In any case, I have asked an expert on Indian affairs to deign to take an interest in your mission. Let us take his advice."

We saw the commanding form of the First Marquess of Ripon making straight for our table.[4] Born in Number 10 Downing Street itself, to one of the first families in England, the former Viceroy might well have aimed higher—at becoming Her Majesty's Prime Minister—had not the call of inner conscience led him to convert to the Catholic faith. However that decision might have been taken, the Queen and her Empire were conscious of the debt owed to the great Whig statesman, who had pacified the warring Afghan tribes and brought them into the circle of England's friends. Seated at the table, and after the first introductions were over, Lord Ripon launched directly into the subject. "Make no mistake, gentlemen," he said softly, but passing his fingers worriedly through his full white beard, "the Shankaracharya has been imposed upon by knaves. We need to find out why, and convince our Hindoo subjects that we mean well by them. Christians we might be—or attempt to be despite our sins—but human respect we accord them and their ways, and there shall be equality and justice for all while we rule."

We were silenced by the simple dignity of these words. With some hesitation, I answered, "But, Your Lordship, the priest apparently confessed, and said he was guilty."

Lord Ripon looked full at me with his limpid eyes. "Sir," he said, "what does a policeman understand from a mystic's statement? Undoubtedly the Shankaracharya said he was guilty, but guilty of what? Of not being efficacious in prayer to prevent the foul murder of a temple servant? Of mistaking his man, and trusting where he should not have? Or guilty of not understanding the Will of God? I know the Shankaracharya, and have disputed with him on the nature of the Trinity. The Hindoos, believe it or not, have a similar concept, but clothe the spiritual essence in human form. That brings them nearer the Truth. We ourselves are brought to Salvation only through the dear form of Our Redeemer." His Lordship's piety was equalled only by his political acumen. He continued, "We have been aware for some time that a certain Power, bloated by military victories, is trying to disturb the equanimity of our rule in India. Large sums of money are being transferred to that country, apparently as Christian charity, but what lies behind this gesture? Jamshed Tata, a personal and honoured friend of mine, was himself approached to be the conduit of these funds, with the bait thrown in that the house of Krupp itself would help his infant industry. He refused, and, gentleman that he is, promptly informed me. Find out for me, gentlemen, what is behind all this mask of Christian virtue, and you would have earned a nation's thanks. You must also help this innocent priest—for of his innocence I am fully convinced, by Nature and by experience in the affairs of men. I have already written to a valued friend, Dr William Miller, Principal of the Madras Christian College, who will await your arrival. I trust him as no other."

Before Lord Ripon left us, Holmes, who had been mostly silent through the evening, asked one question. "Sir, we go to Madras at the invitation of the Ranee of Kanchee. What advice do you have about her?"

Ripon gave a thin smile. "The Ranee is ambitious, very ambitious, for what I don't quite know. Like others among the princely families in India, she has adopted a son to carry on the line, having none of her own. Dalhousie's disastrous Doctrine of Lapse alienated several friendly princes, and memories last long in the East. Perhaps, she wishes to earn our gratitude by showing an excess of loyalty." After a pause, he continued as he donned his hat and cloak in the hallway, "I have met her but once. A woman's mind is hard to read, especially an oriental potentate's, and one who is out to conquer you. But I think you can deal with her easily."

With that we all took our departure. For the next several hours, mundane matters connected with leaving our home in London occupied our attention, and I had no time to reflect upon his wise words until we were halfway across the Bay of Biscay. I kept coming back to Lord Ripon's words and our mission, but the future seemed as dark and confused as the chilly winter evenings in the choppy seas of the Atlantic. We passed into the calmer waters of the Mediterranean, and while I would spend the day on deck lazily perusing some popular modern novel, Holmes was busy consuming the considerable library on the Tamils and south India that he had brought along. In fact, I had remonstrated about the need for such a large trunk of books in our cabin, but as usual Holmes had his way. Mr Ayer rarely put in an appearance on deck, and that always swathed in heavy woollen shawls, even when we were off the steamy coast of the Levant. He seemed to gather energy and interest only as we passed through the Suez Canal, the marvel of the modern world.

We stopped at the Port of Ismailia on Timsah Lake to take in fresh vegetables, after passing through dreary salt marshes. It was a port only by courtesy, being no more than a disorderly collection of ramshackle mud houses alternating with stretches of Arab tents, with Bedouin tribesmen jostling each other to sell their wares to passing ships and their passengers. Captain Petrie, a young British officer in charge of a small garrison guarding that stretch of the Canal, came aboard to inspect and, finding English compatriots interested in his flea-bitten part of the world, invited us to join him for a camel ride to view the Roman remains of a long disused part of the Canal connecting the Nile to the Red Sea. Holmes and I were both happy to disembark for a while, and readily accepted the invitation. As we expected, Mr Ayer declined the invitation, politely saying he would like to purchase a few mementos for his wife.

We set off eagerly enough, accompanied by a few British soldiers and a string of Egyptian sepoys spread out in a wide circle to watch out for any who may dispute our way. We knew that there had been unrest in the land—only a few years ago, General Charles Gordon had been martyred in Khartoum by a mob of crazed religious fanatics. Petrie explained that although he was the target of an occasional attack, he had the place firmly in hand, and anticipated no trouble. The Ptolemaic remains themselves were a trifle disappointing, and there was not very much to see. Nonetheless, we spent some time admiring the ancient brickwork, and returned slowly, sobered by the thought that even under relatively modern conditions, a few thousand men had died on site, while excavating several million cubic feet of earth under M de Lessep's watchful eye.

A cool desert breeze had sprung up from the west when we sat under a sprawling canopy for a dinner of roast lamb served over spiced rice. Petrie's soldiers tried to shoo away the horde of Arab hawkers who surrounded us, but tired as we were, we paid them scant attention. One swarthy fellow, a snake charmer, wanted to amuse us, and kept waving his pipe in Holmes's face, but the soldiers pushed him aside, and he squatted a few feet away in the sand. Captain Petrie produced a good bottle of port he had been preserving for some such occasion, and we had settled down to discussing animatedly the value of the Suez Canal to imperial trade when, glancing down, I saw a long black cobra about to coil itself round Holmes's leg. With a cry of warning, I whipped out my revolver and shot the reptile into two writhing pieces. It was only at the end of the commotion that followed that we realized that the snake charmer had disappeared. We took leave of Captain Petrie, who was full of apologies for what was not his fault, and got back on board, having wished him all success in his Egyptian explorations. If Holmes made light of the incident, Mr Ayer put a different, sinister interpretation on the evening's happenings, and insisted on standing guard all night outside our cabin door.

"Come to think of it, Holmes," I said, just before

falling to sleep, "it does look sinister—*meant*, if you take my meaning."

"Certainly, it was meant," said Holmes from the opposite bunk, "but the question is, what was meant? As they were clearing away the reptile, I noticed that it had been defanged, and hence was harmless, Watson. If it was an attempt to scare us away, it was a puerile effort."

Telling myself I would never understand the oriental mind, although I had spent half my life among natives, I fell into a restless sleep.

We stopped at the great port of Colombo for three days, for taking on coal and fresh victuals. Mr Ayer, who seemed to know the island of Ceylon well, suggested we go up to the ancient capital of Kandy. Nothing could suit us better than to explore that beautiful island under balmy skies. Verdant growth surrounded us on all sides as we rode up part of the way. Later, we transferred to elephants, for a quicker and spectacular journey through the dense forests on the hills of Kandy. Parakeets screamed over us, large flowers scattered their pollen over our shirts, and the occasional deer broke through the undergrowth as we went up the mountain paths single file. Holmes's elephant was in the lead when, as we entered a clearing just short of Kandy, a wild grey tusker broke cover and made straight for Holmes. For horrified moments, none of us knew what to do. Suddenly, a female elephant carrying our effects and ridden by a mahout, calmly interposed herself between the charging tusker and Holmes. Trumpeting, the tusker reared back, and then swinging to the left, dashed back into the forest. He had come within inches of goring Holmes to death.

The story lost nothing in the telling, and Holmes and I were fêted that evening at the Kandy Club, with officers telling many a story of near escapes from charging elephants. We were given a room in the officers' quarters, and as we turned in, I could not refrain from commenting once again on Holmes's narrow escape. He remained silent for a long time, and in the dark I could see only the glow of his pipe, as he relaxed in an armchair by the window.

At long last, I heard him sigh. "It was a very strange experience, Watson," he said. "The tusker was a white elephant, an intelligent, well-trained sacred animal, playing his part extremely well in scaring us half to death. Now why would anyone want that done?"[5]

This, like the other mysteries of our mission, remained unsolved, although they weighed on my mind as we steamed into Madras Harbour. Despite being December, the clammy heat of the morning drenched us in sweat as we struggled ashore, followed by coolies carrying our few belongings and Holmes's large trunk of books. A short, spare, balding officer greeted us on the wharf. "Mr Holmes and Dr Watson, I presume," he said. "I am Colonel Pickering, Commissioner of Police in Madras.[6] Please follow me and we will go straight to my carriage. After some thought, I have booked you rooms in a garden house that once belonged to a boxwallah. His widow rents it out as a guesthouse. Very near the Madras Cricket Club, for I thought you would like not only the comforts of a decent hotel, but privacy as well. You will also meet some jolly good chaps at the Club, whenever you want companionship."[7]

Mr Ayer, after formally taking leave of us on the wharf, took off to pay his respects to his patroness. We rode in the Colonel's buggy through the wide, pleasant roads of Madras, with the Colonel pointing out various landmarks of interest. The Cricket Club in Chepauk fronted as lovely an oval green ringed by shady trees as one could expect to find in England. Near the Club, we found our 'garden' guesthouse built in the Eastern colonial style, low and large, with wide verandahs. It was furnished simply but elegantly, with floors of smooth cool stone; and rooms protected by a second mesh door, which allowed a breeze to enter, while keeping out insects. Punkahwallahs, mere striplings, crouched in the verandahs ready to pull the huge punkahs, or fans, which hung from the ceiling of every room. Bare-foot bearers stood by with tubs of hot water for our ablutions. When we had washed, we found it was still too hot to wear anything but plain white drill trousers and thin cotton shirts, with the sleeves rolled up sporting fashion. After eating a few piquantly spiced, hot curry dishes, we strolled across to the Club, and settled down with glasses of whisky and soda at the bar.

Colonel Pickering, who had promised to join us there, briskly got down to business. "Gentlemen, there is no mystery in this at all," he said. "We were warned by London a while ago to investigate transfers of large sums of European money to religious institutions, ostensibly for charitable purposes. On the face of it, there was a perfectly good reason. A gigantic tsunami—in the words of the South Sea Islanders—hit this coast in 1883, following the volcanic explosion in Krakatoa, immediately west of Java. Imagine, if you can, thirty-foot tidal waves lashing the coast with the speed of an express train. Several fishing villages were wiped out, unnoticed deaths occurred by the tens of thousands. We are still working in most places to help the natives recover. But London was worried, and rightly so. As I investigated, I saw all was not as it seemed. I have a certain felicity for native languages, which permits me to enter the oriental mind and understand nuances of meaning, which would escape a straightforward Englishman. Tamil, in particular, poses certain interesting problems to the modern European scientist, not only with its extensive use of conjunct doubled consonants, but through vowel sounds unique to itself. Accented inflections alter meanings very interestingly. I hope to solve such problems with the help of Professor Higgins, the undoubted expert in my field.

"But coming back to the case on hand, I had the priest closely shadowed—he is not really a priest, but a monk, who has renounced the world—a sanyasi, in fact, but still in charge of a very wealthy monastery. Such people take no interest in worldly affairs, considering what happens in life to be maya, or a shadow of cosmic reality. But the Shankaracharya became suddenly, and curiously, interested in education. He started coming out into the world and giving lectures on the need for natives to receive a good education! This thought, if spread among excitable natives, is in itself dangerous. By policy, we have seen to it that educational institutions should be developed only by British Christians, who can instil proper values in their charges. I see you are to meet Dr Miller, an excellent man.

"To continue—I had him shadowed by Khan Sahib, my thanedar at the Royapettah Police Station, a man on whose loyalty and acumen I would stake my life. The estranged relationship between the Shankaracharya and his accountant was common bazaar gossip. Khan used to follow them discreetly. He was present at his viewing post the night when the Shankaracharya went to the quarters of his accountant; their meeting ended in an ugly quarrel. Later, the culprit was seen returning to the scene, entering the quarters where the murder took place, and then leaving at a dead run. There is no doubt in my mind that the monk killed his man. Psychologically he had already returned to this world—we see that he was interfering in educational institutions. Why he killed his accountant we still do not know, but we will find out. Since the natives are greatly agitated by this arrest, I have been careful to see to it that the police do not apply the usual methods for extracting a confession. Otherwise, all would have been known in half an hour!"

I found Colonel Pickering's careful summary of the case quite convincing, and felt disappointed that Holmes had been dragged all the way from London by a crime that did not seem to merit his interest.

"I should like to meet the Shankaracharya," said Holmes after a pause.

"Certainly, this very day. I had expected you would want to meet him. I have placed a buggy completely at your and Dr Watson's disposal. The coachman understands English instructions, if spoken slowly and clearly."

We left for the Royapettah Police Station after tea, at which we were served fresh cucumber sandwiches, well-buttered toast, and a pleasant jam made of mangoes. The buggy threaded its way through a noisy evening market, with crowds of colourfully dressed men and women spilling out into the streets. The muezzin's call to prayer cut through the ringing of temple bells; street urchins ran along with our carriage, mostly in a spirit of fun, trying to get some bakseesh from us. The police station, hemmed in on both sides by shops, was a rather gloomy building, with red-brick facings, but was whitewashed inside. An immense police officer sat behind an ink-stained desk covered with dusty brown files. His height was accentuated by a high khaki turban, from the folds of which sprouted a grizzled beard. His twinkling eyes belied a first impression of ferocity.

He stretched himself to his full height, and came forward slowly. "I am Imtiaz Khan, Thanedar of the Royapettah Police Station," he said, speaking with an unmistakable Pathan accent. "Colonel Pickering has instructed me to await your orders." Then, as we stepped into the light of the kerosene lanterns that dimly illuminated that dark room, he thrust his beard into my face and said with growing excitement, "Can it be? Dr John Watson, Sir, do you remember Khan of the Khyber border post...I welcomed you as you galloped back?"

Indeed, I remembered the good fellow then; he had on his own initiative stolen forward through the Khyber Hills, seen the plight of our retreat, and run back under fire to bring up reinforcements.

"Jamedhar-Major Khan!" I cried. "How can I forget the man who saved my life? I never expected to see you in Madras, in charge of a police station!"

He had been honourably discharged from the army after an Afghan bullet chipped his left hip, leaving him with a permanent limp. Highly recommended by his superiors, he had sought employment with the police, and was transferred to a warmer climate. Over cups of hot sugary tea, Imtiaz Khan corroborated Colonel Pickering's account of the case in every detail. "But come, Sir," he said, jumping up. "You shall see the man yourself! We have him in our custody, right here in our cells. The case will be heard in the High Court in three weeks' time. The kafir priest has refused to employ a lawyer in defence, but Mr Norton has taken it upon himself to plead his case pro bono. Mr Norton, although English, is liked by the Hindoos here, for coming to their rescue more than is necessary or seemly."[8]

He led us through gloomy corridors lit dimly by hurricane lanterns hung on nails. We crossed a narrow courtyard with a few sad potted ferns, and then came to a narrow cell, a little removed from the others.

"We keep the priest apart from the other prisoners, out of respect for the kafir's caste distinctions. They will all go to hell in any case. We even allow a Brahmin to bring him cooked food, twice a day. There he is!"

Through the gloaming I spied an orange figure, hunched on the ground of the cell like a great orangutan, mouthing gibberish. "My God, Holmes," I said hoarsely. "He has gone mad!"

"No, only saying his prayers," said Holmes quietly. "At dusk, a good Hindoo must say the sandy-vandannam. That Sanskrit prayer, Watson, predates the British Empire by a full three thousand years! Let us wait until he is finished."[9]

Soon, the ritual was over. The monk, who I saw wore an ochre wrap around him, crossed himself in reverse order, like the Devil himself, poured water all round him, and looked up at us. Imtiaz Khan opened the cell door and stood back. Before entering, Holmes whispered to me to take off my shoes. "The floor on which he sits is sacred ground. Let us not defile it with our shoes," he said.

We stared at each other in silence for a moment. The monk startled me by saying quite intelligibly: "I guilty!" Holmes nodded, and then spoke to him slowly in a strange tongue. The monk's eyes lit up, and he responded with alacrity. Words poured out of him rapidly. Holmes occasionally questioned, nodded, and gave short answers. After ten or fifteen minutes of this astonishing intercourse, we rose to take leave of the monk. Holmes bent down deep with folded hands as in prayer; the monk held up his hands and incanted something. Imtiaz Khan, who had stood outside the cell, looked rather disapproving of all this, I could see, but he said nothing.

On our way back to the Club, I could no longer hold back my curiosity. "I didn't know you could speak Tamil,

Holmes," I said with some asperity. "It is not like you to dissemble to your friends."

"I was speaking Sanskrit," said Holmes mildly. 'At school, I had a very able chemistry teacher, who had returned after several decades of service in India, and was full of local lore about the efficacy of wild plants to cure most of the modern world's illnesses. We took to each other, and after school hours, he taught me more chemistry than is known in our universities, and Sanskrit for good measure. But I was unsure I could hold a conversation with the Shankaracharya, to whom it would almost be like a mother tongue. As you saw, I did not have to do much speaking. He told me all we need to know." And after that I could not get another word out of Holmes.

I went to bed early that night after a sumptuous dinner of mulligatawny soup, quails' eggs, and roasted leg of mutton, washed down with passable claret, followed by a fruit salad of papayas, some excellent coffee, and black Trichnopalee cigars. It had been a wild goose chase, but on the whole not arduous. I promised myself that I would explore Madras in the morning, since in my mind the case was solved. The good Imtiaz Khan had himself caught the man red-handed, and like Colonel Pickering I would have trusted him with my life—indeed, had done so a decade ago during the Afghan War. But I heard Holmes pacing in his room restlessly as I dropped off to sleep.

I woke early from a troubled sleep of strange dreams, in which orangutans chased Holmes and myself through a forest full of snakes and elephants. I went out after a perfunctory wash, but found no sign of Holmes. After a light breakfast, I left for a sightseeing tour on horseback, guided by Lieutenant Guha, one of the first Indians to receive a Queen's Commission. He was a bit of a scholar as well, and he informed me with a modest flush that his studies might be noted later, when the economy had developed, for certain percipient insights into subaltern working conditions during the colonial period.

We ambled through several coconut groves, past curious temples, and ended up further down the beach, where I could see for myself the damage inflicted half a dozen years ago by the tidal wave. The debris of large native houses lay strewn all over the sand. Whatever was useful, or had still been intact, had long ago been collected by the poor, whose hovels lined the beach. My friend called over a few of the men who were sitting under palm trees, and asked them to narrate for me what had happened that fateful day in 1883. The day had dawned hot and preternaturally bright. In the still hours of the morning, they had heard their boats grinding loudly against each other. Rushing to the beach to see what had happened, they found that the sea had rapidly receded almost out of sight, all along that gentle shelving coast, and that the boats were grounded on the sand. Some ran down to inspect the damage, when others saw a long black line growing on the horizon. Soon they discerned the crest of a huge wave, taller than the palms, coming at them with a terrifying, grinding noise. They ran for their lives, but few escaped. One man claimed he had been lifted by the wave and deposited atop of a tall palm, to which he clung for a full day, sharing it with cobras that coiled all round him. Later, in the months to come, white fathers had come—no, they were not English, but other whites—and told them that Yesu, who had saved them, had instructed the white fathers to help them. They were now all Christians, and these fathers were now everywhere, rebuilding their humble homes, educating their children, and running clinics to treat the sick and the aged.

After distributing a few annas among the poor and thanking them for telling us what had happened, we turned back, for the day was getting unbearably hot. The subaltern, like a good soldier, had packed a few sandwiches in his saddlebags, which he kindly shared with me, and also the lemonade from his canteen. Back at the guesthouse I lay down for a siesta, and must have dozed off until I heard Holmes rattling my mesh door to wake me. "Tomorrow morning, we have an appointment with Dr Miller of the Madras Christian College," he said without further ado, "so don't go anywhere. Well, I must be off now."

I lay back on my drenched sheets, and cursed my wretched punkahwallah for letting me get all hot and sweaty in my sleep. I tried to imagine what Holmes could be about; the case was solved, any fool could see that. Giving up on such fruitless speculation, I reached for a nearby cane, gave the punkah a huge yank to wake up the youth whose duty it was to keep me fanned, and dropped off to sleep once again. That evening, I dined sparingly on some river fish, and an omelette garnished with fried potatoes, baked tomatoes, and basil, and had no more than one glass of port.

The next day, on our way to the Madras Christian College near George Town, I related to Holmes my adventure of the previous day, and told him I had myself seen the damage done by the tidal wave, and listened to the gratitude of the simple beach folk who related in detail all the help given by the Europeans.

"Dash it all, Holmes!" I said. "They are European Christians, they have helped the wretched of the earth, and converted them to God-fearing human beings. There is nothing at all sinister in all this, no matter what Whitehall thinks!"

"The path to hell is paved with good intentions," said Holmes mysteriously, to which I deigned no reply.

The college was a rather ugly red building, set in a tidy garden. Since Christmas holidays had been declared, it was free of students, and we were conducted through quiet halls to the Principal's office. The appearance of the place was one of order and tidiness. Dr Miller himself was dressed in rather old-fashioned clothes, the elbows of his jacket had somewhat frayed patches, and his cuffs were too worn for a man of his standing. He welcomed us courteously in a pronounced Scottish accent.[10]

"It is an honour, Sir, to meet a scholar with your dedication," said Holmes formally, "one who has sacrificed the comforts of family life to bring education to the natives."

Dr Miller lifted his eyebrows. "How could you guess I am a bachelor?" he asked in genuine surprise.

"Pardon my presumption," said Holmes. "Being a bachelor myself, I am aware that sometimes my attire shows signs—as a lady acquaintance once remarked—of manly neglect, which would not be tolerated by a wife."

Dr Miller smiled. "I am happy to meet with such a keen observer of the human condition," he said. "It is a similar personal interest that sustains me in a climate so different from that of Edinburgh. I believe you are here to investigate the sad affair of the Shankaracharya. Why the man would allow himself to be treated so is well beyond my Christian comprehension. It's a farce in the worst possible taste, I tell you, and has already damaged years of my work among the Hindoos. They are a tolerant people, but there is only just so far you can push anybody."

His support of the Hindoo monk took me by surprise, but Holmes asked with equanimity, "Do you have proof, Sir, that the Shankaracharya is innocent?"

"Proof, Sir! What proof do you want more than the character of the man?" cried Dr Miller. "Would you hand the Pope over to the police on suspicion, or your Archbishop, or even a Deacon from my own Church— although about some Presbyters, the less said the better. Look you, Sir, you have enraged the peaceable Hindoo, and that is a dangerous thing to do. How could a giant of a Muslim policeman hide himself without the whole world knowing, I ask you? And how would he know on a dark night who impersonated a kafir priest? It does not hold up, Sir, it does not; and I am very much afraid Mr Norton will once again make the police look like a parcel of fools, when he takes up the case!"

This put a different complexion on the case for me. But before any more could be said, tea was brought in, as is the invariable custom in any meeting in India, of however fortuitous a nature.

As I took a sip, Dr Miller continued. "Aye, you might be surprised that I, a Christian and head of a Christian College, should take up so vehemently the case of a Hindoo sanyasi. But let me tell you, I am an educator before all else, and Scotsman though I am, a supporter of the British Empire as a creation of Almighty God Himself! I have come to know the Brahmins as I know my own Churchmen, and hold them in equal, if not higher esteem. We have no future in this country, I tell you, none at all—even if some preen themselves that we are over the worst after 1857—unless, and mark my words, unless we bring the best Brahmins within the fold of British education. That is my mission, and I will not allow simpleminded policemen to wreck it."

I could not hold my tongue after this, and put before Dr Miller every argument advanced by Colonel Pickering and Jamedhar-Major Imtiaz Khan, which he rebutted by sowing doubt at every stage as to what was meant, or what was seen. I was shaken in the opinions I had previously formed, and could begin to see how easily a skilled counsel—as Mr Norton was reputed to be—could change the mind of a judge.

"Come, we are debating mere conjectures," said Dr Miller at long last. "In fact, none of us know the facts that lie behind this extraordinary case. I must help you get at the truth, but whether that is what the Ranee of

Kanchee wants is more than I know. No one can help you get closer to the people and events than my star pupil, Srinivasa Chari. He comes from the highest ranks of the Brahmins of Madras; he is a syamachari, which in simple language means he has hereditary powers to set up a temple or monastery in his own right and have a following of thousands. He is an orphan—but no more, since he is all the son I want; find him, tell him I sent you, and that he should help. It is Christmas break, or I would have produced him before you in a moment."

Dr Miller could not help us with clearer directions where we were to find this paragon save for pointing us towards his native village. He might have gone there to look after his lands, but, Dr Miller added in haste, he cared not a tuppence for them. Where else the boy might be found he did not know, or was unwilling to tell us.

The next morning, we received a note from Colonel Pickering, who had kindly sent a rider to the boy's village. He was not found there, and an aged relative had said the boy had not been seen for several months, and that we should enquire at Dr Miller's. We were at a dead end. Finding ourselves at something of a loss, that afternoon we decided to take up the invitation of the Club cricketers, and joined them for a practice game. I remember Holmes, who was quite useful with slow leg-breaks, got two wickets, one bowled round the legs and the other stumped. I am not very good with the ball, so I spent most of my time in the outfield. The shades of evening were upon us when it came my turn to bat, and after a couple of lusty drives to long on, I was happy to retire to the pavilion for a long draught of local beer.

Before we turned in, an orderly delivered a large white envelope to Holmes, and I could see it carried a curious red seal. Holmes read it with interest, and then tossed it across to me. It read:

> Mr Sherlock Holmes is in search of truth, which is an infinitesimal part of the Whole Truth. One must go to the Source, even in mundane matters, but what he dabbles in reaches Beyond to Occult Mysteries. To find, first he must seek—and that only at the Door of Esoteric Knowledge. I shall await his coming hither for elevenses.

I almost laughed aloud at this bombastic message, with its ridiculous conclusion, but Holmes was smiling, and said: "Well, I was wondering when we would get a summons from Madame!" I then learnt that a crazy but colourful member of the lower Russian aristocracy, one Madame Blavatsky, had started a new religion in Madras, as if India needed any more, and her coterie of eccentrics were called Theosophists.[11] We had apparently been summoned by this lady, and what was more astonishing, Holmes was intent on keeping the appointment.

The next morning, we undertook the long journey to Adyar, where the lady had established her sect. We carried umbrellas to shade us from the sun in our open carriage, and it was good we did so, for I was perspiring freely by the time we left civilization behind. We drove past rich paddy fields and young Tamil women in bright saris tucked up almost to their waists. Such visions of limb and figure may have been a sight for the Gods had they been white. As it was, I was slightly affronted by the bold looks they cast at Holmes's fine aquiline face, but he seemed not the least discomfited. Leaving the fields, we entered the heavy woods of Adyar and passed a troop of spotted deer, before crossing the fresh and sparkling Adyar river.

We soon entered spacious wooded grounds and saw, up the driveway, a large mansion fit for a European princess. There was little doubt that this Madame Blavatsky was treated as royalty by her minions. After being made to wait for a while, we were ushered into a large dimly lit room, made yet dimmer by the heavy incense fumes floating around. The lady, of uncertain age, with the unmistakable broad face of a Slav, reclined on a pile of richly embroidered velvet cushions. We were summoned by the imperious wave of a jewelled hand. After a leisurely scrutiny carried out by her languorous eyes, the hand once again waved us to sit down. I was irritated by this play-acting, and would have left, but had no wish to spoil Holmes's game.

"I see that Dr Watson is irritated by what he thinks is play-acting and would leave us," drawled the lady, "but I beg his patience. We are united in the Cause of Causes."

I must confess I was a little discomfited by this fortune-teller's trick, but before I could come up with a rejoinder, Holmes broke in with polished ease. "Indeed, Madame is right, as always. We all seek the truth. You have summoned me to reveal it. And I am here."

Madame Blavatsky smiled. "Dear Mr Holmes, let us play no games. Come, have some tea—I assure you it is excellent—and some cakes as well."

She was right, for the tea was pure and limpid, without the art of sugar or milk, but spiced so delicately as to be almost pure leaf from Hangchow. The baklavas dipped in honey were as perfect as those on the Bosphorus.

"I want to know the truth about what has happened to the Shankaracharya," said Holmes, after he too had spent a moment appreciating the tea. "I know he is innocent, but I do not know why he is innocent. Everything points to his having committed the crime, except that it is clear he would not have done so. I come to you, then, for enlightenment."

"Ah, you reason like a Theosophist, who lifts the mantle of maya to espy the distant path to Nirvana, which might be no path at all, but the ground under one's feet all the time. *Everything in the Universe, throughout all its kingdoms, is Conscious,* so if you wish, you can cognize It. Have you studied the Upanishads?"

"Madam, I was exposed to their virtues at an early age, when I was yet too young to recognize the worth of what I was looking at," said Holmes with ease.

The answer pleased the lady. "Good, Mr Holmes, you are on the path to the conquest of ignorance by the revelation of *secret, spiritual knowledge.* But they have now ceased to reveal it. If it were otherwise, the Upanishads could become accessible even to the Mlechchhas and the European Orientalists."

"Madam, this still leaves me sitting at your feet, and

nowhere near where I might get at the truth," said
Holmes with patience.

"Good, again," said the lady, licking the sticky
juices of a baklava from her fingers. "Remember, *every
Shankaracharya is a Shankara reborn.* And when has a
new Shankara to be 'born'? When a Shankara has to
be born, naturally every one of the principles in the
manifested mortal man must be the purest and finest
that exist on earth. *Shankara, the first one, was a Buddha,
most assuredly, and has not the astral essence of Gautama
attached itself to the body of every new Shankara since
then?* Is renunciation of life in a holy one necessary to
sustain the world?"

"But why is he caught in this horrible crime?" asked
Holmes.

"Good, very good, we understand each other," said
Madame Blavatsky. "It is a mystery which cannot
be unravelled without the insights of some Esoteric
Knowledge. I said at the beginning you do not need to
travel, but study the ground at your feet. The Smartava
Brahmin sect, founded by Shankara, is still very powerful
in southern India, and is now almost the only one to have
real initiates at their head in their Mutts. On the other
hand, there is no sect in that desperately exclusive caste
of the Brahmins more exclusive than is the Smartava;
and the reticence of its followers to speak of what they
may know of the occult sciences and the esoteric doctrine
is only equalled by their pride and learning."[12]

"Yes, much is now clear," said Holmes, rising. "You
have enlightened an European Orientalist, who is truly

grateful. I leave you, Madame, but in a deeper, inner sense, I never leave your presence."

We were seen out graciously after this fulsome gobbledygook, and I was chuckling to myself at Holmes's tact in getting away from that crazed woman, when he surprised me by saying, "I am so glad we came, aren't you? She has almost led us to a solution."

This was so outrageous that, after casting a sidelong look to see if he were pulling my leg, I lapsed into silence. The return journey was completed with each of us immersed in his own thoughts.

The heat of the afternoon made a prolonged siesta indispensable. Dinner was eaten in the boisterous company of the local cricketers, who were preparing for a visit from the Colombo Cricket Club. The fine points of the game were discussed threadbare, Dr Grace's name taken more than once to make a point, and fielding strategies explained over pints of beer, with samosas—an Indian version of a mutton patty—laid out as a field. I had never had a happier time, and soon forgot our visit to Madame Blavatsky and Holmes's curious attitude.

Next morning, Colonel Pickering joined us at breakfast. "So, how did your séance go?" he asked cheerily. "She is mad as a hatter, but in this country, God bless them, it passes without notice. Thinking about her, I suddenly realized that the first thing I should have organized is a visit to the Mutt, the monastery's headquarters in Madras. After all, that was where the fellow presided, and after a fall-out over money—there is too much of it sticking to holy fingers in this country, I can tell you—he got rid of his man, and the reasons of his quarrel with him. A visit will make all things clear."

"Indeed, I wish to go to the Mutt, directly," said Holmes with a little smile. "Strange as it may sound, Colonel Pickering, that is exactly what the lady recommended, in her own peculiar way, of course."

On our way to the Mutt, Colonel Pickering told us that we would see the place at its best, since the month was dedicated to music and dance, sacred to the Gods. The very best of musicians vied with each other to perform before the holy of holies, as did the great courtesans of the land, the devadasis, who if the Colonel was to be believed, plied their trade within the very walls of the temple compound, a veritable town within a town. I was astonished at such profanity, but not after I came in sight of the magnificent temple that rose like a carved mountain from between a bedrock of houses and lanes. Woodwinds poured out their sonorous music, as men, women, and children hurried in and out of the many temple gates. My earlier service in India had been entirely in the Punjab and on the Frontier, where the Mussalman is as austere as the Low Church Christian in England. Hence, nothing from my previous experience prepared me for a sight of that massive temple, which rose pile upon pile to the top of its carved eminence. And what carvings of Gods they were, portraying every aspect of human emotion and experience! Beside the figures giving benediction rose figures of awful form, tearing and destroying their enemies; and above and intertwined were Gods in congress with their consorts—

figures to chill the soul of the hardened soldier, or shame the practised harlot.

Imtiaz Khan and his sepoys cleared a way for us through the crowd until temple officials came running to receive us, bowing meekly before Colonel Pickering. He picked out one bare-bodied man he seemed to know, and conversed briefly with him in Tamil above the din of the keening music.

"There is some confusion in the Mutt," he said, turning, "since the titular head is in custody. His successor has not yet been chosen. That is a task the Shankaracharya performs when he finds his end is near. However, there is an acknowledged 'favourite' novitiate, one Ramachandran, the son of a poor widowed sister. We are requested to meet him, before we are taken around."

We were taken to a bare room within the temple complex, where a bearded, sturdy young man, wrapped in white, sat on a deerskin in meditation. In front of his closed eyes was a picture of a frail white-haired old man. Although we could not recognize the picture, Colonel Pickering whispered, "He is praying for the well-being of the Shankaracharya." As if by intuition, the man opened his eyes and got up easily, the muscles of his powerful thighs rippling under the thin cloth. He stood with folded hands, a picture of submission, and yet, I could not help feeling, of menace as well.

Chairs were hurriedly brought for us, while the young monk seated himself once again on his deerskin. The other temple officials, all in simple white dhotis, sat in a circle round our feet. The conversation was conducted in Tamil, with Colonel Pickering giving us the gist every now and then. At a word, one of them brought forward a long ledger—clearly the monastery's accounts. We were informed that the Department of Religious Endowments had gone very carefully through the figures, made a physical count of the money, notes, cash, and jewels donated to the Mutt, and found the accounts to be in order. The monks, officials, and other devotees, we were told, were disturbed, and prayed that they be arrested instead of their head. At the end of the meeting, the young monk ceremoniously prostrated himself before Colonel Pickering in supplication, his broad, powerful back, covered with wiry black hair, rippling with muscles. His humility was found most affecting by his followers, who went out wiping their eyes.

After walking through a veritable rabbit's warren of numerous courtyards, where monks and officials viewed us with patent curiosity or distrust, we left the temple, the Colonel going back to his duties, and Holmes to a nearby museum where there were antiquities he wished to look at. I chose to wander through the narrow, crowded streets, jostling through the crowds the festival had drawn, and impressing on my mind the sights that might cheer my reflections later in cold, wintry England. Turning a corner, I found myself in the midst of a host of musicians, drummers, flutists, and clarinetists, all streaming away somewhere. Over their heads I spied a narrow housefront where a slight altercation seemed to be in progress. A tall, handsome youth stood barring the entrance to a larger, older man, covered from head to foot in a brown worked shawl. Although I saw only his shoulders from the back, covered in thick black hair, I knew the older man could be none other than the young novitiate we had interviewed a few hours ago. As if sensing that he was now almost alone on that street and noticeable to all, the older man drew his shawl tightly round himself and hurried away into the crowd. The youth gave me a long, steady look before withdrawing inside. A soldier's instinct told me that there was dirty work afoot, and I reminded myself to inform Holmes of what had occurred at the first opportunity.

Colonel Pickering had earlier told us that we should not miss turning up at the temple later that evening to watch the performance of a most promising danseuse, a girl from Bangalore, who though in her teens, was already considered an ornament of the devadasi community. I made my way to the appointed place as night began to fall. The dance stage was brilliantly lit by gaslights, and dhurries had been spread over a large courtyard, on which several hundred natives, almost all men, were squatting, their legs tucked under them to accommodate their neighbours. One end of the dance area was occupied by the musicians and the female singers, who had already begun their performance, when Colonel Pickering, Holmes, and I settled into the chairs that had been provided for us right in front. While that was my first, and I suppose will be my last, experience of a temple dance, I cannot ever forget the mesmerizing effect the dance and the music had on me. The young girl seemed to fix her eyes on me alone as she

spun round the stage—and what deliriously lustrous eyes
they were, rimmed with kohl; sometimes she came close
enough for me to see every detail of the most expressively
beautiful face I have ever seen. Diamonds sparkled on the
wings of each delicate nostril, and sapphires ringed the
edges of her ears. For the first time I realized that some
ears can have a sensuous quality unseen in others. Long
filigrees of gold studded with stones dangled from those
ears and brushed her shoulders as she swayed. Pendants
studded with precious stones were strung round her neck
and hung over her forehead. A long, thick plait of hair,
twined with flowers, moved in counterpoise to her sinuous
body, a figure in full bloom, sheathed in blue–green silk,
and yet drawing homage from the viewer rather than a
vulgar gaze. Neither my age, nor my religion, would have
mattered a whit if she had wanted me; I was her slave by
the time her dance ended.

The others seemed strangely unaffected, with Colonel
Pickering already discussing some administrative matter
that demanded his urgent attention, when the youth I
had seen earlier on the street pushed his way towards
us through the departing crowd, and said in excellent
English, "Bangalore Nagaratnamma presents her compliments to our new visitors, and invites them to join her
for some light refreshments."[13]

He looked straight at me. In the gaslight, I got a good
look at him. A youth of some seventeen or eighteen
years, and as handsome as a young Roman, he was bare-
bodied and clean-shaven, including his head, save for a
long tuft of hair he wore tied in a knot at the back. The

sacred thread of the Brahmins ran across his firm body. A simple white dhoti and sandals were all he wore. Holmes seemed undecided, but the young man quickly put all doubts at rest by saying: "I am Srinivasa Chari, a student of Dr Miller's, who has sent me word to meet you."

Holmes shook hands warmly with him, and we proceeded to follow, when Colonel Pickering drew me aside, and said with a wink, "You have made a conquest. Good luck to you." It was no surprise to me that we ended up in the narrow house where I had seen Chari that very afternoon. The house was really quite large, as we saw when we entered, a rather dark front hall giving on to a couple of open courtyards flanked by rooms, before we were led to a comfortable room, almost opulently furnished. Even as we seated ourselves on cushions, Miss Nagaratnamma entered, having divested herself of most of her jewellery, and now clothed in a dark silk sari lined with four inches of gold border. She had changed her earrings to large emerald studs, and only a single, intricately worked gold chain adorned her neck. Even then, she was enchanting, a dusky perfume rising from her body that I found irresistible. She sat next to the youth, familiarly leaning her hand on his thigh as she extended plates of refreshments to us. She spoke no English, but conversed in low tones with Chari, while he translated effortlessly for us.

After a few formal compliments in praise of her performance, Holmes turned the conversation to the case of the Shankaracharya. Chari agreed that the matter was grave, but not irreparable. "This unfortunate turn of events might have been avoided, but for the even more unfortunate occurrence of the tidal wave," he said. "Help was needed, and help poured in, thanks to Christian generosity and Christian conscience. But money in this case, as in any other, remains the root of all evil. The Mutt accounts undoubtedly show that all money received and *banked* remains accounted for. But what, Sir, of money that was never received through regular channels? In the aftermath of the disaster, everyone was so grateful for any help we could receive in this province that no controls were applied. Nor would controls have been accepted in the mood of that hour."

"Where would you say the money has gone?" asked Holmes.

"I would think, Sir," cried the youth, "that the money has gone nowhere. It sits as a financial *mass-de-manoeuvre*, to be called into life when the moment arises."

"Ah! I understand you," said Holmes. "It is kept against a future eventuality, to sway or earn support for whichever party holds the purse strings."

"Yes, or as a token promise of more patronage to come," said Chari.

"Where could it be now?" asked Holmes.

The young man looked straight at him. "Where could it be, Sir?" he asked in return. "Where would it be safe, and who could have control of it?"

Miss Nagaratnamma broke in with a low comment. Chari said she wished to know our first impressions of the temple and its festivities. I spoke of my own perceptions, and how different I found the southern part of India from its sterner north, but I was still labouring under strong emotions, and cared not to think if I made any sense at all that evening. The conversation became general, and we came to realize with astonishment how well educated the young lady was, and how perceptive her opinions were on a wide variety of subjects. When I blurted out something to this effect, she looked straight but kindly at me, and said a few lines of verse that Chari translated as follows, adding hastily that the poem was not her own, but Muddupalani's, a famous scholar–courtesan of the previous century, whose life she was researching:

> Which other women have
> Felicitated scholars with gifts of money?
> To which other women are epics dedicated?
> Which other women have won
> Such acclaim in each of the arts?

Even Holmes was moved to reach out and spontaneously press her hand. She smiled gently, and told us a lot more about southern Indian temples and their architecture. They had been places not only of prayer, but also of refuge in the past, when their country was attacked. Secret tunnels connected them to chambers, where the kings or their children could be safe, and openings in forests or on river banks helped them to escape at night. After a few desultory remarks, she rose and indicated she would rest. Chari ushered us to the door.

As we were having a nightcap in the verandah of the club, I mentioned to Holmes that Chari and she would make an attractive couple. Holmes gently shook his head. "The caste system makes it impossible for them to be anything but lovers. He is probably already married, and may even have children. He may be her first love, but most certainly will not be her last."

The stress of the previous days, if not the highly spiced food I had eaten, kept me to my rooms for the next two days. Holmes was very busy with something, but always called in to enquire how I was, before leaving and after he returned. On the third day the agony passed, and I was able to muster enough courage to go down to the dining room and eat a little quail, followed by a heartening glass of brandy. At the table I found a formal invitation for me and Holmes issued by His Excellency, The German Consul in Calcutta, to the Adyar Club, to attend Graf von Keyserling's presentation of a large gift from the German Christians to the tidal wave victims of the Madras Presidency. Von Keyserling—as the letter mentioned—was a well-known writer, philanthropist, and head of the Lutheran church of Saxe-Coburg-Gotha.[14] I realized with a start that the function was for that evening. Inside the envelope of the invitation, I found a scrawled, ironic note from Colonel Pickering:

> I hope you can come. If the mountain will not come to
> Mohammed, Mohammed will come to the mountain.

The Adyar Club was a spacious Georgian structure, once the property of a boxwallah, and its grounds and building were brilliantly illuminated for the occasion. Holmes and I arrived late, and found the circular central hall full of the English elite of Madras, with almost no Indians, for whose benefit the evening's entertainment had been arranged, save for a few Parsee ladies, who arrived on the arms of their military escorts. A handsome man in his early fifties, Graf von Keyserling, stood at the end of the hall, a head taller than the adoring circle of ladies. Fashionably dressed, he seemed unconsciously to carry himself with the bearing of a Junker, his auburn beard almost reaching his waist. He spoke so softly of his concern for the tsunami victims that it was hard to catch his words above the hiss of the blinding gaslights.

"Ladies and gentlemen, this is the land of the Buddha, the land of Wisdom," he said, flashing a warm smile round the room. "Today, I bring only gifts from the German Christians to this land, but I take away a lot, a hope for the future; a future when peace will reign in the world, as the Buddha wanted. A world where we will reward only right livelihood, as my friend, Baron von Uexküll, demands so often, rather than military might."

A round of applause greeted these worthy sentiments.

"I am overwhelmed by your kindness," he continued. "With such palpable kindness, what need is there for an unwanted German..." He held up a hand on hearing 'no, no, no,' cooed around him. "...I mean it, there is no need for any outside interference, I mean, intervention, when so good people are near at hand. I come to share in the feast of human goodness you create to help our less fortunate brethren."

Fervent applause drowned out the rest of his words. We saw the cheque he handed over to His Excellency, the Governor; and the large packages of clothes, toys, and other presents from German Christians, which he gave to the ladies, to present to the unfortunate Indians. There seemed to be an awkward moment when Holmes was introduced to him, but after a moment's hesitation, von Keyserling said, "But of course, Mr Sherlock Holmes! What a pleasure to find you so far from the scene of your exploits! Your name is as well known in Berlin as in your own native land. I recommend you visit the temples of Madras while you are here. They bear—so much of interest, that we in Europe can never begin to fathom," and with that he passed on.

I was dreaming of orangutans that turned into bearded German aristocrats, when I woke to find Holmes holding a hand over my mouth and warning me to be silent. He was fully dressed and, signalling me to dress as quickly as I could, he went outside. In a few minutes I joined him on the verandah, deep in shadow, and we tiptoed past the sleeping servants. After keeping close to the hedges, we gained the road in a few minutes, where we spied Colonel Pickering seated impatiently in his buggy, and accompanied by a troop of armed sepoys. We moved forward with the greatest stealth until we were clear of the building, and then, Colonel Pickering giving the order to advance, we moved forward at a fair clip. To my muffled queries I received no clear answer until we reached a small river that flowed past the temple buildings. The order to dismount was given, and rapidly the force took cover behind some bushes. An interminable wait ensued, and I had almost dropped off to sleep, when with a loud cry the sepoys sprang forward, and the torches lit in a trice showed the young novitiate Ramachandran held effortlessly in a vice-like grip by Jamedhar-Major Imtiaz Khan. A box was retrieved from the young man, and when opened, glittered in the fading moon with the light of hundreds of diamonds.

"The matter was simplicity itself once I had the right clue in my hand," said Holmes next morning at breakfast. "Large sums of money were flowing. That much Whitehall knew from its agents on the Unter-den-Linden. But how were they getting past our surveillance? We knew the gifts to the tidal wave victims were somehow involved, but we never thought it would take the form of diamonds from German Southwest Africa. These diamonds were mined in blood, Watson, and have resulted in blood. Whether von Keyserling was a willing tool of Berlin's, and whether he knew diamonds were hidden in the stacks of gifts, we will never know, but men of the highest probity have been known to commit crimes in the cause of national interest. The Shankaracharya was a thorn in the German side. He had to be eliminated, as well as his loyal accountant. We now know that they disagreed on how to regard the peccadilloes of the Shankaracharya's favourite. The old man kept hoping he would mend his ways, and hence his expressions of guilt after the murder. The young man was prey to his own strong passions, and became a tool in German hands. He agreed to be a willing conduit, and bribe the Ranee. That greedy woman loved wealth, felt no sense of loyalty to the Crown, and was willing to switch allegiances if future events and German strength made it feasible. The Khan Sahib had been spotted in his hiding place on the night of the murder. It was the work of a moment for the young man to don ochre robes, hunch his shoulders, and whiten his hair with powder, to make the policeman believe it was the Shankaracharya he saw. Remember it was the dead of night, and Khan already suspected the Shankaracharya. The murder was not necessary, but maddened by passion for Nagaratnamma, Ramachandran was willing to commit the ultimate crime to gain enough money to possess her."

I shuddered at the thought. "You are brilliant, Holmes," I said simply.

Holmes shook his head. "That young man, Chari, had it all worked out, and waited only for me to work out his and Nagaratnamma's purpose."

I was still full of questions. "But how did you know where to nab the tricky devil?" I asked.

"That was elementary, Watson," said Holmes. "When you were in bed with an upset stomach, I contacted some of the fisherfolk you had met earlier on your ride to the beach. With patience and the help of Chari, and the right amounts pressed into the right hands at the right moment, I learnt about all the suspicious movements of the recent past. From their description, I knew we had found our man. They knew where the tunnel opening was in the river bank."

Holmes paused, then added: "The poor know everything; they watch their betters all the time, but keep their counsel. If you win their friendship, many a crime can be solved, and many a disaster averted."

"And what was all that business with the defanged cobra and the trained elephant?" I persisted.

Holmes gave a rich laugh. "Oh! That was just the oriental mind of Mr Ayer, gilding the lily," he said. "We have a score to settle with that gentleman. He wished us to believe that powerful dark forces opposed the Ranee's plans to free the Shankaracharya. By such subterfuges he hoped we would never find out that the Ranee really wanted the old man put away, and a more pliable man put in his place."

"Well, what now, Holmes?" I asked.

"I don't know," he said thoughtfully. "Keyserling, of course, cannot be touched. The arrest of the young novitiate will cause too much scandal. He has agreed to depart for Benares, where he will remain a holy recluse for the rest of his life, watched carefully by the police, of course. The old man will be released, and the police will eat humble pie, but your Hindoo is a forgiving chap, so we anticipate no trouble from that quarter, except for a few marches to Town Hall by a few young, hot-headed lawyers. The problem is the Ranee. She should know we know, and be scared enough to toe the line in future."

Chari paid us an unexpected visit next morning. Perhaps conscious of the white man's decorum, he wore a shawl over the upper part of his body. "Mr Holmes, I have a great favour to ask of you. It is presumptuous of me, but I know you will understand. Ratna has left for her home in Bangalore. In parting, she gave me this priceless gift." He held out twin strings of large, intricately carved corals. "She would not let me refuse her gift. She left it as a gift for my wife. She is very mischievous, but as you know, extraordinary. I cannot throw them away—they are too precious, and I do not have the heart. I cannot be seen with them at college. So I thought I would give them to you. You have done me, and her, a very great service, for which we will always be grateful. I know you will dispose of the corals wisely."

Instead of protesting, Holmes calmly pocketed the jewels, and then held out his hand. "Mr Chari, you are an extraordinary young man. It is you who have done the Empire a great service. I have friends in high places, and by your acts you have earned their gratitude as well. With a letter of recommendation from Dr Miller, of which I am sure, perhaps I might be able to find you a scholarship and a place in one of our colleges at Oxford."

Srinivasa Chari gave him a slow smile. "Sir, you do me honour," he said. "Under Dr Miller's tutelage, I have learnt a British—a Scottish—sense of duty to my fellowmen. He has taught me, and I must teach them. But I thank you for your kind offer." With a formal bow, and after shaking hands with us warmly, Chari took his leave.

The rest of the day was spent at the police station where our many depositions were noted with slow deliberation. What might have occasioned no more than a half hour's work in England took the better part of the day in India. But Holmes, in the midst of all that paperwork at the police station, must have managed to send word to Ayer, for next morning he arrived soon after breakfast, spry as ever, to conduct us to take formal leave of the Ranee. Holmes was in high humour during the drive to the palace—but the saturnine Ayer responded to his sallies with only short, albeit polite, answers.

Large untidy grounds, overgrown with weeds, greeted us as we swept through the rusted gates of the palace. Ayer was at pains to point out that the princely estate was much diminished through British taxation and the munificent generosity of his patroness. The palace itself could have done with a touch of paint. Green patches of moss and lichen ran up the damp walls. Mouldy furniture, of unfashionable design, littered the rooms. Ayer led us to a small intimate room where the Ranee was to receive us. This was much better furnished, and quite clean.

We had been sitting for no more than a quarter of an hour when the Ranee was announced, and an enormously fat lady, shrouded in a rich Kashmiri shawl, waddled into the room, supported by two ancient maidservants. Ayer was all obsequiousness, arranging cushions for the Ranee.

Tea things were brought forward, while the Ranee, in halting singsong English, formally and cheerlessly thanked us for freeing the Shankaracharya, which had been her dearest wish. Holmes in turn made suitable protestations of mutual esteem, and said he had been expressly charged by Lord Ripon to thank the Ranee for her loyalty to the British Empire, and her world-renowned generosity to British subjects. A smirk broke across her fat face, and she made some indication of her continued adherence to the British cause. At a signal from the Ranee, a woman came forward carrying a silver salver piled high with gold mohurs. This was laid ceremoniously before Holmes. With a slight smile, he gracefully declined the gold, and suggested to the Ranee that she might seek the advice of Colonel Pickering as to the proper recompense his services, such as they were, had deserved. Requiring no further persuasion, the Ranee quickly dismissed the woman, who silently withdrew into the inner chambers with the gold. A slight pause ensued.[15]

Holmes brought out a packet carefully wrapped in brown paper, and unwrapped the corals Chari had given him. "These, Your Highness, are a gift from Lord Ripon to yourself," he said unctuously, "as a token of gratitude and high esteem. After due worship, these were given for this purpose by a holy English seer of Queen Victoria's, so that the corals would ever protect you, and keep you and yours safe within the strong walls of the British Empire!"

A tissue of bigger lies I had never heard, but the Ranee took it all in, and after superstitiously lifting the corals to her eyes in prayer, she eagerly twisted them round a very fat neck. Holmes seemed to hesitate with embarrassment, and then blurted out quickly. "Your Highness must forgive me for being unable to convey to you with proper discretion a matter of the utmost delicacy. Lord Lansdowne, our Viceroy, is unwell."

All of us looked blankly at Holmes at this surprising statement. He continued with effort. "Lord Ripon is most agitated…would do his utmost to prevent…even Queen Victoria wishes you to be warned of danger…"

The word "danger" galvanized the Ranee, and she

leaned forward, extending a lukewarm cup of tea towards Holmes. He informed her rather reticently that Lord Lansdowne carried a deep pent-up grief, having lost his father during the treasonable sepoy uprising in 1857. Consequently, he was beginning to suspect the most loyal of British subjects. However, he could not be removed because of powerful family interests, hinted Holmes. The Ranee nodded knowingly. "What is worrying Lord Ripon, Madame," he said at last, "and causing him sleepless nights, is the Viceroy's confusion. He confuses the respected name of the Ranee of Kanchee with the traitoress, the Ranee of Jhansee. And when he heard that you too had adopted a son, it seems he swore, in a fit of madness, to march at the head of his army on to your lands. The situation is very grave…"

The Ranee enquired breathlessly what was to be done. Holmes appeared perplexed, and shook his head. Then an idea seemed to dawn on him. "Your Highness should do something the Ranee of Jhansee never would have done," he said slowly. "Yes, that might clear the Viceroy's mind of his misapprehension. You have expansive lands in Tambaram, lying unused, and of no value to you as they are salt lands. Why not gift them, Your Highness, to the Madras Christian College, as their future site? It would please Dr Miller, who is close to Lord Ripon, who would exert himself more in your cause…although God willing, nothing untoward will happen."

The Ranee readily agreed, twisting the corals like rosary beads. We took leave of Her Highness with deep bows.

"And what might be equally efficacious, Your Highness," said Holmes from the door, "is to gift the incomparable services of Mr Subramany Ayer to Mr Cecil Rhodes, who needs his able assistance in the wilds of Africa. Lord Ripon has many commercial interests in Africa, and will never forget the gesture."

"And that puts paid to the wily Mr Ayer," said Holmes with a chuckle as we drove away, leaving behind a grim and unhappy Indian. "And thus ends the case of the Saint of Kumbakonam. I am afraid that henceforth the name of that town will always be associated in the minds of Madrasis with double-dealing."

"What should we do next in Madras?" I asked.

"We must try for a cabin on the starboard side of *The Coromandel Star*," answered Holmes. "I believe she steams home the day after tomorrow."

The Bite Worse than Death

On the eve of the departure of *The Coromandel Star*, we were relaxing in the bar of the Madras Cricket Club, narrating the stirring events of the last few days to an admiring circle of the Club's members, when Holmes received a hastily penned note from Colonel Pickering. After scanning it, he handed it to me.

"Can you make anything of this, Watson?" he asked. It read in part:

> Urgently request you to consider delaying your return home. A great service may be rendered to the Empire by Dr Watson. Will meet you early tomorrow morning with esteemed guest. Yours, etc. Pickering.

We were both greatly in Colonel Pickering's debt, for all the hospitality and kindness shown to us. There was nothing for it but to cancel our berths on the homebound liner, and await his arrival next morning with some curiosity, not unmixed with mild irritation at having our plans changed so abruptly.

The Colonel arrived promptly next morning, even as we were finishing a bracing breakfast of kippers and sausages. He was accompanied by an oriental grandee of the first water, a large, stout middle-aged gentleman, in a long flowered silk sherwani, and a large pink turban, pinned together with an antique jewel piece of small pearls and diamonds clustered round a large uncut ruby. He greeted us with several deep salaams, a large jewelled hand almost sweeping the floor before being lifted up to his white goatee.

"Dr Watson, Mr Holmes, I am a humble emissary of Asman Jah, Amir-i-Kabir, Azam ul-Umara, Umdat ul-Mulk, Bashir ud-Daula, Nawab Sir Muhammad Mazharuddin Khan Bahadur, Rifa'at Jang, Knight Commander of the Indian Empire, Chief Minister of the State of Hyderabad—Melkote, Shankar Narayan Rao, at your service!"

There was a moment's astonished silence, when Colonel Pickering broke in smoothly: "Diwan Sahib Melkote is a highly respected barrister of Hyderabad, who has undertaken a confidential mission for Sir Mazharuddin, Chief Minister to His Highness, the Nizam of Hyderabad, the Premier Prince of India."

Melkote bowed again, but clearly found this additional introduction unsatisfactory. "Sir, I am the humblest subject of His Highness Rustam-i-Dauran, Arustu-i-Zaman, Wal Mamaluk, Asaf Jah VI, Muzaffar ul-Mamaluk, Nizam ul -Mulk, Nizam ud-Daula, Nawab Mir Mahbub Ali Khan Bahadur, Sipah Salar, Fath Jang, Nizam of Hyderabad, Grand Commander of the Star of India, Kaiser-i-Hind." And then, with great solemnity, he added: "Invested with Full Ruling Powers in Person by His Excellency, the Marquess of Ripon, Viceroy of India."

After more salaams and a few simple English hand-shakes, we sat down to coffee and the strange request of our resplendent guest.

"Dr Watson, God, while showering my ruler with many blessings, is also testing him cruelly," said Melkote, wiping away an imaginary tear. "Sahibzada Mir Faruq Ali Khan Bahadur, who was to be the light of our world, died last year at the age of three. And now the remaining male heir of our gracious ruler, Sahibzada Mir Osman Ali Khan Bahadur, who is not yet three, is ill with the dreaded disease of malaria. Dr Watson, all of India knows of your skill in curing Her Majesty's soldiers. When Sir Mazhar heard that you were in Madras, he sent me straight to you, Sir, to entreat you to come to our aid, restore our prince to health and earn the gratitude of our beloved ruler, whose name itself is 'Beloved', and indeed of the millions who benefit under his kindly reign!"

I was rather pleased that, for the first time, an appeal was being made to me for help, rather than to Holmes. As I looked hesitantly in his direction, he leaned forward and said with a smile, "Watson, we cannot turn down an appeal for succour, and couched in such gracious terms. By all means, let us straight away go to the aid of the infant prince. India has not yet exhausted its fascination for me!" And so it was settled that we should entrain that very afternoon for Hyderabad.

The Paigah Prince, who conducted the affairs of the State of Hyderabad, had sent us his own railway saloon, a string of three long compartments done up sumptuously with gilt mouldings on the sides of the bogies, and with carved teak furniture inside, all covered in red velvet. Elegant chandeliers hung from the low ceilings of the living and dining rooms, which were flanked by our own bedrooms. One of the bogies contained the kitchen and servants quarters for our liveried attendants.

We were rather amused to see that all the heavy wooden shutters were pulled down as we skirted Blacktown and the Leprosy Hospital to the left, and we could not get a view of the countryside until we had pulled out of Perumbur. At Arkonam, we took the newly laid north-west line of Madras Railway, climbing the Eastern Ghats towards Poona. Gangs of workmen, with their wives and children, and their hastily constructed thatched shanties, lined the tracks, as the train puffed its way through the forested hills. It was slow going, but we were engrossed in the beautiful countryside that opened up before us. The windows were flung open, which resulted in a fine powdering of coal dust settling upon everything in the compartment. The servants would wipe the whole area clean every hour, while we took a shower in the wooden bathrooms to refresh ourselves. Later, as the daylight dimmed, we reached Guntakal, where the Great Indian Peninsular took charge of our saloon. We lowered the glass shutters, and settled down to as good a dinner as can be had as guests of royalty in India. I excused myself early, and left Holmes and Melkote discussing the excellence of the railways over port and cigars. The railways were the latest wonder in the country, and Melkote, throughout the long journey, kept up a detailed commentary on its many virtues. Sinking into a luxurious bed, I soon fell asleep, lulled by the gentle rocking of the train.

Around noon the next day, high on the Deccan Plateau, we inched over the new bridge spanning the Kistna, and reached Wadi where, alighting from the Bombay Express, we boarded new saloons attached to a special locomotive of the Nizam State Railway. We reached the Secunderabad Station in good time. As we pulled in, welcoming fog signals exploded under our wheels, the noise mixing with the clash of cymbals of the military brass band that had struck up. Melkote had made punctilious but florid arrangements for our welcome. Garlands of roses and marigolds were thrust round our necks, and obsequious flunkeys escorted us down a red carpet to the carriages that awaited us in the portico. We drove past a lake, said to have been built by a prince three hundred years ago, past gardens, and across the charming Musi River in which elephants and buffaloes were being bathed, and down an avenue wider than any I had seen in London. Glittering shops, topped by the shuttered residences of their owners, lined the way, which led to a magnificent four-pillared structure, whose minarets disappeared towards the sky. This was Charminar, built by a Muslim ruler, several hundred years ago, to commemorate his love for a Hindoo lady, after whom the city was named. In the retelling of this fable, we discovered a fairly pronounced romantic streak in our new-found friend.

Our guesthouse was the Chow Mahalla, or the "Four Palaces", grouped around a gracious garden, with

fountains in the Moghul style. It had been a former
residence of the Nizams, until the present ruler moved
back to an even older palace. We were shown into the
Aftab Mahal, a lovely long building with Corinthian
columns, Melkote needlessly apologizing for any
discomfort we might experience, and adding that he
would have felt happier to accommodate us in the
larger Afzal Mahal, but which, he was happy to say,
was being readied for the expected arrival of His Royal
Highness Prince Albert Victor—so named by Her
Gracious Majesty Herself, thankfully coming out of a
long seclusion of mourning—a prince, the heir of the
Prince of Wales, and the joy of Hyderabad, of India,
as much as of England. Thanking Melkote equally
profusely for all his hospitality, and assuring him that
we would not dream of incommoding the Duke of
Clarence by occupying Afzal Mahal, we shut the door
behind us, and after partaking of a light repast, went to
bed. I fell asleep wondering if I could save the infant
prince without all the support that an English hospital
could provide.

The next morning, Melkote's carriage met me soon
after breakfast. A short ride took me back towards the
river and the Purani Haveli palace of the Nizam, a large,
low U-shaped structure. The ailing child was in one of
the long wings to the side, skirted by a wide verandah
and shaded by low semi-circular arches. To keep the
sickroom cool, khus-thattis, made of a thick thatch
of aromatic roots, had been fixed to all the doors and
windows, and an attendant continually splashed water

on to them from large casks placed near the doors. Two other boys sitting in the verandah were pulling on punkah ropes to fan the prince inside.

As I descended from the carriage, a European who had been working at a low table set in the verandah bustled towards me with an outstretched hand. He was short and spare, with greying hair and moustache, and dressed in a plain white shirt and shorts. "You are very welcome, indeed, Dr Watson. I can't tell you how relieved I am to have some help, especially from a distinguished fellow doctor. I am Dr Lawrie, in charge of medical services in the State of Hyderabad. The condition of the prince is a cause of much concern, I can tell you."

The Scottish doctor's reputation was already well established in Indian medical circles, and I told him I was surprised I had been called in when he was at hand. He waved away what he took as a compliment, refusing to notice my discomfiture. Lawrie was also known to be a hard man to work with, authoritative and set in his views, and not taking kindly to help, or new ideas.

"I have been waiting these thirty minutes for your arrival," he said testily. "I have to make my rounds of the hospitals. Do go in and examine our patient." And with that brusque leave taking, he strode out of the room.

Liveried servants announced me into the sickroom, where three or four veiled women were looking after the invalid, stretched out in the middle of an enormous canopied bed of carved mahogany. On a divan beside the bed sat a beautiful lady, who dropped a muslin curtain as a veil on my entrance. She spoke to me slowly

in halting, heavily accented English, in what was clearly
a prepared speech.

"Dr Watson, I bid you very welcome. You come to save
my son, and for this act of kindness, His Highness and I
are always in your debt. I have already lost a son, my little
Faruq—it was the Will of God. We place every trust in
Dr Lawrie, but you are an expert in curing malaria, no? I
beseech you, kind Sir, to help me and my child. You will
find me not wanting in gratitude."

I was touched by the graciousness of this Indian lady,
who I knew from past experience would have found it
more natural to order than to request. I explained as best
as I could that, while we were all in God's hands, the
fell disease was a result of inhaling impure air, and great
care must be taken at all times to protect little children
from inhaling noxious airs—alas, too common in Indian
settlements. I said I was glad the room was redolent with
the heavy scent of attar. I felt the distended spleen of
the child as he lay feverish and drowsy, and confirmed
that it was indeed malaria that he suffered from. After
writing out a dietary regime for my little patient, I took
leave of the princess with a rather ungainly salaam, and
went out of the room and its cloying scents. A loud buzz
of mosquitoes rose from the water cask at the door,
and I brushed them away in annoyance, but not before
receiving a couple of bites on my face.

The rest of the day was spent in the company of
Holmes and Melkote, clambering over the ancient pile
of Golconda Fort, and examining its ingenious system
of aqueducts and cisterns. Melkote explained to us that

the famed Kohinoor diamond had been found in the now disused mines of the fort. The next day, I found my patient to be a good deal better, the fever having left him. With greater cheer, I mounted one of the ponies Melkote had left for me, and rode out to look at the beautiful tombs of bygone kings, which lay beyond a little wood on the outskirts of the city. After several dreamy hours spent in the Indian countryside, which I loved dearly, I returned to my rooms as dusk fell, a little more tired than I expected to be. Even as I sat for dinner, I knew I was getting a little fever, the course of which that night convinced me it was an attack of malaria. I took a strong dose of quinine at two in the morning, and fell into a deep sleep as dawn broke.

The next three days were spent in bed, but not idly. I puzzled over how the disease could have resurfaced just two days after my first visit to the sick prince. I had had malaria many times years before, during my military campaigns in the north of the country. It was known to linger years in the body, and emerge during bouts of weakness, but I had been very well, never better. I had had great successes in curing Her Majesty's officers and other ranks, by dispatching them immediately to the Himalayan foothills, where the pure air repaired the injury wrought by the fetid fumes of the cantonment. No matter what measures I took to keep the barracks clean, the unhygienic nature of the natives gave rise to unhealthy fumes. But the palaces of the Nizam, and my own quarters, were as clean and healthy as anyone could hope for in this world, so how did I contract the disease?

Could the breath of the child prince have caused it? This started me off on a new line of enquiry. The problem, more than malaria, gave me several restless nights.

Husein Khan, a young compounder, had been deputed to attend on me during my illness. He was very intelligent, knew instinctively when I needed something, and listened to me very attentively. I took him along, when I went back to visit the sick prince. I was perhaps a little irritable, having only just recovered myself. So I was unnecessarily harsh to the bhistee at the door, when I was assaulted by another swarm of mosquitoes. "Didn't I order you, badmash, to smoke out these infernal mosquitoes?" I shouted in rusty Urdu.

The man was trembling with fear, and knelt down to touch my feet. "Sahib Bahadur, I have never seen Huzur before!" he wailed. "It must have been that thief, Ramsingh, he never told me. He has taken the illness himself, and has been off duty for three days."

I brushed him aside and went in. The little prince was better, sitting up, and taking beef broth, which pleased me very much. As I left, I asked directions for Ramsingh's quarters, determining to visit this other patient.

The question that puzzled me now was: how had the bhistee Ramsingh caught the disease from the prince? He had never been permitted into the sick-room, his duty station being the verandah, to keep the khus-thattis wet and cool. The servants' quarters were a cluttered row of little rooms, but not as ill-ventilated as I had expected, nor were there open drains nearby. There was no perceptible stench, as is common in native quarters.

I examined Ramsingh, who was delirious with a high fever. After prescribing the necessary dosage of quinine, and after repeating my instructions slowly and clearly to his tearful wife, who stood with her sari pulled over her head and caught respectfully between her teeth, half hiding her face, I proceeded to inspect the area. The place was kept clean and washed, as I was told, by the orders of the Nizam himself. A large metal tank, filled with water, was used for this purpose. As I lifted the lid, a pestilential swarm of mosquitoes rose out to attack me. Angrily batting them aside, I told the clutch of servants round me to use an incense burner with sambrani, or frankincense, to drive them away, and instructed Husein Khan to see to it personally that it was done. Before I left for my residence, Husein Khan quietly pointed out the wriggly larvae of the mosquitoes in the tank, and suggested that standing water should not be allowed near homes. His remark kindled old memories.

That evening, as I sat over tea in the cool of the verandah outside my rooms, I drafted an urgent telegram to our landlady Mrs Hudson, at 221B, Baker Street, to send me posthaste certain papers and notebooks I kept in my drawers. The illness of the little prince, and of the bhistee Ramsingh, and my own surprising attack of malaria, had stirred certain doubts in me, and recalled to my mind certain long-forgotten case histories and half-completed experiments. I wished to refresh my memory by going over my casebooks of over twenty years ago.

The very next day I ordered that all the water casks on the verandah outside the prince's sickroom should be removed, and that after the khus-thattis had been fumigated by sambrani smoke, fresh water to keep them cool was to be brought in small earthen pitchers by a string of porters. Husein Khan seemed pleased. I thought no more of my instructions, until a furious Lawrie accosted me two days later at the Purani Haveli.

"I see, Sir, that you have countermanded my orders," he said abruptly. "To what purpose, pray? All the water casks have been removed, and the prince will stifle in the heat. I had not expected that a seasoned military doctor would be as squeamish about mosquitoes as a young woman fresh out of England!"

"I assure you, Dr Lawrie, I have instructed them to keep the room cool at all times," I said, biting back an angry retort at his needless innuendo. "I am following a particular line of enquiry, and do not wish to have insects around the sickroom."

"I am astonished, Sir, astonished, that an English doctor will forsake science for whims!" said Lawrie, who was beside himself with anger. "I will not tolerate such methods, Sir, I can tell ye. Sir, I shall speak my mind to the Nizam! If His Highness prefers your services to mine, then I wash my hands off all consequences that may befall the prince!"

I would not have brooked such insolence from a lesser man, but his unquestionable service to medicine came to mind, and bowing stiffly, I turned away, convinced that I should be politely asked to return to Madras before the day was out.[16] I was informing Holmes over dinner, rather ruefully, about my falling out with Lawrie, when

I received a large envelope with the Nizam's seal on it. Telling Holmes that this would be our dismissal, I opened it to find, to my astonishment, a very cordial invitation from His Highness, to join him and Her Highness a week from that day for tea, so that they might both thank me for the saving of the young prince's life.

We were warned by Melkote to expect something of a grand affair, and so it turned out. A host of young British officers from the garrison had also been invited. We were received rather formally in the durbar room, in the central, European part of the palace, with the princely couple at the head of the hall, and the child, who had fully recovered by now, on his mother's knee. His Highness, in European dress and a pink turban, was a large man with fine black whiskers framing a florid face, dominated by a long regal nose. The Begum was veiled, but her exquisitely moulded hands and large black eyes spoke of an unusual beauty. The Resident, Sir Dennis Fitzpatrick, a tall, saturnine man with a drooping moustache, put in a brief appearance, took a cup of tea, and then bowing to the royal couple, excused himself to attend to matters connected with the impending visit of His Royal Highness the Duke of Clarence.

The Nizam seemed to relax perceptibly upon the Resident's departure, and taking the toddler by the hand came up to me, saying, "Osman, child, you must thank the saviour of your life." The small child looked up wonderingly, and lisped his thanks, upon which I could not resist picking him up and kissing him. When I set him down, he gravely wiped his cheek with his hand,

and ran back to his mother. Everyone laughed, and the ice was broken.

"Dr Lawrie begs to excuse himself, Dr Watson," said the Nizam in an unnaturally hearty voice. "He is so busy attending to our hospitals."

The Begum of Hyderabad's eyes twinkled. "I have had prayers said in all our mosques and churches, and sent gifts to all our Hindoo temples. You must have some of this prasad, this offering from God. Did you know that my grandmother was a Hindoo, Dr Watson?"

"Zahra, we are all Hindoos until we see the light," said the Nizam, turning to his wife. "Indeed, Dr Watson, my Begum is the last gift left to me by the late Sir Tawab Ali Khan Bahadur Salar Jung, who was more a father to me than a Diwan. But come, the officers are anxious to present their wives to you, Zahra!"

A plump young Englishman came up to me hesitantly after the presentations, with an equally plump young wife, in a dress as blue as her eyes. "Dr Watson, it is an honour to meet you, Sir," he said. "I am Dr Ronald Ross, Acting Garrison Surgeon from Bangalore, and this is my wife, Bessie. We were married a few months ago in England, and she is very new to India, Sir. I was born here, in Almora, in fact."[17]

I looked at him with interest. His father had conducted himself with great honour during the Mutiny, and I said I was very glad to meet the son of such a distinguished man. "Yes, the pater's name is rather well known in these parts," he said with shy pride. "I believe, Sir, you saved the life of the heir to the Hyderabad throne. I, I look forward to learning some medical skills from you, Sir. My own methods are rather rough and ready. Oh, enough for our hardy boys, no doubt, but what I learnt at St Bartholomew's doesn't seem to have much application here. As a matter of fact, I was a rather bad student."

I laughed at this ingenuous admission, and seeing that Their Highnesses had withdrawn, we settled round an occasional table to feast upon the splendid repast in front of us. Dr Ross had come up in anticipation of the Duke of Clarence's visit, along with some polo players from the Bangalore Garrison. He had hesitated at the thought of bringing Bessie along, but had decided that she might enjoy the tamasha, so they had risked it.

"Oh, you are perfectly safe here, my dear," I said, now that we seemed on such easy terms. "Hyderabad is a very clean city, let me assure the both of you. But you should follow the Begum's example, you know. Wear a veil, and you may have no fear of malaria." I left them on that cryptic note, Ross declaring in a loud voice to his wife that I was one of the old Anglo-Indian hands, the very salt of the earth.

At my request, His Highness had quickly ordered a small laboratory to be set up next to my rooms. Husein Khan proved to be an excellent and knowledgeable assistant. Every day I would ride out to my patients among the servants' quarters in the Purani Haveli. I had been unable to save the life of Ramsingh, but I was determined to let no other person die. Apparently, he had first caught the disease after attending a cousin's wedding near Mir Alam Lake. I rode out to this beautiful lake, and visited Ramsingh's cousin's basti, at the rear of which was a large compound of milch water buffaloes. These large black animals seemed somehow to symbolize India—ungainly, impassive, resistant to all change, and yet strangely comforting. One day, I hoped, some modern Indian researcher would give them their due as the true symbols of India, rather than cows, which are an indifferent lot. The gowlas proudly showed me round the sheds. A few large buffaloes, imported from the Punjab, were kept in special sheds, where they were fed almonds to produce special cream for the Nizam's palace. While the animals placidly switched their tails from side to side to fan away flies and mosquitoes, I was constantly distracted by the insects, and as soon as possible made my way out of there. As a precaution against bites, Husein Khan had suggested that I cover all visible parts of my head under my sola topee and my hands, from my riding gloves to my cuffs, with a smelly paste of neem oil, rather repellent to me but unnoticed by the herdsmen.

The good Mrs Hudson had promptly dispatched my notebooks, and reviewing my earlier work, I was more convinced than ever that I had stumbled on the true cause of the disease. I spent several frustrating days in my laboratory, abandoning Holmes to his own devices.

Over dinner one evening, he let me know that he himself was preoccupied interviewing the Nizam's soldiers and their old fathers. It seemed he was intent on writing a monograph on the famous Battle of Assaye, which might throw fresh light on the real reasons why Wellington had been able to win such a crucial battle.

"Surely, Holmes, we need look no further than the Iron Duke's genius," I had said, dipping into a superb crème caramel pudding. "My dear Watson, more than genius is needed to achieve victory, certainly such a signal victory that settled the fate of hundreds of millions," said Holmes, who preferred the local mango to any work of art from the Nizam's kitchens. "You must remember that the Peshwa's large army had previously been thrashed by a smaller Mahratta force. Then, this same victorious Mahratta force was destroyed at Assaye by Wellington's miniscule army, supported by native irregulars. Historians have given most of the credit to the 78th Highlanders, as Wellington himself did. I take away nothing from their courage or honour, but the real victors were the 'Mahars', the untouchable irregulars, who fought under the British banner to settle scores with all those who treated them as less than animals."

Lighting his pipe, Holmes continued, "The strength of Empire rests on the forgotten shoulders of those made invisible by this caste-ridden Hindoo society. And now in the era of our English laws and letters, the poor in spirit are inheriting the earth. As a good Christian, you should surely appreciate this fact."

Consoling myself that Holmes was equally interested in staying on in the city, I fell to work attempting to unravel the mystery of malaria, trying to use the processes of logic so often demonstrated to me by my peerless friend. Husein Khan's quiet remarks had engendered a train of thought that convinced me that somehow the mosquito conveyed the disease to man, but how did it do it? Indians have always, good humouredly, thought us to be mad, and my antics they put down to English madness. However, every one of my instructions was faithfully carried out as if it were a commandment from on high. Several bags of annas were spent by me on volunteers who would agree to be bitten by the mosquitoes, which an army of ragamuffins collected zealously for me. Even the servants of the palace would come up to me with ill-concealed grins and sleeves rolled up, ready to be bitten by the insects. One greybeard even suggested that the Sahib might find it more interesting to have dancing girls bitten in certain luscious parts of their bodies. Records of every one of these volunteers were faithfully kept by Husein Khan, who seemed even more frustrated than I was becoming.

Ross had gamely tried to be of assistance, but his heart was not in the research, and he soon excused himself to join his bride at all the parties that his fellow officers arranged, as leading up to the British Prince's visit. One day, Husein Khan confidently said that only female mosquitoes drew enough blood to hatch their eggs. Upon examination I found this to be true, and congratulated the bright fellow. But all my dissections of their little bodies, carried out at all hours, over cups of hot coffee supplied in a constant stream from the kitchens, showed me nothing in particular. After some persuasion, and the expenditure of silver rupees, I had been able to extract blood samples from sepoy patients. The fear these brave men had for the hypodermic needle never failed to astonish me, but their resistance weakened as the fever took hold, and Husein

Khan and I were able to ascertain that the red blood cells of malaria patients contained a minute parasitic protozoa not found in healthy people. If the mosquito bite did not introduce these parasites, perhaps an enteric form of the disease entered their bodies through infected water I thought, although Husein Khan did not agree with this hypothesis. I drowned the insects by the hundreds, and my increasingly unenthusiastic volunteers lined up every morning, although no Hindoos would come, whatever the blandishment, for a decoction of the polluted water. But no one fell ill, and I began to be conscious of being pointed out in the streets to suppressed laughter as the "pagal", or mad, Sahib.

The arrival of the Duke of Clarence and his entourage was the magnificent event of the year. Several committeees of notables had gone over every event of each day of his stay with a fine-tooth comb. Every event had been rehearsed several times over. My powers of description can do little justice to the imperial grandeur of the occasion. The Prince's father, the Prince of Wales, had paid an official visit a dozen years ago to commemorate the Declaration of Her Majesty as Empress of India. Although his son was not on so official a visit, there was all the more occasion for several garden parties, polo matches, dances until dawn, drives into the countryside, and tiger hunts. All of the lavishly refurbished palaces were occupied by his vast retinue.

Holmes and I attended the parade at which he took the salute of the British troops in Hyderabad. The Prince was the very likeness of his grandfather, the late Prince

Consort, although of slighter build. Behind him stood
his close friend and equerry, Sir Frederick Challoner,
who at a distance could have been mistaken for the
Prince, possessing as he did the same Saxe-Coburg
nose and the deep-set brooding eyes. Prince "Eddie",
as he was affectionately called by the popular press, and
Challoner had been coached as boys by the Reverend
Dalton, later Canon of Windsor, and both had served
together on the *Britannia* as midshipmen and later
shared digs at Trinity College, Cambridge. They were
said to be inseparable, and this had caused comment, not
always wholesome. Challoner's unmistakable likeness to
the Prince, the Prince of Wales's romantic adventures,
a source of common gossip in the yellow press, had led
to rumours that the commoner was one of "Bertie's by-
blows". An incautious comment uttered in Challoner's
regimental mess had resulted in a meeting one morning
on a beach near Lisbon, from which only Challoner had
returned. Although applauded by the wilder sort, he had
had to resign his commission, but the Prince had insisted
graciously on taking on his friend as equerry.

Later that evening, at a garden party given by the
Resident, we were introduced to the Prince. "Mr
Holmes, Mr Sherlock Holmes?" enquired the Prince.
"Sir, we needed you in London, to solve these damnable
murders committed by Jack the Ripper. That monster
must be found, but with you in India, we all live in fear
of our lives!"

"Your Royal Highness does me too much honour,"
said Holmes smoothly. "At Scotland Yard's explicit

request I did attempt to use my poor powers to lay the villain by the heels, but with little success, Sir. He is a cold-blooded murderer, but so far he has preyed only on fallen women, God forgive them!"

A shiver ran through the circle of ladies around the Prince. "I am very glad I am in Hyderabad," said a high-pitched voice, rather careless of the implications. The Prince questioned Holmes, who gave clear but short answers about the sorrowful events we had left at home. Jack the Ripper, as he was fearfully called, mutilated the wretches he killed in a chillingly skilful manner. Holmes had taken me along one night in 1888, to look at the body of poor Annie Chapman, slaughtered in a narrow fog-ridden lane in Whitechapel. I had examined her body with horror, by gaslight in the police mortuary. For all her sins, she had not deserved to come to such a terrible end. If a crazed surgeon was the culprit, Holmes had hoped I might recognize a colleague's handiwork by examining the incisions. It was clear that they had been expertly done—although for some twisted, ghoulish purpose— but who had done it I could not say, save for hazarding a guess that the perpetrator could have been left-handed. The memory of that evil night still haunted me.

The Prince turned to lighter topics, and as I moved away thankfully, I saw Detective Inspector Burrows, who was in attendance on the Prince's entourage, give me a strange fixed look that I was to recollect later. As night fell, brilliant fireworks were set off in front of the beautiful Georgian structure of the Residency, to the great delight of the ladies. Sir Dennis, the Resident, then invited us into the building, where we were served cocktails, even as a regimental band struck up. A very pleasant evening followed for all the young people. After escorting a couple of ladies to the dance floor, as was my duty, I settled down in an antechamber to play bridge with some older officers. We soon discovered we all had mutual friends, and recollections of older times took us well past midnight.

Feeling the need to sustain the inner man, I had gone to the dining room, where several hundred excellent dishes were laid out, when Ronald Ross came looking for me in some agitation. "Dear Dr Watson, I have been looking for you—to take your advice. I really don't know what to do. Beyond my experience, y'know, but Bessie is very uncomfortable, and I must collect her, without giving offence, y'know? Devilish tricky to know what to do, y'know?"

I could see the young man was in the throes of acute jealousy, and he would not listen to my advice to eat something. The Prince had been dancing with Bessie, had danced several dances with her, in fact, and Bessie, a little—a lot—out of her depth, had cast despairing glances at Ross. With Ross in tow, I went in search of Melkote, whom I found laughing happily in the middle of a circle of admiring ladies. Extracting him from their care, I marched towards the dancing Prince, and heedless of etiquette, I interrupted him.

"Your Royal Highness, permit me to present Diwan Sahib Melkote, Shankar Narayan Rao," I said in an unnecessarily loud voice, much to the annoyance of the group around him, but I did not care. "He has single-handedly taken it upon himself to clear Her Majesty's domains of the scourge of malaria, and I am here to assist him. And this is Dr Ronald Ross, Acting Garrison Surgeon from Bangalore, and the husband of your charming partner."

The Prince was all accommodation. With a gracious bow to the lady, and a word of praise to Ross about his wife's exquisite dancing skills, he turned gravely to Melkote and plied him with questions about the dangers posed by malaria to common people. In a few minutes, others led the Prince away, and we rejoined the Rosses to find Bessie mildly remonstrating with her husband. "No, really Ronny, His Royal Highness was all graciousness, truly. He, he was very good—in fact he rescued me from—from, well, Ronny, you won't understand. But let's go home. I am tired."

The flustered young doctor could get no more out of his wife, who just laughed, thanked me eloquently with a look, and firmly guided him towards their carriage. I wouldn't have given it a second thought, had I not caught Detective Inspector Burrows fixing me again with that strange look of his. But I was tired, and my brain a little befuddled with wine; so I hardly made out what Sir Frederick Challoner meant when he hallooed to me as I got into my carriage.

"Watson! An old campaigner like you should know enough to keep the 'baggage' and savants in the middle of a well-guarded square when on the march. Look out next time!" With a raffish laugh, he flung himself onto

his horse, and galloped away recklessly into the night.
As I was driven home, wondering about Burrows and
Challoner, I dropped off in the cool night air, and had to
be helped to bed by my syce.

The Nizam's entertainment of the Prince was even
more lavish. Synchronized invitations were issued by
all the Nawabs and Rajahs under the Nizam to parties,
outings, musical concerts, hunts, and dances. Merriment
was organized for every moment of the waking day, and
often for most of the night as well. India's wealth of
craftsmanship was poured at the feet of our visitors, with
jewellers, tailors, carpet weavers, and gunsmiths taking
their orders in the morning, and returning by evening
to delight their exalted customers. Whatever puritanical
values I had inherited from my strict Low Church
upbringing had long since eroded under indulgent Indian
skies. As I turned in, in the wee hours of morning, my
ears would continue to ring with the sounds of the sitar,
the sarod, or the veena, and even in sleep I seemed to see
and hear soft, naked female feet twirling on the parquet
dance floors.

With dogged determination I kept to my research,
ignoring as many invitations as I politely could. A rash
of malaria cases had broken out in a slum to the south
of Charminar, mostly among construction workers
building a majestic new palace on a hill for the Paigah
noble, Nawab Vikar-ul-Umra Bahadur. I had visited it a
few times out of curiosity. The palace was in the classical
European style with a two-storeyed colonnaded verandah,
with Ionic and Corinthian columns. At the rear, a six-

hundred-foot-long courtyard led to a round hall, or Gol Bungla, and a glass-roofed verandah overlooked the expanse below. The interior was being furnished in the style of Louis Quatorze.

However magnificent the building, the workers and stone cutters lived in deplorable conditions, with malaria carrying away many a person of sturdy constitution. While attending to my patients, Husein Khan happened to notice a strange-looking mosquito, with dappled wings. A few landed in a glass jar I had left open, which he quickly sealed and carried back to our laboratory. Some instinct made me dissect the insects carefully, micron by micron. But I found nothing. When I was resting, I heard a sharp yell from Husein Khan. He showed me through the microscope a perfectly formed circular cell in the stomach of the last mosquito, a cell I had never seen before. I tingled with excitement. Could this belong to the parasitic protozoa I had found earlier in the men ill with malaria? If so, how did it develop within a mosquito, and how did the insect transmit it to man?

Husein Khan called my little band of "malaria irregulars" to the laboratory, showed them the dapple wings, and said they would be richly rewarded for all such insects they could gather. Within two days I had as many as I needed. As I fell to dissecting them, I was soon assured that this had been no chance discovery, but that this mosquito, which stood like a dart about to inflict a bite worse than death on unsuspecting persons, indeed carried a parasite in its body. But was it the malarial

parasite I had found in people? I could not sleep at night
for worry and excitement.

Around three o'clock one morning, after restlessly
tossing in my bed, I went out into the large garden in the
middle of our four palaces, and sat on a marble seat by
the fountain to reflect calmly how I might establish facts,
one way or the other. I had long since ceased to pay heed
to the sounds of laughter, squeals, and running feet that
filled most of the nights with youthful merriment. But
my reverie was suddenly broken by a piercing scream,
a scream of mortal terror, which came from behind a
curtain of bushes not far to the left. I stumbled towards
it, when rounding a tree I saw a short, sharp tussle
among figures in the dark, and then a shape broke away
and fled into the night, but not before a gleam of light
flashed on the back of a Hussar jacket. As I came up, the
figures resolved into those of my friend Melkote and the
trembling form of a swooning girl he was holding up.
Holmes had also appeared suddenly out of the darkness,
and without a word we carried the girl back to my
laboratory, which could double as a surgery.

In the yellow flare of the gaslights, I saw that the girl
was none other than the vivacious Meherunnissa, the
famed Kathak dancer from Gulbarga, who had been the
toast of Hyderabad over the last three weeks. I feared for
her life as we laid her down on the table, for she had bled
copiously, drenching her own silk dress and Melkote's
sherwani with her blood. But I was soon reassured—the
wounds were not life threatening. Her jewelled jacket
had been ripped apart, exposing a part of her left breast,

but except for an abrasion there she was uninjured. A superficial cut above the jugular in her neck had caused the most damage, but she seemed to have saved herself by instinctively flinging up an arm, her gold bangles taking most of the blow.

I gave her some laudanum to ease the pain and shock, and then quickly stitched up the wound, bandaging her neck with fine gauze to staunch the bleeding. Her terrified eyes rolled from one of us to the other; she was clearly in no condition to answer our questions. Within minutes, her own attendants had arrived, and without a word to us, they carried her away. As Melkote made to follow, I mumbled some incoherent question. He turned to me with a strange, wild look. "Honi soit qui mal y pense, doctor," he said, before vanishing into the night.

As Holmes turned to leave, he asked me quizzically, "Notice anything about the cut?

He knew as well as I did. "Surgical type incision," I murmured. "Undoubtedly left-handed."

Who had the mad assailant been? I thought I had seen the red jacket of a Hussar, officer or soldier, but I could not be sure. If I had glimpsed the facings, I would have spotted the regiment in a trice. The thought that hesitantly crossed my mind as I drifted asleep was whether it might have been the Prince's own.

The next morning the city was told that the beautiful Meherunnissa and her large troupe of musicians, dance masters, cooks, and attendants had left for Gulbarga, without a word of farewell. Neither the incident, nor her departure were ever mentioned again, and the merrymaking continued as usual, but I sensed a certain tension in the air, a brooding darkness that none of us were quite able to shake off.

Fearing the questions that came unasked to my mind, I plunged into my work like a drowning man clutching at straws. Husein Khan rediscovered in the blood stream of my patients the round or oval cells we had first seen in the stomachs of my dapple wings, which had clearly sucked them in with their meal of blood. I saw these strange cells fertilized, and Husein Khan showed me that they penetrated into the mid-gut wall of the mosquito to form a cyst. I saw the cysts rupture and release spores. Did these spores reach the insect's salivary glands, and could they, reinjected into people, recreate the malarial parasitic protozoa? I needed more time, more instruments, and above all, more luck to be sure.

An invitation from Melkote to enjoy a party and witness a play broke into the morbid train of my thoughts. On the few occasions that I had been to his devdi before, I had been cordially entertained in a cosy little room downstairs, with much of the mansion shuttered and in darkness. On the eve of the party, however, it was ablaze with light, and strains of violins wafted from the windows. As we trooped in, we were delighted to find every part of the house a sample of intricate craftsmanship, from the carved balustrades to the mosaics on the walls, and the colourful tiles on the floors. Level by level, Melkote led us through a house that was more a museum than a residence, until we reached a large open courtyard on the third floor, with deep, covered verandahs on all sides.

The verandah at the end was clearly decorated as the stage; the one on the right had divans for the musicians, and the other on the left had large tables laden with refreshments. Chairs were arranged in the middle for the guests who would form the audience for the evening's entertainment. Since the Prince was not expected for some time, we moved about laughing and chatting, while servants carrying trays of canapés and drinks stood at our elbows. The gaiety of the evening drove away the devils of the day before.

Wishing to explore the roof of this old devdi, I went up a curved wrought-iron staircase, to emerge under the stars of a beautiful evening. I was surprised to find that my only other companion on the roof was a short, dumpy girl, of about ten, in an old-fashioned long-sleeved, full-length frock, sitting on a ledge beside a flowerpot, and busily scribbling into a notebook.

"Hello!" I said softly, so as not to alarm the child. "I didn't think anyone would be here. I am Dr Watson, a friend of your papa's."

The child looked at me gravely, and without the least trace of embarrassment. "I think you mistake me for one of the Melkote children," she said easily, in perfectly good English. "My papa is a very distinguished man, whom I don't think you know. He is Professor Aghoranath Chattopadhaya, the Principal of the Nizam College, the best in the country. I am Sarojini. How do you do, Dr Watson."[18]

We shook hands gravely. Not wanting to be snubbed by a chit of a girl, I said, "And what are you doing here all by yourself, Sarojini? Someone should be here with you, you know?"

"Well, you are with me," she said matter-of-factly. "I am here because I want to compose a poem about Hyderabad at night. A poet must actually experience, and not just make up things, don't you agree? My father says so in any case."

I agreed that her father was a wise man, and asked to hear her poem.

"I am still struggling with some phrases," she said, jumping up. "But I think I know how to end it. Over the city bridge, Night comes majestical, borne like a queen to a sumptuous festival. Just the right note, don't you think? Dr Watson, will you lead me downstairs? I so want to see the play."

With this strange serious child on my arm, I went down to the sound of the arrival of the Prince. After refreshments and another round of drinks, we seated ourselves in a semi-circle to watch the play. Melkote, a man of varied parts, declared himself devoted to the amateur stage.[19] To please His Royal Highness, the Little Theatre of Hyderabad would stage select scenes from Dumas' masterpiece, *The Three Musketeers*. A loud and carefree hurrah went up from the audience, who were almost all from the forces, and we settled down in expectation of slapstick and farce. Melkote's production did not disappoint us. Gales of laughter welcomed him and the other musketeers clip-clopping across the verandah on gaily beribboned hobbyhorses. The slapstick and the loud theatricals were everything one could wish for on an evening dedicated to thoughtless enjoyment. But imperceptibly the mood seemed to change, grow more serious, more contemptuous of the audience. The giggles and the sniggers subsided until in utter silence, we watched the final scene of retribution for Madame de Winter. The stage darkened, and the ominous figures of the musketeers gathered round the red-clad figure of the lonely woman with drawn swords. As a knife flashed upwards, and the actress screamed horribly, the Prince sprang up with a loud cry, asking for a light.

A hundred lamps were lit instantly, and Melkote was at the Prince's elbow, with a solicitous glass of brandy and soda. "Ladies and gentlemen, I beg your pardon," said the Prince shakily. "I took the shadows for reality. You must admit, Mr Melkote, it was all too realistic by half! Wretch as she was, she did not deserve to die so…"

The mood was broken. Everyone soon discovered they needed to go home. With hurried goodbyes, we thanked Melkote, and made our way out of the mansion. "What did it all mean, Holmes?" I asked, as we said a sober goodnight on the verandah outside our rooms.

"Oh, Shankar Melkote is a thespian of the highest order." said Holmes. "I am sure he knows his *Hamlet* better than most Englishmen. And the play is the thing, right, Watson, to catch the conscience of the king?"

It is not only women who overeat when they are unhappy. Unconsciously, I started to gorge myself on every dish that was brought to the table. Spiced Nellore fish, roasted quail, pattar-ki-gosth, mutton biryani, mirchika-salan, aubergines in Hyderabadi gravy, Lucknowi shish kebabs, and khubani, that delicious comfit of gently stewed apricots under an inch-thick layer of fresh cream, all followed one another, until I went down with a touch of liver. Luckily, my robust constitution saved me the ignominy of a stomach pump, and as I sat, three days later, nursing my conscience and my liver, Husein Khan suggested that that long-suffering part of the body held the clue. Religious sentiment forbids the performance of autopsies in India, but luckily for science, the poor and nameless also die of malaria. Husein Khan and I found what I was looking for in the liver cells of a dead man. The circle of infection and death was clear to my mind. I was now sure that malaria was not caused by poisons in the air, as hitherto thought, but by a parasite that infected a person's red blood cells. Further, my assistant Husein Khan had helped me to see that the parasite was transmitted from one sick person to another through a mosquito bite, enabling it to travel through the bloodstream to the liver, and then extend its deadly infection to all red blood corpuscles from there.

Before I could gather my thoughts and findings, which I wished to place before Ross, we were swept away to an elaborate tiger hunt organized by the Nizam himself. A keen sportsman, he had draped half the walls of his palace with tiger skins, while several more skins were laid end to end to lead up to the throne. The hunt was to be taken up on the heavily forested Srisailam Hills on both sides of the Kistna, a few days' march from the city. The encampment for the shikar was itself a splendid city on the move. All the luxuries of the palace were provided in our tents. We walked on Persian carpets, ate at tables groaning with silver and crystal, slept on the softest beds under fine linen, and hot water was available for a wash at any time of day or night.

The royal elephants, stripped of the finery in which they were decked in the city, carried shooting howdahs to which we could clamber up by short ladders slung on the elephants's sides. The howdahs were wickerwork affairs, from which one could shoot, sitting or standing. Bags of sandwiches and flasks of tea could be strapped to the sides. Five or six elephants would lead the hunt, with the most important personages on them, while gunbearers and shikaris followed in close order. As the elephants pushed through the heavy undergrowth, a line of beaters, local villagers who were paid an anna a day, would make enough noise to raise the devil at the other end of the forest, driving the animals towards the hunters. The trick was to let the small deer, and even the leopards, leap past, and wait until a tiger broke cover.

Over the next ten days, we hunted a very considerable number of tigers. One chase was particularly memorable. Even in death, the animal was magnificent, measuring twelve feet between pegs. No other gun but the Prince's, averred knowledgeable shikaris, could have fired the fatal shot, and at the Nizam's insistence, the Prince graciously accepted the kill. A spur of the hills had never been shot over, so it was decided against better judgement, during the last days of the shikar, to try combing up the hill. The dense forest soon separated our elephants,

scattering us almost out of sight of each other. Before
the experienced could call us to order, a most dreadful
incident took place.

The Prince's elephant was in the lead, and was
struggling to clamber over a large granite rock, when
a tiger hidden in a cave underneath sprang full upon
its neck with an awful roar, pulling down the hapless
mahout. Even as the Prince fired unhesitatingly at the
beast, his elephant stumbled, pitching him almost on
top of the wounded animal. His gun knocked out of his
hands, the Prince grappled with the tiger, desperately
slashing at the beast's neck with his hunting knife. He
could not have long sustained the unequal encounter,
but for rescue from an unexpected quarter. Holmes's
elephant, a tusker that stood nine feet at the shoulder,
was fifty yards away. At the instant the tiger appeared,
he turned and charged, bearing down on the tiger like
an express train, only to come to a rock-steady stop
upon command. A tall, dark soldier sprang from its
howdah, and swinging under its upraised trunk, with a
hand on a tusk, shot the tiger through the head in the
coolest manner.

The Prince was on his feet even before we reached
him, covered from head to foot in the blood of the beast
and the dead mahout. He was badly shaken, but game.
"Ah, Dr Watson, see if you can do anything for that
poor wretch of a mahout," he said with a nervous laugh.
"I am all right, thank you. How I wish I could save lives
like you, but my profession as a prince, it seems, is to
take life." And with that, he flung away in disgust the

knife he held in his left hand. Turning to Holmes, he asked, "And who is my saviour, Mr Holmes? Surely I would be dead there, between the tiger and the mahout, but for him."

"This is Subedar Ambadvekar, of the Mahar Regiment, Your Royal Highness," said Holmes soberly.[20] "A soldier and a scholar, and among the best in Her Majesty's army. In my short stay here, I have learned much from him, and now he has saved the future King Emperor himself!"

"Thank you, Subedar Sahib," said the Prince, shaking hands with his deliverer. "Would you please join me for a cup of tea this evening in my tent?"

The Subedar bowed with dignity. "Your Royal Highness does me too great an honour," he said slowly, but distinctly, in English. "Perhaps it is right I inform you that I am an untouchable?"

"Sir, none but the cowardly and the treacherous are untouchable," said the Prince in an emotionally charged voice. "There, I have left blood marks on you. We must be brothers."

A shikari held up the dead tiger for all to admire. "His Royal Highness almost killed it single-handed," he exclaimed. I saw that the knife thrust had almost severed the animal's jugular with a neat surgical incision.

"Well, one learns something, dressing deer in the Highlands," said the Prince carelessly, and so ended a momentous day. In celebration of the Prince's miraculous escape, a tribal dance was arranged the next evening, in the clearing of a nearby village. The drums and the dancing, and the heady mahua toddy that was handed round in mud pots, sent several of us into a hypnotic trance, in which the past and the present appeared to have fused together. For a moment I thought I was in the arms of my dead wife, miraculously restored to life, but the hay on which we lay pricked my nose, and I saw it was only a laughing bare-breasted tribal belle who was making sport of me. She went away good-naturedly, and I shut my throbbing eyes to sleep it off.

I was rudely shaken awake, and found Holmes, Burrows, Ambadvekar, and Melkote staring down at me. "Watson, we need you, if we are to avert a terrible tragedy," hissed Holmes. "Come, man, pull yourself together." There was no time for questions. The five of us were to comb the surrounding woods as noiselessly as we could. The campfires had almost all died down, a few village dogs barked far away, and I could see that most of our party had ridden back to our camp. So I simply could not understand what we were doing that cold silent night, walking through the black forest around a distant tribal village. Treading carefully, lest I step on a snake, I made my way softly through the trees, uncertain what I was supposed to look for.

A sharp cry, and a loud hallo, ended all uncertainty, and I ran as fast as I could towards the thrashing sound of heavy bodies struggling in the undergrowth and cursing furiously. In the waving light of the lanterns held by Holmes and Melkote, I saw that Ambadvekar had the Prince pinned helplessly to the ground, no—by God! It was Sir Frederick Challoner, wearing a Hussar jacket of a bygone era! Under a tree, an almost naked tribal girl was sobbing, trying to stop the blood flowing from deep incisions over her breasts.

"She never loved me, she never cared!" howled Challoner. "The pater gave up long ago. God! I tried...but it was no use, she never stayed home, she never cared!"

Even as I was tearing up my shirt to bandage the poor girl, Holmes went across and slapped Challoner twice sharply, to stop his howling and frustrated cursing. Melkote took charge of the girl, and led her gently away, back to her village, his pashmina shawl draped around her body.

"Challoner, I suppose you know what to do," said Holmes coldly. "You don't want to sully your family name any further."

"Yes, I know there was a Challoner at Hastings, and another at Crecy," said the man listlessly. "God, it was always being thrown at me, don't you know? And the bishops on every side, but bloody hypocrites, all of them! And the mater, with that awful man..." He was weeping inconsolably now.

Holmes looked at the wretch without pity. "Tomorrow it must end, Challoner," he said.

"It is not all that hard, Sir," said Burrows gently, "and it will give you peace, I know." With that, the four of us walked away, leaving Challoner slumped against a tree.

After the tribal dance of the previous night, none stirred in our party until after lunch. At teatime we decided to shoot some ducks at a nearby lake. They came in curving flights as the sun was setting, and we must have shot a few hundred brace, when a most unfortunate

accident occurred. Sir Frederick Challoner, in his haste
to reload, forgot that one chamber was already loaded.
The shot took him in the mouth. The Prince responded to
the death of his friend with fortitude. We buried the
pitiful remains under a wooden cross on a hill overlooking
the lake.[21]

All festivities were cancelled for the period of
mourning, and the Nizam ordered that flags would fly at
half-mast for a week. The Prince felt compelled to shorten
his visit, the Nizam understood with heartfelt sorrow, and
the royal entourage departed for Calcutta to keep their
appointment with Lord Lansdowne, the Viceroy.

We had taken our leave of the Nizam and his Begum.
Holmes, Melkote, and I sat in the bar of the Nizam Club
the next evening, to share a farewell drink.[22] I broke the
long silence with some effort.

"What went wrong, do you think?" I asked of no one
in particular.

Melkote did not speak a word. Holmes smoked in
silence for a long time. "You may remember I spent a few
weeks recuperating in Switzerland a few years ago, after
my encounter there with Professor Moriarty," he said at
long last. "I was nursed back to health in the home of my
old friend, Pastor Johannes Jung of Kesswil. During a
select supper for some other religious men and doctors,
I presented a monograph of mine on that strange organ,
the human mind. For some time I had been trying to
understand the mind of that evil professor, and the
other criminals we had brought to book. Was there a
way of curing them? Early on, I had come to realize

we cannot change anything unless we accept it—that condemnation does not liberate, it oppresses. I said at that supper that there is a vast outer realm and an equally vast inner realm; between the two stands Man, now facing one way, now the other. We have little knowledge of our unconscious mind. Our conscious mind bobs around on a vast sea of passions, of fears, of ideals, that sometimes rise unbidden, to overwhelm us. In each of us is hidden primitive archetypes of bygone ages, untamed by civilization, resentful of hurt, willing to kill. No one took me very seriously at that supper, except, perhaps, the dreamy son of my friend, who, child though he was, wrote down almost everything I said.[23] This case brings my remarks back to mind. Being sniggered at as 'Bertie's by-blow'[24] must have hurt Challoner somewhere deep in his unconscious; he longed for his mother, but she had no use for her boy, or her husband, for that matter. She would rather be the royal mistress. Where love rules, there is no will to power, and where power predominates, love is lacking. The one is the shadow of the other."

"I wish we had understood much earlier," I said. "We might have prevented a great deal of misery. All those poor women..."

"Yes, the devil of it is that women don't trust men, they don't believe we can understand, and most times we don't," said Holmes sorrowfully. "Even Bessie Ross wouldn't tell us that night, at the Residency, that she had been rescued from Challoner's dangerous advances by the Prince. She would rather not speak of it than get Ross working himself into a tizzy."

"Why was he wearing that strange old jacket?" asked Melkote thoughtfully.

Holmes sighed. "It was his father's military jacket. He was acting out some mad fantasy. God keep us all sane." And with that, we went in for a silent dinner.

Before turning in that night, I said, "Holmes, my work is completed, and I am ready to leave for Madras. Are you? Is your monograph on the Assaye ready?"

"Oh, it is ready. Has been ready for some time," said Holmes casually. "But I shan't be publishing it, or reading it in any learned society. The world is not ready to hear that the lowly win battles without the help of the great, or that they can get along without most of us. I have given the manuscript to my friend, Subedar Ambadvekar, and one day it may help his people write a truer history of their country!"

I delivered a large trunk full of my notes to Ross next morning, as he and Bessie were trussing up their luggage to leave for Bangalore. I explained as carefully as I could the details of my investigations into the causes and progress of malaria. I emphasized to him my full belief that the dapple wing mosquito was the vector for the disease. Ross listened to me respectfully, but a little blankly.

"Ross, don't throw away my notebooks," I said with a sigh. "If I stayed in this country, I would go on to prove that malaria is caused by a particular mosquito bite. I would prove it in every medical forum. But my time is past. As you examine your patients, you may come to see that there is some truth in what I say."

"Treat your notebooks with the greatest respect," stammered Ross. "Like an heirloom, in fact. Greatest respect, although, as a matter of fact, right now it does look as if noxious fumes have some effect, what? I mean to say, malaria, bad air, all that sort of thing?" he added with simple honesty. I wished them both well, kissed Bessie, and reminding her to wear a veil, made my way back to my rooms.

My effects were packed by lunchtime. As was my custom before a long journey, I had ordered a lunch of thick mulligatawny soup, steak and kidney pie, an omelette, some cheese and fruit. "Holmes!" I yelled. "Lunch is served, and if we don't want to miss the Madras Express connection at Wadi, we had better start as soon as we finish lunch. Melkote has kindly arranged for a saloon and engine to be readied for us at the station."

Holmes entered the dining room with a strange young fellow, wearing very thick glasses and a floppy brown moustache that fell over his mouth. I remembered having seen him at several parties, but we had had no occasion to meet.

"We may have to change our plans and go north if Mr Kipling is to be believed," said Holmes wryly. "Oh, this is Mr Rudyard Kipling, assistant editor of *The Pioneer*, published from Allahabad. He was here ostensibly to cover the Prince's visit, but in reality to carry out an extraordinary mission. But perhaps, he should speak for himself?"[25]

Over lunch, Kipling explained that he had undertaken a secret mission for the Chief Commissioner of the Central

Provinces, Sir Alexander Mackenzie. The great forests
of Central India stretched far down into the Nizam's
domains, their tribal populations shared a common
culture, worshipped the same primitive Gods, and owed
allegiance to the same leaders. What he had learnt very
discreetly in Hyderabad had confirmed the worst fears
entertained by Sir Alexander, and his government.

"There is something brewing in the forests of Seoni,"
said Kipling soberly. "We don't know the half of it. The
tribals are arming. They are getting money, and, worse,
some unknown religious leader is fanning their hatred
against the Crown. If it erupts, or rather *when* it erupts,
it will be far worse than 1857. No white woman will be
safe between Calcutta and Madras. The Crown needs
your help, Mr Holmes, and yours, Dr Watson. You have
an enviable reputation for finding the criminal, and there
is no greater one than the fiend who is fanning the flames
between Damoh and Rajnandgaon!"

I had been looking forward to putting up my feet in
our little study in Baker Street, but you can always get
around an old soldier by appealing to his patriotism.
I nodded unwilling acceptance of this new task, in an
unknown part of the country, far from even the figment
of civilization offered by Madras, but that, as Kipling
would say, is another story.

The Naga Baiga of Moogli Hills

Kipling, Holmes, and I informed the stationmaster that we would be leaving a little later for Wadi, not to catch the train for Madras, but the one going up to Bombay. This was certainly the long way round to Nagpur, but there was as yet no rail link between Hyderabad and Nagpur. It gave us a couple of extra days to rest from our latest exertions, and listen carefully to the extraordinary tale Kipling had to tell. The police under the Chief Commissioner of the Central Provinces had declared themselves baffled, although reports had reached them from several quarters, mostly late at night, through informers who feared for their own lives, that an insurrection was being planned on a scale never before envisaged, or thought possible, in the remote vastness of the Central Indian jungles.

The insurrection, if indeed one was being planned, was being organized with skill and secrecy, well beyond the powers of the simple feudatory Indian Rajahs and Zamindars, who ruled over their vast estates that covered about half of the territories under the command of the Chief Commissioner. A European hand had to be at the bottom of it; and yet the only foreigners in those remote

and trackless parts were a few German, American, and
Scandinavian missionaries, all of whom had been put
under close surveillance after reports of the planned
insurrection were confirmed. No incriminating evidence
was found, even after the most thorough of interrogations
was carried out with the help of some informants in their
congregations. The Chief Commissioner was convinced
we had to look elsewhere for the source of the mischief,
but in what direction, and for whom? Certainly, reports
indicated that "religious symbols" were being used to
promote disaffection among tribals, and this was itself an
extraordinary train of events; for the tribal, be he Gond,
Baiga, Korku, Muria, or Khond, follows simple animistic
beliefs, which do not lend themselves to the kind of
proselytizing for war that the Mahdi had been capable
of, leading to the martyrdom of "Chinese" Gordon a
few years ago in Khartoum. Even more unbelievable was
the possibility that the two million or so tribals in the
vast jungles of the Central Provinces could be brought
under one banner, especially for revolt, since it was well
known that they kept to small groups of families even
within their own tribe; that cooperation between tribes
occurred only in the pursuit of customary practices; and
that any protest against authority was always made by
these simple people in a straightforward manner, by one
or two leaders who never showed any deceit or secrecy
in their dealings. In fact, it had been their honesty of
practice that had led, in a few cases, to their exploitation
by unscrupulous Indians living on the plains, which
British officers had been ever vigilant to prevent.

Once in Bombay, we thought it would be only courteous to call on Baron Reay, the Governor, before proceeding inland. We were given immediate permission for our visit, most cordially received, and closely questioned about the unfortunate events leading to Sir Frederick Challoner's death. Baron Reay listened to Kipling with close attention, on being informed of the purpose of our journey, and formally offered all help that lay in his power.

The railway track at Bhusawal splits into two branches, the northern section going to Jubbulpore, while the southern arm extends to Nagpur. East of these two cantonments, the Bengal–Nagpur Railway was being extended to link up to Allahabad in the north, as well as make a direct rail connection through the trackless jungles of Chattisgarh to Calcutta. But so far only a narrow gauge line had been built between Nagpur and Rajnandgaon, well to the west of Raipur. Work was also feverishly in progress on the Umeria branch, which would connect Jubbulpore through Katni with Bilaspur. But the important towns of Nagpur, with a thousand or so Europeans, including the regiments in Kamtee, and Jubbulpore with thrice as many Europeans, depended on one single road over the Satpura range through the dense jungles of Seoni, which could easily be cut by a determined foe, leaving either, or both towns, exposed and in extreme jeopardy.

These were the worries that Kipling had shared with us during our journey, and brought up again, as we waited to see Sir Alexander Mackenzie, the Chief

Commissioner, at Government House, below Seminary Hills in Nagpur.[26] Summer had set in early, and we felt the heat even in the deep verandah as a sheet of hot light reflected off the red murram gravel. The chaprasi came to fetch us, and we entered a large, cool office, where twin brocaded punkahs fanned out water particles from dripping khus-thattis.

The Chief Commissioner came straight to the point, laying out what information he had at his disposal, the various conjectures made by his subordinates, and the precautions he had ordered to be taken. "Mr Kipling, the information you gathered in the south, while visiting Hyderabad, only confirms our worst fears. Somehow, someone has been able to influence the sentiments of our varied tribal populations; imbue them with a spirit of disaffection, and defiance to authority; and even more surprising, and equally alarming, this person, or gang of unscrupulous persons has managed to organize so many disparate tribes into a potential army. Despite our best efforts, we have still no inkling of their plans; and we do not know when or where they will strike. Our most exposed lifeline is the long, tortuous road over the Satpuras connecting Nagpur with Jubbulpore. It can be cut at a thousand places at any time. My forces are stretched to the utmost. It is just not possible to protect such a vast region without additional British troops. Rumours have it that there are a hundred thousand armed tribals—clearly an exaggeration. A fourth of that number in insurrection, and I would lose the Central Provinces, and six thousand European lives! I have appealed to the

Viceroy, but Lord Lansdowne has informed me in no uncertain terms that I may expect no troops from him, the state of the borders demanding his full attention."

We had discussed all this on our way, and so we remained gravely silent, with nothing to add to the Chief Commissioner's comments. "I am indeed very grateful to Mr Holmes and Dr Watson that they accepted your invitation to join us at such a dangerous juncture," said Sir Alexander with a gracious nod in our direction. "The Empire needs your help, gentlemen, as never before. More than six thousand British men, women, and children are at grave risk in my domains. I dare not warn them, for that would create a panic. To remain silent, with the knowledge I have, is morally indefensible. You are the only cards left in my hands, in addition to Mr Kipling's undoubted skill in entering the native mind. I depend upon you to find out as quickly as possible who is behind this treacherous plot, and what their plan is, so that we may strike them, before they can do any harm!"

Sir Alexander rang a bell to summon his private secretary, a pleasant young civilian. "Robert, I want you to bring these gentlemen copies of the confidential report you prepared on the famine persisting in certain districts."

He gave us time to look through the details before continuing. "As you will see, gentlemen, that report contains sad news about conditions in the Jubbulpore and Chattisgarh divisions. Rains have failed us for three years running; the crops withered last year; several thousands have perished; there are well over a thousand orphaned

children in Jubbulpore town itself; there is acute distress
in the land; wells have dried up, and others are polluted;
villages have been depopulated by cholera, following on
the heels of famine. I have no spare resources to alleviate
the suffering, which forms a natural hotbed for sedition
and revolt. Once danger to the Empire is allayed, we
can try and take special measures to ease the suffering.
I have never had more than ten or twelve percent of the
provincial revenues available for public works, and with this
additional threat to our security, I am forced to draw upon
those slender resources for paying police informers."

I asked why work, like felling trees for railway sleepers,
or road construction, had not had the salutary effect
of arresting impoverishment, at least to the extent of
affording ready cash to the poor to buy grain.

Sir Alexander bit his lip in vexation. "In a way we
have brought this crisis upon ourselves. My ideas for
reform and rent fixation met with stiff resistance from
the military members of the Provincial Commission. It
was argued, and I must say with justice, that landlords
in our malguzari system raised rents only when the land
became more productive, and that if the land slipped
into more affluent hands, that could only result in better
revenues for the province. To create artificial barriers to
economic process was against the genius of British policy.
Some District Officers have raised land revenues even in
ryotwari lands, so that there is parity, and no 'injustice'
is done to peasants living under landlords. Mind you,
the extra money thus collected has been spent for good
purposes, such as opening new schools, a development

which I cherish. However, the number of the landless has swelled steadily, and now when the rains have failed, we are faced with catastrophe. The spectre of the Irish famine looms in my mind!"

Assuring the Chief Commissioner that we would count our lives well worth lost if, in any way, we could lay these scoundrels by the heels, we retired to the dak bungalow to work out a plan of action. Clearly, the first step was to meet some of the first Indian families in town to glean some new information. Mrs Chitnavis was at home, her husband being away on business, and she gladly shared her worries over tea.[27] Yes, the rumours had reached them too, more from anxious enquiries made by the government than through any other source. She was glad the Lancashire Fusiliers were at hand at Kamtee. Kipling returned late that evening from Itwari Bazaar, saying that one or two grain merchants had confided to him that the rumours were certainly based on dark facts, and that they and their friends had already started to store away grain and gold in secret godowns known only to a few trusted servants of their own caste. A sense of unease and fear prevailed, sending up prices of essential commodities beyond the reach of all but the wealthy. Roadside mithai-wallahs had complained that they were being ruined, for no one had money even in the richer Shukrawari bazaar to buy jalebis.

We took two days to drive to Seoni, sometimes leaving our carriage to ride out to nearby villages to assess the situation and gather news. The land was dry and dusty, with bare trees poking out of a messy carpet of brown,

withered leaves. There seemed to be no work going on
in the villages, and many mud huts were empty. A few
old men crouched under a tree told us many had died,
others had migrated. There were almost no children to
be seen. I saw an emaciated baby in the lap of a woman,
who was probably still in her teens, but looked older than
forty. She held up her child, but I could see the child was
beyond all medical help.

Seoni was almost like a ghost town. The only sign of
life was around the residence of Ameerchand, the local
grain merchant and malguzar, which was encircled by
men armed with spears. Indeed, as we knew, the surest
signs of grave scarcity among these timid people were
the armed guards at the grain godowns, or at the homes
of the rich. Later we passed the Wainganga, shrunk to
a narrow, indistinct stream, glimpsed between granite
boulders. Even the mighty Nerbudda above Bheraghat
was only a flaccid slow-moving river between broad
sandy banks. Jubbulpore had far better facilities for the
traveller than Nagpur, and we stayed at the comfortable
Jackson's Hotel, with its obsequious servants and cooks
who understood British cooking. Sadr Bazaar boasted of
shops that supplied the simple necessities of an English
household, and there was even a bookshop which displayed
a few English books. Casually browsing the shelves, I was
amused to find a serious study penned by a little-known
Frenchman, who doubted the very existence of British
heroes, such as Sherlock Holmes, named as an apocryphal
example, who according to him had simply been created
by imagination to justify Britain's imperial rule.

Mr Alan Bloomfield, the Commissioner of the Division, lived in a large bungalow of perhaps twenty-odd rooms, overshadowed by a clump of old peepal and mango trees, and surrounded by a well-kept garden of a few acres.[28] When we rode up the gravel path he was busy supervising a number of malees, who seemed to be turning over a line of flowerpots below the long verandah in front.

"Mr Kipling! Welcome to Jubbulpore! And I believe your friends are Mr Sherlock Holmes and Dr Watson. You are all very welcome," he said, wiping muddy hands on a towel a bearer held out. He was a short, middle-aged man, wearing rimless glasses, with a friendly, no-nonsense air about him. "My little daughter called out early this morning that she had pinned a baby python under her stick. Imagine my horror on seeing her hold down a Russell's viper, inches from her foot. I am having these fellows see if there are any more. The snakes like to curl up under wet flowerpots, you know. But come in, and meet another guest who is staying with me."

We found Colonel Montgomerie, the other guest, in the large office, poring over several rather outdated maps, laid out in a sheaf on a side table.[29] He was very tall, and would have been considered handsome in any company, had he cared to be more particular about his dress. "The Great Trignometrical Survey of India is almost complete by now," he said happily. "But as you know the devil is in the details. I have come back from the Himalayas to rework some of our measurements in the Satpura Range, which I rather suspect were carried out in a hurry by my subordinates. Accuracy is everything in mapping, and even more important if our measurements are to aid astronomical work."

We were amazed to hear that the geodesic work he was launched on would one day fix with great accuracy the curvature of the earth. Upon hearing that Kipling was a writer, who in addition to editing *The Pioneer* in Allahabad, also wrote children's stories, Montgomerie laughed in a most friendly way. "Oh, I wish you could meet my young Canadian niece, Lucy, Lucy Montgomery—spells her name with a 'y' in the new style. She is prolific in her correspondence, asking my advice about her stories, all very engaging, I must say, all about a girl called Anne who lives on an island somewhere there. I am sure you would be able to help her, Mr Kipling. I am only a plain geographer."[30]

The morning passed in the exchange of interesting anecdotes between Kipling and Montgomerie. Holmes and I half listened to their stories while pondering over the complexities of our mission. After a simple if not stark lunch, which Bloomfield said he insisted on in view of the grave famine stalking his lands, although the British community had an ample stock of every necessity and quite a few luxuries besides, he led us back to his cool office to discuss the situation.

"I shall go against our policy," he said with determination. "Oh, I know that far better heads than mine have thought it all through, and decided that the market must not be interfered with, but, gentlemen, this is India, where historically different values have been applied in society. The most vicious of Rajahs have opened their granaries to their people in times of scarcity. It would be unchristian to do less, when we all know that it is our policies that have brought this blight on people. This evening I shall try to take corrective measures, although they may be too late to save several, and I shall do it without putting one word down on paper!"

That evening, soon after the blinding sun had dipped below the horizon, although heat waves continued to shimmer upwards from the scorched earth, Bloomfield drove past our hotel to collect us. Leaving the civil lines behind, we crossed the railway tracks to the north, and entered dense native quarters, where lamps were being lit in the shops, although a cursory glance showed little business activity. Most owners just sat on their steps, fanning themselves, and chatting with the people hanging about in the streets. After several twists and turns down narrow gullies, we walked through wrought-iron gates set in a high wall, and suddenly found ourselves in a spacious garden, fronting a mansion set well back and hidden from view of the crowded bazaar. We were at the residence of "Rajah" Gokuldas, one of the country's richest Marwari businessmen, belonging to the powerful Malpani clan. Bloomfield had informed us during the drive that few in India had an accurate assessment of the extent of his empire, or his wealth, perhaps not even Gokuldas himself. Business was conducted across the length and breadth of India through a select army of loyal Marwari henchmen, whose instructions arrived on small slips of paper covered with Gokuldas's cryptic hieroglyphs, which only they could decipher, and which they carried out in implicit obedience. Although originally the honorific of "Rajah" had been informally used in recognition of his great power and wealth, the government had lately confirmed the title since he and his nominees in any case owned several hundred villages, and their lands spread across the districts of the province.

We were seated in a cool, shady part of the garden in large cane chairs, our feet thankfully resting on a freshly watered lawn. While some servants continued to fan us, others served tea, cakes, and sandwiches, as well as several Indian delicacies. Rajah Gokuldas himself appeared shortly thereafter, accompanied by a large retinue of assistants, who were dismissed with a wave of his hand after preliminary introductions were over. He conversed easily in Hindoostani with Bloomfield, whom he seemed to regard as a respected and valued friend. After they had enquired about the health and welfare of everyone in each other's families, they fell to discussing a variety of trivial subjects under the sun with polite attention. In the process, the Rajah's eyes would casually pass over each one of us, and we sensed every time that we were being assessed by an expert master of men.

Suddenly, the Rajah asked, as if the thought had just come to mind, if he could be of any service to his respected friend, the Commissioner? Bloomfield seemed to consider the novelty of the question, and then as an afterthought said the famine was causing him great concern. The Rajah nodded solemnly in concurrence. "Rajah Sahib, your munificence to our people is known throughout the world. You have helped the poor whenever they needed you. You have poured money into their hands, and thousands bless you and your family. You have brought up generations of orphans." Gokuldas nodded solemnly in agreement.

"One of those orphans Commissioner Sahib was pleased to adopt as a son," reminded the Rajah.

A shadow passed over Bloomfield's face. "Unfortunately I lost him, but I pray one day he may return," he said. "Rajah Sahib, the people need grain. With the rains failing for a third year, all of the grain, as you know, has been moved to distant towns and cities, where people still have the money to pay high prices. Many have died around us, and many more will, unless grain at low prices appears in the shops. None can make this happen but you."

Gokuldas contemplated the stars that were beginning to peep out at us through the dust haze. "Commissioner Sahib, as you know, I am not an educated man. I have never been to college, but can somehow, through God's grace, carry on a little business. So, what do I know how to run a district, or a division, or a huge province? I watch with admiration how all this is done by you, Sahib, and the Chief Commissioner Sahib Bahadur. I am told the old ways were all wrong, that it is against British policy to bring grain at low prices to the bazaars, for that would upset the market?"

Bloomfield fidgeted. Finally, he burst out: "What can I hide from an old friend, of twenty years' standing? What you say is even so, but the harm of letting the famine go

on will be immeasurable. We must act, you and I, for
we belong here, while many great sahibs come and go. I
think if the grain returns to the bazaars now, when the
years of prosperity return, the farmers will only sell to
your munims. I shall remind them of the gratitude they
owe their protectors."

The Rajah suddenly realized that the four of us had
remained silent, and that we had been sorely neglected
during this exchange. Begging our forgiveness, he gave
loud orders that sherbet and sweetmeats should be offered
to us for our delectation, and begged to be acquainted with
our interests and work. Kind enquiries were made into
each of our family histories. As we were about to leave, he
called an assistant, scribbled a note on a small slip of paper,
and respectfully saw us off at the door. As we drove back,
I commented that it was unfortunate Gokuldas could not
see eye to eye with us, to which Bloomfield replied to
my great surprise that, on the contrary, everything had
been agreed, and he expected to see grain in the shops by
the very next day. And so it was. We were all amazed to
see how quickly and efficiently the writ of Gokuldas was
obeyed by all the lesser dealers.[31]

Confident that the worst phase of famine would soon
be brought under control by his informal understanding
with Gokuldas, Bloomfield turned with energy to arrest
the spread of cholera. We rode out south through the
worst hit part of the district. At least half the people of the
villages we visited had died of the dreaded disease. Only
the lack of victims seemed to halt its spread. Villagers
were advised to drink only boiled water; to wash their

hands before and after meals; to eat only hot cooked food, and let no flies settle on it. Bags of potassium permanganate were supplied to all the naib tasildars for free distribution, to protect the yet unpolluted wells. Once we passed downwind of a long, sad procession of the dead on their way to the burning ghat, and Bloomfield quickly ordered all Europeans to wrap scarves round our mouths and noses. It seemed he had lost a young officer some years ago within two days of his inhaling detritus dust from one of the corpses.

At Narayanganj, we came across the tents of Dr France, the Assistant Civil Surgeon, and found him drunk and asleep in his camp chair at four in the afternoon.[32] His shirt, stained and smelly, stuck to his body with sweat. He jerked himself awake on our entering his tent, and smiled at Bloomfield without bothering to leave his chair.

"Sir, I know I am drunk, that's why I'm alive," he said, his eyes passing over us without recognition or interest. "I'd advise you all to do the same, or you will die of cholera, or of dehydration. You can help yourself to my whisky on that side table there. The best medicine I have in the chest. Not enough to get everyone drunk though!" He laughed stupidly, and with that his head fell back, and he was snoring again.

His Indian compounder, a short, thin man of about fifty, came in, lifted the taller man with ease, and laid France out on his camp bed. He told us brusquely that France had worked round the clock for six days without sleep or rest. With nothing to say, we went outside and came to a long tent, in which the dead and dying were laid out on dhurees, with hardly an inch of space between any two. The sickly sweet smell that enveloped the tent, and the black stains of vomit and faeces, told their own tragic story.

Mandla Fort itself seemed free of the disease, and we breathed freely for the first time in days. The little town of no more than five thousand souls was perched on the right bank of the mighty Nerbudda, which flowed past several bathing ghats, cooling the town even in the height of summer. Beyond the left bank, there was unbroken forest as far as the eye could see. After a hot bath at the dak bungalow, we made our way to the kutcherry to be told that the Deputy Commissioner, Mr Comrie, was out visiting a recently opened school. Since education was one of Bloomfield's passions, we set off as a group to the school, only to find the DC standing at the blackboard of a large schoolroom, cane in hand, while several respectable men stood precariously balanced on the benches at the back.

Comrie threw down his cane upon seeing our open-mouthed entry, signalling to the men to get down. "And mind you don't break my furniture, while you are about it!" he said to them. "What can I do, Sir? I am plain exhausted with frustration, I am," he added to Bloomfield. "The children are not coming to school. So I changed the curriculum to make it more meaningful to them. Agriculture, accounts and bookkeeping, and English are all they have to learn, but the classrooms are mostly empty. The bania children will not attend classes in agriculture, the kisans will not take up bookkeeping, and none will come to a class in English. So, I have got all their fathers to stand on the benches and repeat after me twenty times, 'I will send my children to school!'"

We all laughed at the discomfiture of the men as they filed out shamefaced, but later Bloomfield gently reminded his subordinate that perhaps more sympathetic means should be adopted to get children into school, since none of us wanted to offend the sensibilities of the natives. That evening we had gone to the little Officer's Club, not far from the river, for a bit of tennis and a drink, when Comrie came up, invited us into the billiards room, and said bluntly: "Mr Pierce, the Deputy Superintendent of Police, has just received a telegram from Jubbulpore that Rajah Gokuldas's men have been making particular enquiries about your guests. Can you make anything of it, Sir?"

We sat on the side benches, and over glasses of whisky and soda, we told him of our mission. Until that moment, Bloomfield had shown little interest in the fears of the Chief Commissioner, his whole attention being focused on measures to mitigate the severity of the famine and the pestilence. At this new piece of information, he turned to us with a worried frown. "Mr Kipling, I have heard such rumours before, and I put the latest batch down to exaggerated fears at a time of great privation—indeed, my efforts were all to mitigate the suffering of my people. However, your presence here, and this latest report that Gokuldas is making pointed enquiries about your mission, make me fear that I might have been remiss in not securing the safety of my division a little earlier.

But the idea of a great tribal insurrection seems quite preposterous! Who can have the power of bringing all of them together, the vast family of Gonds, the Murias, the Abhuj, the Bison Horn, the Halbaa, the Batra, the Dhurva, and then the Baigas, the Bhinjwaras, the Barotrias, the Narotrias, and even the Khonds? These people are brave beyond question, but they do not come together for political reasons, I tell you; that would be quite against their character. I have known them to come together only occasionally, and that only to perform a major religious ceremony."

"Indeed, Sir Alexander is of the same opinion, Mr Bloomfield," said Kipling gravely. "But someone has stirred an ancient animistic belief—they seem to be answering a call from the very origin of creation."

Bloomfield now turned to his deputy, having made up his mind. "Comrie, you have a company of English soldiers here under Lieutenant Hazard. Good. Mandla is peaceful, it has only plains people. A small contingent of the Indian police is sufficient for their protection. We shall take our soldiers and march southeastwards into Dindori tehsil, towards the Maikal Range. Luckily, Colonel Montgomerie is here on a scientific mission, along with his orderlies, with measuring chains and theodolites. Nobody will suspect a thing. We shall also enquire about shikar. The tiger is a scavenger—with so many people dead, and the poorest lying unburied, the oldest among the cats may have turned man-eaters. The Gonds will be happy to lead us to good hunting sites, and we may be able to learn a lot around campfires. The

Rajah of Chuikadan sent me a message earlier, inviting me to a Keddah operation he is conducting in the Maikal area, to round up two or three large herds of wild elephants that have been ravaging the villages there. I had forgotten all about it, engaged as I was with famine operations. Send him a telegram that we are marching to help with the round-up. The elephants would never have encroached upon farmlands, if broad swathes of forest had not been heedlessly felled to provide sleepers for the Bilaspur section of the railway. I had warned about the consequences in a memo two years ago. Well, there's no use crying over spilt milk. And oh! Andrew Fraser has just taken over as Commissioner of Chattisgarh in Raipur, and he must be a deeply worried man. Invite him in an open telegram to join the Rajah and us in the Keddah work; after all it's on his boundary. With both of us sweeping through the forest, we should comb out any malcontents, who may be hiding in there, and scotch the revolt before it starts. The Gond likes nothing better than a hunt, and he instinctively respects brave men. We will have them all on our side before the month is out!"

Two days later, we were on the march, mounted on several elephants. Bloomfield, and Comrie had their own trained savar animals, with hunting howdahs, with three more carrying their staff and orderlies, while Montgomerie was on the fifth, with his own scientific staff. Six British soldiers were mounted on an old elephant, sitting uncomfortably on a grey dhuree spread across its broad back muscles. Kipling, Holmes, and I sat on a charpoy tied to the back of a young she-elephant.

Two other elephants carried shikaris and some saman of immediate need. Two trains of bullock carts, carrying khalasies and tents, bearers and cooks, chamber pots and cooking vessels for our camp had left a day's march ahead, and would leapfrog one another, so that we always found tents pitched, and cheerful servants waiting with food and water at the end of a day's march. It never failed to amaze me that the clever fellows could find provisions, meat, eggs, and milk, at short notice, in any corner of the jungle. They always pitched camp in the most beautiful spot they could find, so that we looked forward with pleasure to seeing a fine sunset, or a lovely stream meandering through forest glades. The evenings spent in our large tents had their own unequalled charm, for we walked on soft dhurees; ate excellent meals at a table laid out with spotless linen, and gleaming cutlery and crockery; bathed in hot water; and slept between clean sheets. If the occasional krait was found in a tent, we also saw peacocks perched on top, or had koels wake us in the morning.

Early one morning, noticing that we had made do with eggs for a few days, I went out with a fowling piece to see if I could bring back a brace of ducks from the nearby lake. A Gond, trotting up, signalled to me not to fire, and then disappeared into the rushes by the bank. Soon, I noticed a large empty gadda, or earthen pot, float gently towards a flock of ducks that were busy investigating a clump of reeds. There were a few empty pots there already, and the new pot flowed slowly towards them. After it had reached the ducks, I saw a few birds quickly disappear underwater without their fellows noticing, and then the pot floated back to the bank, and a minute later the Gond emerged, smiling and holding four ducks by their feet.

The hunting skill of these wild men is proverbial. We had come across a Gond village almost depopulated by cholera, and haunted by an old tiger, with a limp acquired from an encounter with a careless shikari. He not only dragged away the dead, but also killed the living at will. The Gonds had cut down a heavy sal tree, propped up one end of the trunk with a wooden support, and left a dead body underneath tied to the prop. The tiger, pulling at the body, had brought the heavy trunk down on itself, smashing its spine. A joint cremation of man and beast ended the period of terror.

At the foot of the Maikal Range, we came across a deserted Baiga Chak, or reservation, that the Government had created to pen these wild people of the forests, and prevent them from destroying valuable sal timber by slash-and-burn methods. The tribals had quietly slipped away, and, according to Comrie, most probably settled in the forests of the feudatory Rajahs of Khavarda.

"They are dogged in their attachment to their own ways of life, and refuse the benefits of ours," he said, pointing out the abandoned plough and other materials thought necessary by the Agricultural Department. "It's a waste of the twenty rupees we spent on each of them to pen them in here."

High atop a ridge, we came upon the tents of Mr Percival, Divisional Forest Officer of the district, pitched

near a remote Baiga village.[33] He came striding up the
hillside looking round fondly at his trees.

"Mr Bloomfield, glad to see you here, Sir," he said
heartily. "The forest is in excellent shape, despite all
alarmist views. If you and your guests can spare the time
to walk a transept through these ridges, I would like to
show you how little damage bewar cultivation does to
the forest."

Percival, it seemed, found no harm in the traditional
slash-and-burn cultivation of the Baigas, although the
Government had taken every step possible to suppress
the practice as harmful to forests. After a hearty lunch,
cooked by his servants and eaten in the open under tall
sal trees, he took us on a long walk to visit various bewar
sites. Thick forest growth had spread over all the sites
carefully selected by the tribals to ensure regeneration.
Percival had his orderlies make tea at a recent bewar
site, where the standing khodun millet crop had been
wantonly destroyed.

"Major Reston's handiwork," pointed out Percival
grimly.[34] "Thank God, he's been transferred to Bilaspur.
In a fit of zeal, he thought of this cruel measure to dissuade
Baigas from bewar, but as you yourself saw, it does no
harm at all to the forest. How can it? They have been living
here since before there were men in England. But we are
appropriating most of the forest lands as Government
wastelands, and a twenty-year cycle of bewar cannot be
reasonably maintained on the land we allow the tribals.
So we cannot blame them, or their system of cultivation,
for our failure to understand their cycles of cultivation."

"Percival, we need to sequester forest land for our own use, if we want to generate revenues from this region. You know we need to do that, if we want to set up schools or hospitals that are the least bit good," said Bloomfield mildly.

"True, Sir, I grant you that, but some other way must be found of generating revenue," said Percival doggedly. "A third of our revenues go to support our military establishment. Why should the tribal pay for the army? He doesn't need one here!"

"That's where you are wrong, Percival," said Bloomfield soberly, and told him the real purpose of our drive towards the range.

Percival listened, partly with incredulity and partly in amusement. "I don't believe there is any danger at all, Sir," he said contentedly, after hearing us through. "Oh! I know there is some talk of Naga Baiga having come back to lead his people. He is the founder of the human race, as you know, his eldest child being the priestly Baiga with mystic powers, and his second the kingly Gond. There has been a great famine, and the land needs to regenerate. What better than to pray that Naga Baiga will come back, for does he not carry Dharti Mata's regenerative powers in his teeth? Nothing more to it than that, Sir," he added with finality.

We were all relieved to hear this simple explanation, but it left Kipling and me worried, for there were many unanswered questions, and trained police informers could not have so grossly overestimated the danger.

As if to prove his point, Percival took us to the Baiga

village nearby, in the cool of the evening. It was far neater than many villages in the plains that it has been my misfortune to pass through. Its houses were arranged in a circle around a central peepul tree with a stone platform around its base. The mud walls of every house were beautifully painted in bright colours, with floral designs, or line pictures of animals, birds, and snakes. A store of khodun millet was next to the slightly larger house of the mukhiya. A single short piece of cloth was wrapped round the loins of men and women, and even attractive young women seemed quite unashamed of their beauty.

They crowded round Percival whom they recognized as an old friend. He called us to sit on the platform round the central peepul tree, while he questioned the Baigas. He asked how much khodun seed they needed for a plot. A koru was the answer. How much did they get for it? Ten khandis or two hundred times the seed, came the reply.

"You see, gentlemen, this is a very productive form of agriculture, and it keeps them well fed until the next season. Recollect, the bewar is carried out only on high slopes, above the frost line, which the modern farmer would consider uncultivable."

Bloomfield asked how much a koru was, and we heard that twelve surias made a koru, while three tomas made a suria. How much was a toma, and a giggling girl held out two handfuls. Percival needlessly re-emphasized the scientific nature of their practice. By this time, several girls had come forward to serve us an evening meal of khodun bread and ragi porridge, with some greens. We all drank mahua liquor from the same large bowl, as it would have been impolite to refuse it. An old Baiga priest then came forward with a small earthen pot, decorated with turmeric and mango leaves, and gave the special mahua ceremoniously to Bloomfield, bending down to touch his feet.

"What did he say?" asked Bloomfield.

"That you were the father of his father," replied Percival uncomprehendingly.

Cresting the Moogli spur of the Maikal Range, we came upon the Keddah conducted by the Rajah of Chuikadan. A stockade encircling several acres had been completed. To put final touches to it, slim Gond girls effortlessly carried long bangeys, or shoulder poles, laden at each end with a load of cut timber. The stockade had a single heavy gate, which could be dropped like a portcullis when needed. A broad wooden rim ringed the top of the stockade, on which men could sit and use sharpened poles to prevent wild elephants from ramming the wooden walls. A few wild elephants had already been captured, and bound by every leg to trees within the stockade. Female Keddah animals stood near, to sooth their wild cousins with their low rumbling murmurs. The Rajah's tent was a magnificent affair, no less than a palace under canvas, with rich carpets and tapestry, glittering chandeliers and silverware. Returning from strenuous Keddah operations, he had changed from working clothes to formal royal robes, with a feather-mounted brocaded turban, to welcome Bloomfield and his party. He sat on a makeshift throne, while each of us went up to make our bows. Once the introductions were over, he invited us to the next tent for lunch where a hundred dishes were laid out on the dastarkhan, around which we sat, reclining on long, soft bolsters.

Later that afternoon, His Highness changed into workmen-like sturdy corduroys, and invited us to round up a few more elephants with him. When we spotted a herd, our female elephants went forward, making their low soothing noises. The mahouts were all dressed in black, and had bathed their animals that very morning to remove any human scent. After some time, the female elephants gradually cut out a tusker, and started leading him towards the stockade. A few from the wild herd followed the tusker. Upon coming to the gate, our elephants went in and started munching noisily on sugarcane laid out for them. The wild animals found this irresistible, and followed them in. The gate was dropped and we mounted the stockade, and sat on its rim to watch. The females then stood pressed to the sides of the tusker so that he was unable to move. Men quickly dashed in between their legs and secured him with ropes fastened to trees. The move was repeated with all the other wild animals. If, in the meantime, any elephant approached the walls of the stockade out of curiosity, it was discouraged from coming any nearer with sharp pricks. Once the animals had been safely tied up, our working elephants quickly left the stockade.

Before dawn the next day, Bloomfield suggested that we should try and spot a herd ourselves, without the formalities necessarily connected with the presence of His Highness. Hence we set off quietly, on two elephants. Our mahouts were strangers to the range, and our animals were untrained in Keddah work, or else we might not have wandered negligently within the circle of a large herd. A huge old tusker, standing over ten feet at the shoulder, sounded an alarm at our intrusion, the females retreated to the rear, with their calves protected between their legs, and we found ourselves menaced by a circle of bulls. Our own elephants were now trembling at the danger; and our mahouts were uncertain what orders to give. At that moment, a young Baiga, a head taller than most of his kind, quietly emerged through the rising mists of the morning, and standing near the old tusker, began to give orders to the herd in a thunderous voice. It was the strangest sight we had ever seen, and seemed to last an eternity, until the lead tusker turned back, and led his herd away.

The young Baiga turned to go, but catching sight of Bloomfield, stood transfixed, and then came slowly forward, without any of the shyness exhibited by his tribe. Our Baiga guides had prostrated themselves on the ground, crying, "Naga Baiga! Naga Baiga!" Bloomfield, with a strange tense look, also eased himself to the ground from his howdah, until he stood within arm's length of the Baiga. "Father!" said the Baiga in English, and Bloomfield embraced him, calling him "Krishna", and asking a dozen questions. The memory of that extraordinary reunion between father and son still remains fresh in my memory, bringing in its train a flush of happiness and a depth of sorrow I have never

experienced before or since. We took the Baiga away
to our camp, and learnt from Bloomfield that this was
the very boy he had adopted from among Gokuldas's
orphans, during a famine fifteen years ago. A son he had
named Krishna, and brought up as an English boy, only
to have him disappear mysteriously eight years earlier.

After several anxious, probing questions, the boy
spoke reluctantly and slowly, but without fear or shame.
"I cannot tell you, father, in English, or in any other
language, why I went away. I was called by the jungle,"
he said simply. "I knew this was my home, I do not know
how I found my way. I worked for farmers going to the
market, and they gave me a ride on their bullock carts. I
even rode on the camel of a Muslim seeking the dargah
of a particular saint. By the time I found these hills, I
was weak, and had high fever. But I knew I was home; I
embraced the trees, and they comforted me. Then I lay
down to rest, and slept for a long time. I remember a she-
wolf licking my face all over. I was too ill to fear her, and
many Gonds believe she raised me, but you raised me,
dear father! Since then, for some reason, no animal fears
me, and I know I have nothing to fear from them."

"What did you tell the elephants?" asked Bloomfield
gently of his son.

"I do not know," replied the boy truthfully. "I never
know what I tell them, or the other animals. There are
no words, you see. I feel them, and they feel me, each
in his own way. Elephants, tigers, cobras, they are all
different, but somewhere all the same, and no different
from the trees, or the air."

As if to allow us a glimpse of his world, he held up a hand to the sky, and two long-tailed fly-catchers came weaving through the air to settle on his shoulders. Soon other birds started to use him as a natural perch before flying off again, and we found this distracting as we spoke with him.

Yes, all the tribals had heard of him, although he had done nothing to call them to him. Yes, they thought he was Naga Baiga reincarnated, although he did not know what that meant. Yes, they were together now, many, many, many men together, yes, the Baigas, whether Bhinjwaras or Bharotrias, and Gonds, whether Muria, Halbaa, or Dhurva, and also the Khonds, but none meant harm to anyone, they wished to explain to the Sircar how the forests may be cared for; and they wanted him as the Naga Baiga, the high priest of the priestly Baigas, to talk to the Sahib Bahadurs. They all knew that the great Bloomfield Sahib, the Commissioner from Jubbulpore, and the great Fraser Sahib, the Commissioner from Raipur, were coming together in the home of the Naga Baiga, the Moogli Hills—the whole forest knew—and they were all coming to speak with the great sahibs.

Andrew Fraser's crowd was even larger than the one accompanying us, and the Rajah went through another elaborate court ritual of welcome, introductions, and feasting for the renowned Commissioner of Chattisgarh and his officers. Even as the meal was nearing its end, nervous assistants were whispering to the Rajah, and it soon became evident to all that a large Gond-Khond-Baiga gathering was taking place outside, in the forest

maidan adjoining the stockade. When we came out of
the tents, we were amazed to see two or three thousand
men already encircling the camp, all armed with bows
and arrows, and some with spears. Their arms aroused no
comment, for no tribal went about without his hunting .
weapons, but the unusually large numbers of men caused
grave anxiety. The native soldiers of the Rajah showed
their fear; even Andrew Fraser, known for his fearlessness
in the face of danger, looked pale and drawn.

Chairs were arranged under a large, spreading tree for
the Rajah Sahib, Fraser and Bloomfield. Major Reston,
in charge of Bilaspur district, Comrie, Montgomerie,
and Kipling stood behind the chairs, and I saw them
surreptitiously unbutton their pistol holsters. Holmes and
I sat to one side, below a small tree. A low chant started
among the tribals, and slowly grew in volume until an
anguished roar of 'Jal! Jamin! Jungle! Jeevan!' resounded
through the forest. Behind the few thousand tribals
immediately before us, loomed the mass of many more
thousands, filling up the forest as far as the eye could see.

Suddenly, Krishna appeared between the crowd of
tribals and us. His arms were raised, perhaps to signal
to the men to be quiet. But the roars only grew louder,
and mingled cries of "Naga Baiga! Naga Baiga!" could
be heard. As he turned to face us, his men stood up and,
in a single concerted movement, raised their bows and
spears. Perhaps this was simply a salutation—we will
never know. Major Reston leapt forward, drawing his
revolver. In a flash, Holmes had scooped up a round
stone and, using his large handkerchief as a sling, flung

it with great force at Reston, a trick, he admitted later, he had learnt in Patagonia. The stone hit Reston's wrist even as he was discharging his pistol, knocking it upwards. The ball grazed Krishna's temple, and he fell unconscious to the ground. Absolute silence descended upon the jungle, even as the shot was ringing in our ears. The nearest tribals caught Krishna before his body touched the ground, and in a matter of moments, their hands were smeared with his blood.

Reston stood before us, gesticulating like a mad man and shouting: "Look! Look! He is no Naga Baiga, he is a man, a badmash, he duped you. The Sircar will destroy all such badmashes. You will all meet the same fate, unless you are obedient to the Sircar. Disband immediately, and go home, all of you!" We saw that none of them took any notice of Reston; in all probability, they had not heard a word that he had said. Their minds and hearts were all fixed on the unconscious body of their young leader, whom they held tenderly in their arms. With a deep growl, the great tribal concourse withdrew, carrying their Naga Baiga with them.

Bloomfield was beside himself in grief and in anger. "How dare you, Reston!" he thundered. "How dare you, Sir, try to murder an unarmed boy, without the least provocation! I will have you court-martialled for this!"

Reston regarded him coldly, holding his wrist in pain. "I will take my instructions from my own Commissioner, thank you, Bloomfield. I think I have saved the lives of all of us, and put down a rebellion before it started. I know of your native interests. If you wish for any satisfaction,

I am ready to give it to you, but that would be plain murder, knowing your skill with a pistol!"

Fraser had risen to interpose himself between the two, and while the Rajah signalled to his men to attend to Reston's wrist, Bloomfield said with great dignity, "I will not meet with a man who is not fit to call himself an Englishman."

With that, the two camps from Jubbulpore and Raipur separated, with all of us feeling Bloomfield's anguish. For the first time in our short acquaintance, I saw Bloomfield drink himself into a stupor that night. He cursed the fate that had given him a son, and then had him shot before his own eyes. Would the boy survive, could he survive without proper medical attention, Bloomfield agonized. Would he ever see his son again? Would he ever return to his father after such a reception?

"I am beginning to see that Hume, the chap that started the Indian National Congress, is right after all! We cannot trust the system; it is pitiless. We have to trust the people," said Bloomfield bleary-eyed.

Kipling looked at him with great compassion. "Sorrow comes to all of us, Sir," he said softly. "It is how we live, and what we are, that matters. Your son is a credit to you. He is, in his whole person, what makes us truly human. I am sure his people, so wise in the ways of the jungle, and its pharmacopoeia, will help him recover. I shall write about him."

"No! Kipling, no!" cried Bloomfield. "I'm a father, a grieving father, but I am also a servant of the Empire, which in the final analysis stands for all that is good and noble. A word from you about this tragedy, and all the vernacular papers will be baying for our blood. A thousand times no! You must not breathe a word about what has happened!"

"Believe me, Sir, I won't, not about what the poor lad faced at the hands of that bounder, Reston," assured Kipling. "Your son will live in children's stories, as the very spirit of these Moogli hills, as an eternal boy, who can live with animals and talk to them. He is not just a tribal leader—there are several unfortunate characters for that role. He showed us we belong to Nature, and are a part of eternal Nature, and he will be immortalized for showing us that, I promise you."[35]

Later that night, alone with Holmes in the privacy of our tent, I bemoaned the fact that we had stood by as helpless spectators, and done nothing to change the tragic course of events. From under his mosquito net, Holmes replied, "Our endeavours until now have been to support the laws of duly constituted authority. But what do we find in these jungles, Watson? The laws of the uncivilized are far superior to those of the Government's, and the laws of Nature are better than both."

Kim and Kim Again

Our debt to Colonel Montgomerie was already considerable. Much to our gratitude, but also somewhat to our discomfiture, he insisted that we go up with him for a period of rest to Naini Tal. Holmes and I had been worn out by our exertions in the jungles of the Central Provinces, so we permitted ourselves to be persuaded, after a few weak remonstrations that we were already in his debt, and it would be an unconscionable presumption to impose on him any further. Kipling added his considerable influence to Montgomerie's urging, saying that he would follow soon, as he planned to write a book on an extraordinary protégé of the Colonel's.

We caught the night train to Jhansi at Bina, and next morning, switched to the Eastern Railway up to Lucknow. After a night halt, we resumed our journey north, straight up to Kathgodam. The Colonel's carriage conveyed us the rest of the way to Naini Tal. After the scorching heat of the central plains of India, it was a relief to climb the foothills of the Himalayan spurs. A fresh smell of pine and fir wafted in on the cooling breeze. We could see in the pale moonlight that the road, somewhat better than a cart road but not much more than that, had wound high over gorges, with the tops of swaying trees well below the level of our windows. Certain hairpin bends seemed treacherous, but the horses were surefooted and the coachman experienced. Well past dinner time, by way of the Upper Mall skirting the township, we reached Montgomerie's establishment, Fairlight Hall, high over Naini Tal, and just below the zigzag climb up to Alma Peak. The lake gleamed far below us in the distance.

The large estate had several smaller buildings, which served as offices, storerooms, and machine shops for the Survey of India. The main building itself was spacious, capable of accommodating several officers for long periods. Montgomerie needed to put them up when his staff was called together from various expeditions to consolidate their latest work on the Great Trignometrical Survey of India. The work had been started by the legendary Lambton early in the century, carried on by the irascible Colonel Everest, who never saw the peak that would be named after him, and later expanded over the two-thousand-mile range of the Himalayas by Montgomerie's famous uncle. Our friend had trained an enthusiastic corps of Indian surveyors, dressed them up as lamas, shepherds, and mendicants, and sent them off, with compasses hidden in prayer wheels and measuring tapes in holy books, to map the roof of the world. He told us, during the long ride up, that he was proud to carry on in the footsteps of the great men of science. He had rented the large estate so that he could complete the work of the Great Arc in the peace of the hills, yet not too distant from Delhi or Calcutta.

When we came down next morning for breakfast, we found we were almost the only guests staying there at the time, save for a couple of young lieutenants helping Montgomerie in his office. The air was fresh and cold, and we felt invigorated by the climate, which was vastly different from what we had endured until just twelve hours ago. After a hearty breakfast and a quick survey of English newspapers several weeks old, we were ready to accompany Montgomerie. We were driven down to the lake in a light phaeton, down winding roads, and past cottages full of English families vacationing in the summer. We could easily have thought ourselves in the Lake Districts, were it not for the Indian servants. We drove past the rather pretentious Albion Hotel, down the path on the lake's edge, past the cottages of the important, past the Telegraph Office and the boathouse until swinging past the barracks, we entered thick woods of silver oak and fir. A dirt track took us past an outpost of Gurkhas to a little hunting lodge tucked away among the trees.

An Englishman was sitting in the sun on a small patch of lawn, drinking tea and reading through some papers. Seeing us, he jumped up with a glad cry. This then was Captain Francis Younghusband, of whom our host had spoken so often. He was a smart young fellow of medium height, with a full black moustache under a fine nose, set in the middle of a rather broad face. He was quite unassuming for a man who had been the first to cross over from Kashgar to India over the high Pamirs, and the first to explore the Karakoram Range.

While servants came running out to bring us tea and toast, and escort our carriage round to the back, Younghusband launched into a breezy account of his latest adventures high in the Himalayas. With a small band of Montgomerie's people, he had gone to the source of the Indus, and even stayed as a pilgrim at the Charto Monastery at the river's head. Then he had traced the Sutlej to the Manasarovar Lake, worshipped by Hindoos as the abode of Shiva. There he had encountered some regiments of Thibetan cavalry, and reluctant to provoke an incident, had quickly crossed back to India just east of the Nanda Devi peak, and followed the Kali River downstream. Without omitting any of the details of such a risky undertaking, he yet made it sound no more dangerous than a visit to Brighton.

"How did Kim hold up?" asked Montgomerie rather anxiously.

"Oh, you needn't worry, Sir," said Younghusband. "That boy has a lot of spunk. I had to keep him on a tight leash, I can tell you. He would have led us into rash adventures, if he had had his way. Every now and then, I had to remind him we were only on a scientific mission—well, almost," he added with a laugh.

Montgomerie frowned, and then said after a pause, "Honestly, Francis, I wish we could just keep to science. That is the key object of all our surveys, you know. I don't want our work to be mixed up with what the War Office wants, in any way."

"Quite, Sir, I keep to the line," said Younghusband easily. "But y'know, one just has to oblige the boys. And if the Russians get past us on the high passes, there will be the devil to pay. We will have a full-fledged frontier war on our hands. You remember the Afghan debacle, don't you, Sir? Just trying to keep the Himlayan ranges peaceful, so that we can complete the Survey."

"Yes, I see that. Quite," replied Montgomerie with some conviction. "Ah! There is Kim! I was wondering when that rascal would show up!"

A wiry lad of about twelve or thirteen came running out of the woods to the left. He was dressed in woollen Gharwali leggings and a heavy jacket, and wore an outsized turban. He was as brown as an Indian, and it was only his English that betrayed his British ancestry.

"Hello, Sir! I've been on a grand adventure," he said, dancing up to Montgomerie. "If it hadn't been for me, Francis Sahib would be lying in a ravine with his neck broken!"

A quick narration of the story established that he had indeed held on to Younghusband's horse's bridle when it had shied dangerously over a gorge.

"You rascal, come and shake hands with two very good friends of mine," said Montgomerie, relieved that his protégé was well, and in high spirits. We found the boy to match in every way the description we had been given previously by our host. He had been orphaned a few years ago when his father, Sergeant O'Hara, died of cirrhosis of the liver. With no living relatives nearby, he had been an uncared-for vagrant for a short while, before coming under the care of the Reverend John Budden, and his daughter Mary, in Almora.[36] Kimball O'Hara, or Kim, as he was known to everyone, had received some education at the Mission School in Almora for orphaned boys and girls, although, perhaps, he had been the only white boy among Indian children. John Budden having passed away recently, Mary Budden, now his nominal guardian, had taken Grasmere Cottage just below St John's Church in Naini Tal, and Kim was supposed to be staying with her, although most of the time, he was to be found with Colonel Montgomerie, or Captain Younghusband. Miss Budden, after some faint remonstrance, had given in to the wishes of her headstrong ward, and consoled herself with the thought that the company of officers on a scientific mission was, perhaps, more suited to the interests of a high-spirited boy than a Christian Mission could be.

Sharp for his age, Kim knew that Francis Sahib travelled to the high mountains partly for research, which Kim found acceptable but boring, and partly to spy on the Russians, the Chinese, the Thibetans, the Afghans, and the Khirgiz. He loved the idea of deadly games of hide-and-seek among the highest mountains in the world, where defeat probably meant torture and death, and victory would lead to a chance to tell Montgomerie Sahib of his prowess. We spent the better part of the day listening to his boyish stories, and later giving serious consideration to the scientific and political situation of the region, which left Kim rather bored and drowsy.

The shadows of the trees were beginning to lengthen when we decided to return to Fairlight Hall, dropping Kim off at Miss Budden's. This time we took the other road round the lake, and leaving the dispensary to the right, we went up to Grasmere Cottage, which was behind a high hedge of rhododendrons. Mary Budden, a small-built woman, with a careworn, lined face, thanked us for bringing Kim in, asked him anxiously if he were all right, and then shut the door in our face without further ado.

"Mary Budden has taken her father's death rather hard," said Montgomerie. "She doesn't mean to be uncivil, only with so many children under her wing… and she is particularly solicitous about that boy. I keep telling her he is a high-spirited lad fast growing into a man, and cannot be kept tied to her apron strings. Frankly, I think she has come to see a son in him."

Holmes had kept silent, but when we were alone on the landing before our bedrooms, he said, "Strange, Watson, very strange. That woman wanted us out very quickly. She was afraid—now what could she be hiding, I wonder?"

During the next few weeks, we must have harked back to the decadence of the Regency, for the crowd in Naini Tal thought of nothing but gaiety, fashions, dances, and dinners. It could have been any of the spas of a bygone England, except for the ever-present servants on whom the English depended, and towards whom they displayed an arrogance that would not have been tolerated at home. The Assembly Rooms at the head of the lake could have been at Bath a hundred years ago, with Lady Colvin, the wife of the Lieutenant Governor, as chief patroness. Sir Auckland rarely put in an appearance, and that too—as

far as one could tell—only to please his wife. Captain
Younghusband was an eligible bachelor, and he was much
in demand at all parties. His ease of manner, and his
enthralling stories made him all the more popular with
the ladies, and he seemed as much at home at one of their
parties as he was alone on a high Himalayan range, with
only Kim and a lama for company. Colonel Montgomerie
was also very well known in that narrow circle of imperial
officers, and equally in demand for his skill at bridge.
Holmes and I were made welcome as his guests.

We were on our way to a lakeside tea party, which a
young hostess had thought would be more fun on the
steps of the Hindoo temples beyond the bathing shed
attached to the Assembly Rooms, when we came upon
Miss Mary Budden, seated by a willow, in the company
of a tall, striking gentleman. She looked at us with the
same startled reserve, if not fear, she had displayed on
first seeing us, but quickly composed herself and began
to introduce us.

"Mr Holmes, Dr Watson," she said hurriedly. "How—
how very unexpected. I am delighted to see you both in
the open, and not sitting at a stuffy bridge party," she
continued nervously. "May I introduce an old friend—a
good friend—Mr Gable, from America? He is staying
at the Albion. Mr Gable, these English gentlemen are
friends of Colonel Montgomerie's. Mr Holmes—surely
you have heard of the famous Sherlock Holmes, the great
detective from London?" Even I could detect a note of
subdued warning in her voice. "They know dear Kim,
are attached to the dear—boy, you know, he—he is so

adventurous—heedless of his safety…" Her voice trailed off, and she stood looking from one to the other of us helplessly.

Mr Gable, a man of sixty years, with a shock of white hair, and a white well-trimmed moustache, was dressed expensively in the height of fashion, but with a touch more flamboyance than an English gentleman would have found suitable. He unwound himself to his full height, looked at us with a humorous expression, and then, clamping his cigar to his mouth, drawled, "Put it right there, Mr Holmes, Dr Watson. Call me Clark, I'm Clark to my friends. Can't rightly say I've heard of either of you gentlemen, but the loss, as the lady says, is all mine. I am in the cotton business, gentlemen, and apart from meeting old friends like Miss Budden, I've come to see if I can strike a profitable deal here."

Miss Budden may have wished us to leave, but Holmes had already drawn up a chair, and so, after a little hesitation, I did likewise. Bearers came forward with more tea, sandwiches, and cup cakes. Miss Budden, evidently unaware that I had a fair knowledge of Hindoostani, told them rapidly that we would be leaving soon, and to come and tell the Amrikan angrez in exactly five minutes that a message awaited him in the hotel. I was extremely embarrassed, for I could see she wished us all at the devil's.

"The best cotton you may find far to the south of here, Sir," Holmes was saying earnestly. "I presume you landed at Bombay; further inland to the southeast from there would take you to the best fields India has to show. But I suppose you came all the way north to meet Miss Budden?"

"Yes, that's right. I couldn't miss a chance of meeting Miss Budden, could I now?" asked Gable, with that condescending smile of his, which I was beginning to find rather irritating. "It's hot down there in the fields, the same as in the deep south of my own country. Thought I would stay here in such excellent company—lovely ladies, good food—and wait for it to cool off."

"Well, Mr Gable, you will have to wait a long five months for that to happen," said Holmes reasonably. "And by that time you may even be able to see some cotton. Nothing but bare fields now."

A lesser man might have flushed at getting caught out telling a lie, but not our Mr Gable. "I am a patient man, Mr Holmes," he drawled. "Time well spent, if I get what I want. Will I get what I want, Miss Budden?" he asked, turning suddenly to look piercingly at the little missionary. She jumped almost as if he had hit her.

"I—I don't know, Mr Gable, sincerely, I don't know," she said in a pleading voice. "I wish you every success, you know that, and I will try, and I have tried before..." And then she stopped quickly to look at us, knowing she had said more than she should have.

One of Montgomerie's servants now approached me, and said in Hindoostani that the Sahib desired my company at the card table inside. I nodded, and was rising to leave, for I had no desire to be where I was not wanted, when I saw her give me a stricken look. Obviously she realized I had understood her instructions for a bearer to come with a false message for Mr Gable. With a simple bow and a look, I tried to convey to her that her little secret was safe with me, but her look of dejection told me it had no effect.

Later that evening, back at Fairlight Hall, I asked Holmes what it could all mean. "There is a mystery here, Watson, and she is afraid we will discover it. This Gable is no friend, you can see it from her stiffness in his presence. Oh, I know, missionaries are a stiff lot, but there is something unnatural in their relationship. And both of them were lying, he not even caring to hide it. He is amused that we are detectives, and was almost challenging us. Now, what can the little old miss be hiding, so scared that she doesn't want us anywhere near?"

The thought bothered us both, and so we decided we would take the hill road to Almora, where she and her late father had run a mission school. Montgomerie lent us excellent ponies for our sightseeing trip when we told him of our plan, and the air being cool and fresh, and the views splendid, the fifty-mile ride was accomplished with ease. The Commandant there had been informed beforehand, and our rooms in the cavalry barracks were ready. Discreet enquiries revealed nothing about the Buddens that we did not already know. We inspected the mission buildings and the school, and found them clean and well run, a tribute to the late Reverend Budden, who had been much loved by all. And everyone seemed to hold Miss Mary in even higher regard.

After thanking our considerate hosts, and exchanging cards, we rode back along the scenic cart road back to

Holmes of the Raj

Naini Tal. "Everything is as it should be, Watson, which makes it all the more mysterious," said Holmes, as we rested on a ridge, to drink from our canteens. "The only odd fact I could discover was that Kim's name is nowhere recorded in the registers of the school, but everyone remembers he studied there. I wonder why they wouldn't enter his name?

As dusk was falling we found ourselves within the settlement limits of Naini Tal. Pulling up at a little break between the tall trees that lined the road, Holmes looked at something down in the cantonment to the left, and then silently passed the glasses on to me. Kim's small figure was unmistakable even in the gathering darkness, and he was down by the huts behind the cantonment bakery, hurrying along some sepoys who were carrying long wooden boxes. They disappeared into a hut, re-emerging a few minutes later. Kim locked the door of the hut, and they all scattered rapidly. It certainly looked as though they were hiding something. Was it under Montgomerie's orders, or was Kim playing some foolish prank? Holmes gave no replies to my half questions, and we rode back to Fairlight Hall, whose windows were agleam with friendly and welcoming light.

Lady Colvin, taking a particular compassionate interest in me, saw to it that I was invited to every party, and that I was constantly introduced to charming new people. For Holmes she felt no such responsibility, instinctively recognizing in him the thinker who was happiest alone. The season's grand party, of course, had been organized by her at Government House, and almost all the summer residents of Naini Tal were invited. In the sea of English faces at the party, I spied a tall, handsome Indian, not yet thirty, wearing a faultless muslin turban above a perfectly tailored tailcoat, which he carried with ease, unlike other Indians I have seen. His white bowtie had been tied with elegant precision, and a large diamond stud gleamed on his impeccable shirtfront. The Colvins, like Lord Lansdowne, the Viceroy, openly discouraged Indians from coming up to the summer resorts of the English, but exceptions were always made for a handful of favourites.

Lady Colvin bore down on me. "Dear Dr Watson, I must introduce you to our charming Mr Motilal Nehru, the most famous barrister in India. He is always besieged by the ladies, but I am sure with your experience of India, both of you would have much to talk about. Mr Nehru would rather we all left India. Now, come be honest with an old friend, tell me you would rather see me back in England, cold and hunched over a small wretched fire in a shabby room!"

Mr Nehru smiled down on her, and bent and kissed her hand gracefully. "On the contrary, Lady Colvin, you know I will be desolate, and so would the rest of India. My efforts are to prepare the Indian subjects of Her Majesty to share in the better running of the Empire." Tapping him lightly on the chin with her fan, she bustled away.

Mr Nehru continued to smile. "Dr Watson, I have heard so much about you, and your redoubtable friend, Mr Holmes. I would be very happy if both of you could join me and some friends for dinner, whenever convenient. I have rented Haddon Hall for the season, but most of the time I am down in Allahabad in the interests of my clients. But this weekend I am here, and two of my closest friends will also be coming up."

Before I could reply, I heard the soft froufrou of a silk saree, and turning, saw a beautiful young Indian lady coming up in haste. She was wearing large rings studded with diamonds in her ears, a glittering diamond nose ring, and a matching diamond necklace. Mr Nehru introduced her as his niece, Kasturi.

She smiled mischievously at me from under the brocaded paloo of her sari, drawn over the large chignon that seemed to stand under the silk like a hood. "Dr Watson, let me add my request to my uncle's," she said softly, in the Welsh-like singsong most Indians use. "You and Mr Holmes, about whom I have read so much since I was a child, both of you must come for dinner this Sunday."

I could not have refused such a charming invitation even if I had wished to, and was beginning to ask her why I had not yet seen her in the Assembly Rooms, when Colonel Makepeace Guthrie, the Assistant Quarter-Master General, came panting up. "Miss Kasturi, I have told one of my boys to bring up the gun to the terrace. As I was telling you, it is an absolute beauty. Although, of course, it is not in your class," he added rather obseqiously. "But the new Lee-Enfield has a smooth bolt action, a short magazine, and a short muzzle; the best rifle your sepoy can have to defend the Empire. Come, my dear, so few women can combine beauty and brains like you do…" and he led her away, confidentially whispering into her hidden ear the beauties of the rifle.

Nehru was laughing now, but without malice. "Every man must love something, I suppose, other than women," he said. "Old soldiers love guns. I care for law books. I am sure, for you, Dr Watson, medical records are a passion."

With that, I could not resist telling him about my recent discovery of the malaria-carrying mosquito. He listened with interest, and asked me several scientific questions, which I could answer only with suppositions.

Later that evening, I saw Gable waltzing around the floor with Miss Kasturi on his arm, smiling at her through his moustache, hugging her elegantly at the turn, and somehow the sight left me slightly annoyed. She reminded me of someone I had known, but I couldn't place the name, although I mustered memories of all my past acquaintances, English and Indian. I spent a few hours at the card table, and after winning and losing a rubber, I went out on to the terrace to savour the cool night air. Walking past the formal "Italian garden" I heard a murmur of voices, and then came a girl's voice raised in anger: "I tell you, no! A thousand times no! Now let me go!" Miss Kasturi was on her feet, while Gable lounged on a marble seat, with a restraining hand on her arm.

I find lechers particularly despicable, and I stepped forward with an angry exclamation. "Can I be of service, Miss Kasturi?" I asked, glaring at Gable.

The girl had freed herself by now, and murmuring it was of no consequence, she thanked me and, with an odd little bow towards Gable, ran back to the lighted halls. I was on the point of stepping forward and challenging the fellow, when I saw Miss Budden silently emerging from the shadows behind the seat. She must have been there all the while. With a little exclamation I could not suppress, I turned and left without a word, while his little cat-like laugh sounded behind me.

I was glad to find Holmes in the library of Fairlight Hall when I returned late that night. I had had little opportunity to talk to him for almost a week, for he had busied himself in some esoteric research, which took him away early and brought him back late. I related the whole episode to him, and asked him what he thought it all meant. He would say nothing for a long time.

"What is clear, Watson, is that this Gable is not here to buy cotton, nor is he a friend of Miss Budden. He is here on some sinister business, and we should track it down before he does any mischief."

Holmes and I took up Mr Nehru's invitation to have dinner with him and his special Indian friends that Sunday night. Haddon Hall was a rather ostentatious mansion, and was brilliantly lit for the evening. We were met at the door by a retinue of servants, ushered into a very comfortable study, and plied with whisky and soda, and mutton kebabs. Mr Nehru entered soon after, dressed comfortably in a European lounge suit, and shook hands, hospitably asking Holmes how he, as an Indian, could make our stay more comfortable. Soon, his two Indian friends entered, and stood rather stiffly to be introduced.

"Mr Holmes, Dr Watson, let me introduce two of my very best friends. Both are lawyers, as you might have guessed, and also educators—in fact, they are men of many parts. Pandit Madan Mohan Malaviya, and Lala Lajpat Rai."[37]

They were both very handsome men. The Pandit was the eldest of the three, dressed in a long, spotlessly white coat over a white dhoti, and a large muslin turban, like our host. He wore a chandan spot on his forehead. The Lala, a well-built Punjabi, wore a black sherwani over churidars, and a tall black cap. I noticed that special vegetarian dishes were laid out on a separate table for the Pandit, by a special Brahmin servant, with a long tuft of coiled hair.

The conversation turned effortlessly to India's political situation, the condition of her peoples, the efforts of the British Raj, and the mistakes of individual officials. The services of Lord Ripon were acknowledged with warmth and enthusiasm. When Lord Macaulay's educational policy came up for scrutiny, Nehru supported it vehemently, while Malaviya opposed it with equal vigour. Lajpat Rai had a third opinion, but I could not quite make out what it was.

"Are you of the opinion, Mr Rai," asked Holmes, "that we must have modern educational reforms to suit the times, but that the British system is faulty or insufficient for that purpose?"

"Precisely, Mr Holmes!" said Lajpat Rai enthusiastic-ally. "To hanker after traditional Vedic education, and the spreading of Sanskrit patshalas, as our friend Panditji does, would be to shackle Indians to the past. If there is any benefit at all for Indians from the British connection, it is that these shackles have been broken. None of us should put them back on. But education, as it now exists, is forging a new set of shackles for our people, making them babus, loyal servitors of the British. What Indians want, what they need at this hour, is freedom, and education must prepare them for that freedom, or it is next to useless!"

Nehru quickly distanced himself from that opinion.

"India's future and well-being lies within the embrace of Empire," he said evenly. "The world is not like my friend, the Lalaji, imagines. There are sharks and wolves out there, and we would be swallowed up by nations without a conscience, should the British Government do something so immoral as to wash its hands off India. It is India's fortune that Providence brought the British here when the Moghul Empire lay dying, bereft of money, morals, or fighting men."

Conversation then turned to the recent past, Nehru adding many little known facts from the history of his own family, who had been ministers to the Moghuls for generations. Finally, they turned to the Pandit as arbiter of the discussion.

"I want change," he said slowly. "I am sure these English gentlemen, all men of character, would also wish to see the best for their fellow Indian subjects. I am with Motilal, when he wants a modern India, free of poverty and disease. I am with Lajpat Rai who wants an India that will be the equal of any nation in the world. But I am with neither, when they think all these changes can be brought about by 'foreign' methods. If India is to become great, she can become great only by strengthening her own great traditions, not by aping anyone else."

During the long discussions that raged until well past eleven at night, we did not see any of the household's womenfolk, although we did hear them giving instructions to the servants. I was disappointed not to have the English-educated niece in our midst. She came in briefly only once, before dinner, carrying a baby. Giving us a quick smile, she came straight up to us. Holmes and I struggled to our feet, but both the Pandit and the Lala ignored her presence and, in fact, looked the other way when she was in the room.

"Mr Holmes, Dr Watson, let me introduce little Jawaharlal, the chirag, the light of our house, as we say," she said in her sweet singsong, holding out the baby for our admiration. "He is so like his father, wouldn't you say? He is a son for me too, well, as much mine as Swaroopa's," she added, kissing the baby's tummy. From the set of his shoulders, I could see the Pandit had stiffened, while the Lala tried to distract himself with a magazine. Nehru continued to smile indulgently as she went back to the zenana with the baby.

When dinner was over, we bade a cordial goodnight to our new Indian friends, and refusing to be driven home, decided to walk back. Before leaving the estate, however, I wanted to take a quick look at the greenhouse beyond the fountain, for I could see some beautiful orchids in the pale light of the moon. As I was coming out of the shed, I had a view of the back of the house, and saw Miss Kasturi and Lala Lajpat Rai, whispering together in the darkness by a door, while he quickly passed her an envelope.

Despite the salubrious climate, the little town was beginning to irritate me with its unanswered questions. I needed physical activity to keep my brain from churning round in circles. Consequently, I accepted the invitation of a few young officers of the Gurkha Regiment to do some practice shooting with the new SMLE Lee-Enfields—the "smellies", as they were beginning to be called—the next afternoon after tea.[38] Walking down the Upper Kaladungi Road, I reached the rifle range in the dip of the hills well behind the Christian cemetery. The rifles fired as well and rapidly as Colonel Guthrie had enthusiastically proclaimed at the Government House party. The rifle's action was astonishingly reliable, even when the barrel was hot after several rounds had been fired.

Invigorated by the exercise, I congratulated the officers on acquiring such a splendid weapon, and walked homewards. Passing St John's, it occurred to me I had not been in a church for a long time, and that a little prayer could only do me good. It was empty at that time, with a clean white interior, an indication of an arched roof, and a simple attempt at a stained-glass religious motif behind the altar. The setting sun scattered a pleasing mosaic of colour down the aisle, and choosing a pew by an open window, I bent my head in prayer.

No words of prayer would come easily, as my mind kept returning uneasily to the events and intrigues of the last few weeks. I was aware of the danger that Gable posed, and I also wondered whether it was my duty to inform Nehru that his niece might be entering into an unwelcome liaison with his friend. Who did she resemble from my past, I wondered with irritation. The sound of voices jerked me out of my reverie.

"I was at my father's grave, it's none of your business," I heard Kim say hotly.

Raising my head, I could see out of the angle of the window that the boy was almost pinned to the wall of the cemetery by the tall, stooping figure of the American.

"Don't waste your time here, Kim," said Gable with authority. "What are these people to you? They will merely use you and discard you, as they did your mother. I know the type—the English look powerful, but their days are numbered. They are laughably arrogant, I tell you. It is the little old United States of America that will matter in the future. Come with me, I have money, plenty of it."

"Don't you be bloody arrogant, Clark!" the boy flashed back. "I know what I'm doing. My home is here! I like it here, and I will live here!"

"Yes, I know how you will live, and for just how short a time," said Gable, sneering openly. "I know all about your liaisons with the darkies here!"

"Don't you dare say a word about my Indian friends!" cried Kim angrily. "What do you know of people, you, you disgusting slave owner!"

I could see that Gable was angry now. He grabbed Kim's arm, twisted it with force, pulling the boy close to his chest. "I know what must be done, you idiot," he said into the boy's face. "I want to see you dressed in a skirt, and to act like a woman with me!"

I was shocked and disgusted at the man's depravity, and would have stormed out, but for the proverbial appearance, round the corner of the church, of the harried Miss Budden, looking for her charge. Gable relaxed his hold, Kim shook himself free with a disgusted expression, and placed himself behind the woman.

"Mr Gable, you know I am on your side, but I will not have anyone use force on poor Kim," she said in a firm tone. "We may seem poor and stupid in our ways to a great man like yourself, but this is our life, and God directs us, I am sure. If Kim does not wish it, Kim shall not go to America with you!"

It was said bravely. Kim, suddenly overcome with the release of tension, burst into tears, and somewhat ashamed, raced away in the direction of Grasmere Cottage. With a muttered curse, and without even the courtesy of a nod in the direction of the lady, Gable strode off to his horse, tethered by the cemetery gate, mounted, and galloped off. Miss Budden stood swaying with emotion, her face buried in her hands.

Risking her rebuff, I went out to steady her. Her worn, tear-stained face looked up at me.

"You are very kind, Dr Watson," she said simply. "Believe me, I did what I thought was for the best. My poor sainted father did not approve of Kim's wild ways, how could he have? I stood between his wrath and Kim, knowing what that poor woman had gone through when O'Hara died. She protected her child the best way she knew, among those ungodly men; and...poor woman, she had to sell herself to feed them both, God forgive her. He surely will forgive her. I promised her on her deathbed, Dr Watson, to take care of her child. Kim was already wild by then, willful...God! I see I have erred, I should have been strong right from the start... insisted, brought Kim to see reason...but when Colonel Montgomerie took charge... I thought it might all come out all right later...and now this! I must pray! I must pray for forgiveness!"

Weeping, her face buried in her handkerchief, she ran inside the church.

I was deeply disturbed by her pathetic, incoherent account of Kim's stewardship. It was clear that Miss Budden was no longer capable of taking care of a growing white boy in this remote place. As I walked back, I determined to talk to Montgomerie, Younghusband, and Holmes, so that we could work out a way of sending the boy to school in England. We could jointly support the expenses of his education until he grew up and found a job suitable to his talents. I would certainly not leave him here at the mercy of perverted scoundrels like Gable.

Colonel Montgomerie had been away for some days, on one of his missions to obtain a complete range of geological samples for classification in British universities. A couple of days after the unpleasant incident at St John's, the geological team arrived late in the afternoon, riding alongside several slow bullock carts laden with different kinds of stone and other specimens. When I broached the subject of Kim's education, Montgomerie looked at

me with the vague look of a scientist, and said that it
was certainly important, but didn't I think it could wait
until we had all the samples properly labelled, organized,
and packed for despatch? And right after that, he lost
interest in me.

Kim himself seemed to have regained his composure,
and had become the heart and soul of the geological
group. "Look! Dr Watson!" he would call out, holding
out a piece of rock. "See how beautiful this is? When
I was with Captain Francis, up the Churta Tsangpo,
before it joins the Brahmaputra, there was a whole
hillside that shone like this! What was it called, Sahib?"
He darted back to an indulgent Younghusband. "Yes, I
remember, the Hurkiang peak! Oh! You should see the
sunsets there—the reds and greys turn a golden yellow
for a minute!" Or, it would be: "Oh! Like the pebbles
littering the banks of the lake, before we reached Sang
Sang Giado village. Remember how we were attacked by
those fierce Thibetan mastiffs, and poor Sarat Das fell as
he ran? He would have been torn to pieces, but I picked
up a long Thibetan whip, and cracked it round in circles,
keeping them away until their masters came!"

A week of hard work had most of the rocks and stones
neatly catalogued, labelled, and packed in long wooden
crates, for despatch to Britain. Kim sat astride of one of
them as if it were a horse. "How I wish I could fire this
like a cannon straight for England, and ride it all the way
there," he said, his eyes gleaming.

Considering the moment ripe, I broached the subject
of going to school in England, but he was daydreaming

and would not pay much attention to me. However, I took his interest in England as a good sign, and I was determined to pursue the subject at a calmer moment in the presence of poor Miss Budden.

The day came for the boxes to be sent down by carts to the railhead, for despatch to Bareilly, where, under proper supervision, they would be loaded into wagons, bound for London via Calcutta. Kim begged Colonel Montgomerie to let him accompany the officers in charge as far as Bareilly, and the Colonel, ever indulgent, agreed with a laugh. I myself was relieved that the boy's spirits had not been affected by that cruel meeting with Gable.

Two days after the loaded carts had left, with Kim perched atop one, amusing a platoon of accompanying sepoys by singing a song of the hill people of Kumaon, Holmes took it into his head that he and I should go up north and climb the foothills of the Nanda Devi. Colonel Montgomerie quickly arranged for two ponies that we might use. We declined any escort, saying good-naturedly that we were old enough to look after ourselves. Holmes swung the horses round, the moment we were out of sight of Naini Tal, and led us down the hills at a fast clip, towards the road to Kathgodam. I was surprised at this mild deception, but knowing Holmes and his methods, held my peace, and spurred my horse to a canter.

Leaving the ponies with a shoesmith near the railway station, with promises of a rich reward if we found the horses well cared for on our return, we took a train down to Bareilly. The monsoon rains had broken over the town when we reached it. Fortunately, the long hooded Garwhali coats we had borrowed from our host now kept us dry on the platform lashed by hot rain. Shouldering our saddlebags, we waded across the dirty square before the station, and took refuge under a sheet of tarpaulin, at a dark chaiwallah's. Why Holmes would drag me to this dirty soot-blackened shack, instead of going to a waiting room in the station, I did not know, or ask, leaving him to command the order of the day's work. Sipping sugary tea, and eating hot onion bajiyas, we gazed down the length of the platform. Through the sheets of rain, we saw a goods wagon being shunted to the front, and the figures of the officers, sepoys, and a nimble Kim, supervising the loading of the long trunks containing geological samples. The work accomplished, and the wagons sealed, the team disappeared into the station's restaurant. I made myself as comfortable as I could on the chaiwallah's floor, which was already wet with the seeping rain.

Dulled by fatigue and boredom, I must have dozed off, for waking to change my position, I found Holmes gone. With an imprecation against the rain, I leaned against a sack of potatoes, and fell asleep again. When Holmes woke me, the rain had stopped, although clouds hung dark against a threatening sky.

"Come, Watson, the game is afoot!" said Holmes grimly.

Leading me across the square, he introduced me to a Superintendent of Police, whose face I could hardly see by lantern light, and both then led me to the wagons on a siding. Our friends from Naini Tal must have taken a train back, for none of them were in sight. The order was given to break the locks, and with some difficulty, the long wooden cases with geological specimens were dragged out on to the platform. By then, the first light of dawn was streaking through the clouds, and the station-master had sent round bearers to fetch us cups of tea. A stout, dark mechanic in deep blue overalls prised open the nailed-down lids of the cases, and through the straw we saw the labelled pieces of stone. Holmes ordered the specimens to be lifted out carefully. After several layers had been removed, a thin wooden partition was lifted to reveal several rifles, neatly arranged. The boxes were now torn open in haste, and the orderlies laid out on the platform, as if for inspection, several dozen rifles and boxes of ammunition, still in their original wrappings. The rifles were mostly the older Martini-Henrys and the later Lee-Metfords.

"Look at the markings, Officer," said Holmes, pointing to the guns. "Almost all from our ordnance factory at Cossipore. These rifles must have been sent there ostensibly for repairs, then discarded as useless, stolen, and shipped out in these boxes. They have been careful not to steal any of the new Lee-Enfields, for fear of raising a storm and starting an enquiry. And look at the headmarkings of the ammunition. We find 'KH' for the Khamaria Arsenal at Jubbulpore, and 'DF' for the dreaded soft-nosed Dum Dum bullets. They are a clever network of thieves, all right, and very well organized, for several men must be involved from various departments."

"Well, money can buy many men," admitted the policeman. "Especially if they have fallen in debt, and think one carelessly inspected batch might not matter after all."

"But what is the purpose of this theft?" pursued Holmes. "What nefarious insurrection will these arms aid?"

We turned to the despatch instructions on the boxes. Neatly pasted over the original sheets was the address of the Department of Geology, Trinity College, Dublin. The discoveries had been too rapid for me to understand what had happened. "For God's sake, tell me, Holmes," I pleaded. "What is going on? And how did you chance upon this piece of knavery?"

"I am not yet fully certain what is intended," said Holmes soberly. "Do you remember that evening when we were headed back from Almora, Watson, and we spied some sepoys hastily stashing long boxes in a hut behind the bakery in the cantonment? I knew even then that something fishy was going on. I hid myself near that hut, caught a sepoy red-handed, when he opened that door, and handed the scared man over to his commanding officer. The fellow was terribly afraid, for he knew it was a hanging offence. We got him to tell us all he knew, in exchange for a promise of a fair trial and a lenient sentence, if possible."

Having instructed the police officer to notify the headquarters of the Indian Imperial Police in Calcutta, and put the stolen arms under close guard in the Bareilly Police Station, Holmes said it was time we got back to Naini Tal. His last instructions as we boarded the train were for all the coolies involved in the loading of the boxes to be arrested and interrogated closely.

On the silent journey back, I tried to piece together the facts as I saw them. Clearly this Gable was no cotton merchant but a gunrunner who, in all probability, would collect the shipment in Ireland, through some agent in his pay in Dublin, and smuggle them across to the United States. They would then be given to Red Indians, or worse still, be exchanged for costly buffalo and other pelts. I could see he was the type—quite without conscience or remorse—who would go to any lengths to "make a buck". He had some hold over poor Miss Budden, or more probably had simply terrified her into silence. He was lecherous and perverted, and that I thought was the whole of the story.

It was late afternoon by the time we led our horses to the stables at the back of Fairlight Hall. Montgomerie was nowhere to be found, nor did we look for him. Asking me to bring my service revolver, Holmes set out on foot down the steep footpath leading to the Middle Mall, and when we had reached it, swung right towards the church. We burst unannounced into Miss Budden's living room, to find, to my considerable surprise, Miss Kasturi in animated conversation with Gable. Miss Budden jumped up in fright, but the other two looked at us with remarkable composure.

"Kim! Throw off this stupid disguise, we know everything!" said Holmes in a tired manner.

Even as I looked around for the boy, Miss Kasturi rose sinuously. "With the greatest of pleasure, Mr Holmes," she said in a faultless British accent, without a trace of the charming singsong I had heard before. She tore back the paloo of her sari, and with a sweep of her hand, flung the wig that had formed her large chignon to the floor. Slowly and deliberately, she removed her jewellery, smiling at us, and then, shaking free her short curls, stood revealed as Kim, although still dressed immodestly in a sari! But it couldn't be Kim; there was no mistaking the slim womanly body under the clinging silk sari! I gasped in confusion. Even Holmes, ever imperturbable, was visibly taken aback and at a loss for words.

"Well, Mr Holmes?" challenged Kim. "But where is your Kim? I am Kasturi, and also Kim, Kimberley O'Hara, not the Kimball O'Hara of your imagination! None of you ever dreamt that a girl could do all the things I did, could you? That presumption was my best disguise. My mother was right, poor sainted whore, I could only have survived as a boy among so many rascals. And did it never enter any of your arrogant skulls to ask why a child of Ireland would be loyal to an English Army, when you have eaten like pigs at a trough from our green fields for eight centuries? Had you referred to our sacred history, you would have discovered that the O'Haras are not just cannon fodder for the English, but descended from the high kings of ancient Ireland, when you English had neither God nor language nor learning!"

Her eyes blazed. "God's curse on you, your armies, and your Queen! My grandparents starved to death in Killinkere in the forties, when you killed millions of Irish with your potato famine. And all the while your Castle Irish fed off groaning tables! And when you hanged the Manchester Martyrs, you thought it was the end of the

Fenians, did you? Poor you! We are as strong as Finn McCool himself, and yes, I have sent home guns to kill all you villains!"

"You are under arrest, Miss Kimberley, on the charge of seditious conspiracy and high treason," said Sherlock Holmes soberly.

"And where's your proof, man?" scorned Kim. "Remember, the gunrunner was Kim, the darling boy of the British Army? I am Kasturi, an Indian woman! You cannot even prove I am white. You will have to strip me in public to do that. Do it!" she screamed. "My Indians will butcher every Englishman, if you dared so insult the house of Motilal Nehru!"

"No one would dare touch an American, Kim," burst in Gable. "I'll tell their tinpot Viceroy you are my wife's cousin, daughter of her father's younger brother, and the President himself will speak to their Prime Minister. Come home, girl, enough's enough. We have money and lands aplenty. You will have all of Atlanta at your feet, and more beaus than you can handle. You don't have to end up as a mistress of an Indian lawyer!"

"Who are you, Sir?" I burst in. "What are you doing here, and how are you connected to this young lady?"

He looked at us gravely, and then said with a little mock bow as he got up. "Why, I am in the cotton business, true enough. My wife Scarlett and I own one of the largest plantations in Georgia. I am Rhett Butler of Tara, Atlanta. I chose the name of an actor I once knew, for experience has shown me it is better to travel incognito when on serious business. Scarlett and I have no living children,

and my wife's dearest wish is to adopt this thoughtless
young girl, as the last remaining member of her family.
We took a lot of trouble to trace her here, and now the
wench won't come home!" he ended in comic despair.[39]

"Dear Rhett, I thank you and Scarlett for your kind
offer, indeed I do. It is a kind, generous gesture. But
I am happy here, Rhett, even as you and Scarlett are
on your plantation in Tara. India is now my home. I
am very happy in my relationship with Motilal, and
the position I have in his household," said Kim with
noble poise. She then turned towards Holmes and me.
"And I should like to assure you, Sirs, that you may have
stopped one of my shipments, but others will follow.
And Motilal's little son, Jawahar, will suckle hatred
against the British at my bosom, and I am quite certain
that in good time he will expel you from India. By all
that is sacred, I swear it!"

So commanding was her presence that none of us had
noticed Mr Nehru himself slip quietly into the room
during Kim's little speech. Behind him crowded his tall
Rajput servitors, polite, but ready to do their master's
bidding.

Gently, he said "Come, Kim, let us go home. You
are finished with this charade now. Do not worry, Miss
Budden, I shall make her as happy as is possible."

"Yes, Mary, you must come and visit me often," said
Kim, giving her benefactor a fond kiss. "You have been
mother, sister, guardian, angel, all in one to me for so
many years. We shall never part." And with that she, Mr
Nehru, and his entourage were gone.

We spent a few more minutes in the little room, comforting Miss Budden, who agreed that what could not be mended must be endured. Mr Gable, or rather Mr Butler, said he would leave the very next day, for now that he knew for certain that his mission had been unsuccessful, there was nothing further to delay his return to the only country he cared for.

Holmes and I walked up to Fairlight Hall through a light drizzle. It was a foretaste of the monsoon that would soon thunder upon the hills. On the brow of the Upper Mall, we stopped and looked at the lights twinkling below.

"What shall we tell Montgomerie, Holmes?" I asked.

"We shall tell him nothing," said Holmes decisively. "It is better that he never knows. He will miss the boy for some time, and then like any other dreamy scientist, he will console himself with the thought that he must have run away to some distant mountain village, and will return one day. I don't think Younghusband would really care one way or the other. He thinks only of his career, and his mission. Miss Budden, I am sure, will say nothing. She is too fond of Kim. And as for our romantic friend Kipling, who has been threatening to write a story about Kim—well, let him write about the Kim he knew. There wasn't just one Kim, but several. We saw one just now, Kipling saw another a while ago, Montgomerie a third, and Miss Budden a fourth."

"Aye, and now, let's get in out of this rain," I said.

Art, Crime, and Enlightenment

When we went up to the Government House at Naini Tal to take formal leave of Sir Auckland and Lady Colvin, the latter beamingly presented us with an invitation. It stated that the Vicereine was graciously pleased to ask us to stay with her for a few weeks, as guests of the Government of India, before we sailed for England. "Your services to Empire have not gone unrecognized," said Lady Colvin excitedly. "I am so pleased."

It was more than an invitation—it was a command. We realized that the next few days would be spent attending formal functions, without once having the chance to slip into a smoking jacket. Despite our yearning for some peace and quiet, we consented.

The monsoons had broken over the city, and at the famous Howrah Railway Station, we were received by a dashing aide-de-camp, and seated in a closed carriage drawn by four greys. The carriage crossed the fifteen-hundred-foot-long Howrah Bridge, travelled down by the Hooghly, and turned at the Bentinck Monument on the Esplanade, towards the palatial Government House. We were received at the private entrance on the south side, and taken by servants to our rooms on the second floor.

Despite the early hour, we could discern a bustle of activity around the palace, and by the time we went down to breakfast on the covered circular east-facing verandah, the building had become a veritable hive of activity. Lady Maud was seated alone at the table. We bowed before her, and at a gesture, sat on either side of her deep cane chair. "Mr Holmes, Dr Watson, I have so wanted to meet you, and hear firsthand about your daring exploits," she said kindly. "Here, do let me pour out tea. The kippers could be better—we have excellent fish in Bengal—but I am having this old building completely refurbished, and everything is at sixes and sevens. Fortunately, the artistic work is in masterly hands. Evelyn, my daughter, discovered a modern Florentine master at an obscure gallery in London—well, actually started by one of her friends—and wrote to me that Signor Moresconi was just the artist to touch up the old paintings and generally advise me how we might convert this barn into a liveable home. He is such a dear—here he is!"

Signor Moresconi, looking like nothing but a caricature of the famous portrait of Leonardo da Vinci, came out through the large doors of the Throne Room to Lady Maud's left. He had a large, white, bushy beard, and wore a floppy maroon cap flecked with paint. A long blue apron, generously daubed with paint, covered a gaunt frame, now stooped with age. Two very bright eyes twinkled on either side of a fleshy hooked nose. He stood still for a moment, looking at us, his head cocked to one side like a parrot's. "Your Ladyship! See how charming is the lambent morning light of Bengal!" he said in a heavy accent. "Reminds me of the softer lights around Capri; not like the—the clarity that has made Umbria the universal home of art!"

"Dear Signor, meet my guests," said Lady Maud, handing him a cup of tea as he sank into a chair, guiltily wiping his hands on his apron. "I know you are devoted to art, but you must rest, dear Sir, it is essential at your—at our time of life, especially in this treacherous climate."

He turned towards us politely. "And Mr—Mr Shelley Gomez and the Doctore love art as well? Yes? They are here to advise me, yes, how best to make this most magnificent palace a home, truly, for so charming a woman as Your Ladyship?"

Lady Maud simpered a little at his warm compliment, and reintroduced us, speaking slowly and clearly. Signor Moresconi was profuse in his apologies; he was getting old, and English names were not always the easiest to understand. So we were detectives? Ah, he was relieved, a burden had been lifted from his shoulders, milady's palace had such priceless pieces of art, but everything was sadly unprotected; with us here, he felt braver, he could work without fear. Lady Maud broke into this stream of words to assure him with a smile that no place could be safer than the residence of the Viceroy of India.

After a leisurely breakfast, several bright young officers whisked us away, at the Vicereine's insistence, for a sight-seeing trip around the great city, while Moresconi went back to his paintings. The sky had cleared, and we were

driven down Chowringhee Road towards the Bengal
Club and the Asiatic Society offices, past Dufferin
Statue, round Fort William on Ellenborough Course,
and then back past Dalhousie Square, and through the
charming Bow Bazaar to Calcutta's intellectual centre,
Presidency College. From there, we proceeded to the
bridge, the last stop on our itinerary, where an incident
occurred that would have profound consequences for our
stay in Calcutta.

We had wanted to take another look at the long
bridge at Howrah, inspect its electrical machinery, and
see how the bridge itself opened up to allow steamers
to pass upriver. As we were crossing the square at
the mouth of the Howrah Bridge, an Indian peasant,
evidently quite unaccustomed to city traffic, almost
found himself under the wheels of our carriage. With a
shriek, he grabbed his little son, and both rolled over,
missing our horses' hooves by a whisker. They lay in
a stunned heap in the dust, their meagre belongings
scattered everywhere. We were out of the carriage like
a shot, and while I examined the child to see if he was
hurt, Holmes had the grooms riding behind us gather
the man's belongings together, which they did very
grudgingly. The boy and his father were unhurt, but
badly shaken. We heard the pathetic story so common
in India. The man had lost his two bighas of land to
grasping moneylenders, and had come to the city in
sheer desperation, to look for work. By then our carriage
had pulled over, and we had ordered for cups of tea
for the unfortunate father and son, whose names were

Balraj and Parikshit. The man knew no work other than tilling his fields, so, on the spur of the moment, we gave him some money and instructions, and advised him to purchase a rickshaw to eke out a livelihood. We left him crying out his gratitude at the top of his powerful lungs, while tears streamed down his face.[40]

The rest of the trip was uneventful, and we were back for lunch in the small dining room to the north of the building. Lord Lansdowne received us graciously enough, but we could see that the Viceroy did not have the friendly ease of manner of Her Ladyship, being supremely conscious most of the time that he ruled India in the name of Her Majesty.[41] The only other persons present at lunch were Lord Roberts, Commander-in-Chief of India, and the Military Secretary, Lord William de la Poer Beresford. "Bobs" of Kandahar, a balding soldier with clear blue eyes and a large white moustache, was already a living legend, as much for his bluff, straightforward manner with the men, as for his astonishing victories. He put us at our ease immediately. Beresford, a handsome, delicate-featured Irish bachelor, was the third son of the fourth Marquess of Waterford, and had made his own way through life with his sword, winning a Victoria Cross when he was barely thirty, at Ullundi, in Zululand.

After lunch, when we rose to leave the Viceroy and Lord Roberts alone, the latter signalled us to stay, saying: "Let's have you with us. You are detectives—every British schoolboy has heard of you—and who knows, you may be able to see something an old soldier like me misses!"

The Viceroy did not seem too pleased at Lord Roberts' offhand manner, but he was too magnanimous a man to show annoyance, and with a slight nod in our direction, turned his attention completely towards his Commander -in-Chief. "The state of the borders is a matter of constant concern, Sir," said Roberts, puffing away on a black Trichnopalee. "We have created three lines of defence in the northwest: one around British territories under Direct Rule; the second around the Protectorate of tribal areas; and the third at the very borders of the Amir of Afghanistan, who is under our Sphere of Influence. We have removed the men not loyal to us, who imagined they were strong enough to rule independent kingdoms. At some sacrifice to ourselves, we have disabused the Afghans of any such notion. We have installed an Amir, an ineffective ruler, I grant you, but one who for that very reason will be loyal. The defences are deep, I warrant you, and conditions seem normal enough—if anything can be called normal in those parts, with the Russian bear itching for trouble. Younghusband is a capital fellow, and these gentlemen here have played a signal role in his success—under cover of geographical surveys, he has managed to infiltrate into the high valleys beyond the northern slopes of the Himalayas. Our men are there in Thibet, without the Chinese Empire or the Thibetan rulers being any the wiser, because most are not in uniform. Our writ now runs north of the Pamirs, which is today in our Sphere of Interest. We may soon need to convert that into one of Influence. Thanks to your wise policies, and the proverbial 'whiff of grapeshot', the King of Bhutan has handed over the southern slopes to British India, and our planters will convert savage lands into profitable tea gardens. The folly of the Thibaw of Burma in fining the British–Burma Company for felling forests beyond the concession area has enabled us to incorporate Burma into the Empire. Thibaw has, thankfully, been incarcerated in Ratnagiri. All this is cause for some celebration and ease of mind, but nonetheless, we must devote much further thought to our extended frontiers, for greater security."

The Viceroy was silent, drawing meditatively on a Turkish cigarette. "It is a natural process of history," he said at long last, "for the weaker to give way to the stronger. Spheres of Interest tend to become Spheres of Influence; temporary leases to become perpetual; Spheres of Influence to develop into Protectorates; Protectorates to be the forerunners of complete incorporation. The process is not so immoral as it might at first sight appear; it is an endeavour, sanctioned by general usage, to introduce formality and decorum into proceedings which, unless thus regulated and diffused, might endanger the peace of nations."

"I am a soldier," said Roberts with a grunt. "It's for you to work out the rest of it."

"First, I see the necessity for consolidation at home, within the heartland of India," said the Viceroy. "You may remember there was a time not so long ago when the Mahrattas drew the frontier between us and them. Thanks to the Iron Duke that threat was removed, but I sense a weakness in those parts. The Nizam must be induced to cede Berar into our hands. The sale of Kashmir to a protected Hindoo chief carried the strategic frontier into the heart of the Himalayas. An agreement at Kabul must draw a line between the tribes under the British and those under 'temporary' Afghan influence, which, as long as Afghanistan retains an independent existence, is likely to remain our frontier of 'active responsibility'. We have spent enormous sums fortifying the independence of Afghanistan. On the extreme northeast, the annexation of Upper Burma has brought to us the heritage of a fringe of protected states known as the Upper Shan States. At both extremities, the Indian Empire, now vaster and more populous than has ever before acknowledged an Asiatic sovereign, is only narrowly separated from the spheres of two other great European powers—Russia and France. It is separated from the former by the buffer states of Persia and Afghanistan, and from the latter by the buffer state of Siam. The three powers are still anxious to keep their frontiers apart. This is evident from the scrupulous care with which the integrity of the intervening states is assured."

"What are your intentions, Sir?" asked the Commander-in-Chief.

"We must prevent, at any cost, the building of a railway line, or even a road, from Annam westwards, which could give the French access to the heartlands of Siam, or the Shan States," said the Viceroy bluntly. "We must make it possible for the Americans to create markets in China, and thus distract that dying empire from concerning itself too much with its Indian borders.

We must encourage the Germans to hold the attention of the Tsar to the west of his domains, and stop his advance south at Khiva. If, in any of these worthwhile endeavours, our diplomats fail to reach a satisfactory conclusion, why, Sir, we shall require your active services once again!"

"Are these your own opinions, Sir, or those of the Government's?" asked "Bobs" very bluntly.

"They are the opinions of the Viceroy of India," said Lansdowne grandly. "They will be voiced by any who are to follow me, and would have been the opinion of my illustrious predecessors, save, perhaps, Lord Ripon—he had too much religion, and that too of the wrong sort."

On that grave note, we rose from the table. Beresford then attached himself to us, and led us away to watch an afternoon of cricket, and have a quiet drink later at the club. His ease of manner, his knowledge of Calcutta, and his genuine desire to befriend us soon made him a pleasant companion, whose time, perhaps, we began to monopolize more than we should have. At any rate, whatever time was available to him after the performance of his duties was spent in our company, in the following days.

Two evenings after our lunch with the Viceroy and the Commander-inChief, we ran into Beresford, dressed even more elegantly than usual, and fidgeting impatiently in the long marble hall leading from the Throne Room to the northern part of the building. He was staring at the marble busts of the Caesars. We enquired what he planned for the evening and, flushing, he informed us with a peculiar stammer that he would be

accompanying Lady Evelyn to the Corinthian Theatre
to watch a local performance of *Romeo and Juliet*. Before
we could interject in astonishment, the lady in question,
a slim and pretty young woman of about twenty, came
tripping down the stairs. We were introduced, and she
apologized prettily for having kept herself away for two
whole days, but she had been assisting Signor Moresconi
in his restoration work, and she had little energy left for
entertainment. Beresford led her away, pointedly saying
that old Macaroni had no business tiring her out in
that weather, and that he would put in a word, which
she promptly forbade, a little pettishly. In the days that
followed, we saw, as everyone else did, including her
amused mama, that Beresford was trying to secure his
interest with her, apparently with little effect.

The next morning, Lady Evelyn came down early for
breakfast with her mother and us. Holding out her hand,
she commanded us girlishly to come and see the master
at work, in changing a dowdy old colonial house into a
"temple of art", as he had declared he would.

Moresconi was already perched high on a ladder, on
the staircase leading up from the Council Chamber to
the northeast, with three Indian assistants holding up
brushes, pots of paint, and other artistic paraphernalia.

"Ah! Just in time, fair Diana!" he cried, upon seeing
his young patroness. "We are about to restore the
famous portraits of the very great Duke of Wellington,
and his famous brother, Lord Wellesley, your papa's
predecessor—they should not hang here, no, no, no, a
thousand times no! It should be—yes! I know, in the Green

Drawing Room, but the wall should be brown, I shall change the silk, suiting the colour to the military glory of the Very Great! See—Mr Om-mez, Doctore! These are copies of the original painted by Robert Home in 1804. The Duke of Wellington wears the Star of the Order of the Bath on his breast. His brother, Lord Wellesley, in a scarlet coat with black cuffs and facings slashed with gold, wears the Ribbon and Star of St Patrick. Below this is a jewelled star in the centre of which is a crescent and another star! Behold! They were made out of Tipoo Sultan's jewels, and given to him for his selflessness in refusing to take his hundred-thousand-pound share of the prize money, after the fall of Seringapatam in 1799. The money was then distributed among the army. What generosity! What greatness!"

Moresconi jumped off his perch nimbly enough, and danced up a few steps. "Ah! Here is your dear papa's portrait—um—tolerably well painted by Mr Hall, but how well His Lordship looks in academic robes! So noble! So wise! Power and Wisdom are fused in him. It is a shame to hang this painting where only the staff can cast their eyes upon it; I will have it on the southeast staircase so that every guest can doff his cap at the Master of the Empire. Is that not good, *cara mia?*"

Without waiting for any response from us, he swept us forward on an impromptu tour of the planned restorations. The black pedestals of the Caesars in the long hall had to go. Great God! Who was the madman who perpetrated such a monstrosity? No, only marble pedestals would do; the carpets would be torn away, to expose the dignity of the grey marble underneath. All the portraits of the past Governor Generals would be rehung appropriately, so that the place was no longer— how does Madame say?—yes, a barn, but a house of history, of British conquest. In the Throne Room, Signor Moresconi scornfully dismissed Tipoo's throne—a large cushioned sofa with silver lions for arms; but yes, that red lacquered low seat was Thibaw's Burmese throne—he would work on it. The exercise of listening to incessant learned opinion, while clambering up and down sweeping staircases, and padding through vast rooms, tired us out, although Moresconi was fresh as a daisy. At lunchtime, our lessons in art were thankfully brought to a halt. But Moresconi was not to be deterred. On our way out, he halted below a painting by Zoffany, of Holwell Building, a monument to commemorate the Black Hole sufferers.

"Holwell stands on a scaffolding—like we saw Moresconi himself, yes—and the workmen are below," said the artist. "This painting is very, very special, for milord has bought it himself from Holwell's descendants in Canada, when he was there as Governor General there."

Holmes remarked vaguely that it reminded him of a painting he had seen in Florence, a long time back, by Tintoretta. "No! No! Signor Om-mez, Tintorett-o, the great painter, si. An 'ah' is for the so-charming women, who do not paint, Signor. Yes, I see what you mean— the atmosphere, the tints, yes, Signor as ever perceives everything!" I noticed a quick sardonic glint in his eye as he said this, and then we went in for lunch.

Holmes and I escaped soon after, but Lady Evelyn seemed a willing captive, and went back with the indefatigable artist.[42]

Taking advantage of a break in the rains, we were setting out one day in our carriage, when we came upon an altercation at the gate between the guards and a rickshaw-wallah. He hailed us loudly with joy, and I recognized the fellow who had almost died under our wheels.

"I am Balraj, huzur, do you remember me? Garib-parvar, you bought me my rickshaw, so here I am to take you wherever you want to go!" he exclaimed in Hindoostani. Upon hearing this, Holmes alighted from the carriage with a pleasant laugh, and rode the rickshaw up to the Bengal Club, Balraj gamely trying to keep up with our carriage, and laughing ruefully when we outdistanced him by several hundred yards. Although Holmes could not speak Hindoostani, he had an uncanny ability of communicating with signs, and his easy manners removed any sense of social distance when mingling with the lower orders. He made a regular habit of going off with Balraj every day to look around town.

His romantic pursuits not progressing as smoothly as he wished, Beresford would occasionally be glum, although his good nature was such that he was never grumpy. One day, his forehead was creased with a new worry. "Lord George Harris, the new Governor of Bombay, is coming up to discuss commercial policy with the Viceroy, but I suspect he is really coming to play cricket here, and rub our noses in the dirt. The British in Bombay play regularly with the Parsees and others there, who all have jolly good teams, so they have plenty of practice. Our boxwallahs do not have a good team, I must admit; although they have excellent horses. My own racehorse Myall Kind is peerless—you should see him—he's won both the Viceroy Cup and the Governor's Cup." Rather reluctantly, he returned to the matter at hand. "And if that were not enough, Harris, in addition to bringing his best players—'to inculcate the spirit of Empire through cricket' as he says pompously—is also bringing along Lord Hawke, the captain of Yorkshire! And there is more—Hawke is travelling with a young fellow, Stanley Jackson, who has already made a name for himself at Harrow!"[43]

We agreed it would be a rout, the like of which Bengal had not seen since the days of Robert Clive.

"I have seen the boys of Presidency College at cricket," said Holmes thoughtfully. "They play a sound game. Perhaps you can add a few of them to ginger up your team?"

Beresford looked doubtful, and then his face cleared. "Yes, by God, that's what we will do," he smiled. "After all, Harris is bringing Jackson, who has nothing really to do with any team from Bombay, so I am going to stiffen up our lot with boys from the college!"

The next few days were spent on the cricket grounds, studying form, and discussing the merits of various youths on the field. Unfortunately, there were no demon bowlers to be found; in fact, pace was totally lacking among the college bowlers. Many fared very well as batsmen, and

Beresford hazarded a guess that with proper coaching, some could hold their own in any county. Seeing our continued interest in their game, a few of the boys came over, and Beresford put the problem to them collectively. Their polite indifference turned into fiery zeal upon realizing that Beresford's purpose was to uphold the honour of Bengal. Yes, they would join in and show Harris, Hawke, and the rest of the world, what Bengali men were made of.

Sarbadhikary, a good leg-spinner, was a natural leader, and we left it to him to bring in the best of his friends, and start net practice with Beresford's team. Matters were a little stiff in the beginning, for the boxwallahs really did not wish to rub shoulders with Indians, while the boys stood on their own dignity, but soon the desire to win or, at least, to put up a good show against a formidable team, won the day, and everyone tacitly decided to play together as politely as possible until the match was over.

A worried Beresford, Holmes, and myself would watch and comment on net practice every evening on the college grounds. We insisted that they play on even when it drizzled, for we did not know what the weather would be like on the day of the match. While most of the boys were good players, there was no one that we could spot with match-winning genius, save Sarbadhikary, and possibly another friend of his, one Ray, whose father owned a sports shop at Bow Bazaar, and who, in honour of the forthcoming match, had assured a free supply of excellent bats, pads, and balls for the team. Ray, a dark, squat chap, had a maniacal devotion to the game, and would tirelessly bowl his off-breaks, good length balls pitched exactly on the off stump or just shaving it. He could pin down an average player, who in exasperation could be tempted to mishit him; but we feared that for experienced players, such as the team Harris was bringing along, he might have few surprises.

One evening, Holmes went up and asked him to bowl round the wicket, pitching around the leg stump. It seemed a pretty pointless exercise, and a negative one, at best. "When I was at school, I devised a way of fooling good batsmen," said Holmes thoughtfully, taking the ball. "I am not sure I still have the hang of it, but let me try the off-spinner's googly."

None of us had heard of such a thing and, bemused, we watched Holmes bowl several off-breaks going away from the leg stump, until one broke back and hit the stump. An amazed shout went up from the watching cricketers.

"Try it, Ray," advised Holmes. "It is difficult to master and one needs a strong wrist, but you can do it, I am sure. It gets the conventional batsman out every time. When things started going badly, my captain would call me up, and after a few overs, signal me to bowl the 'other one'. Here, I will show you how it is done. Watch: it is bowled from the back of the hand with a lot of top spin, but with the wrist moving clockwise, so!"

Seeing Holmes's success at coaching the boys, I thought of a trick I had been taught at school. I went up to Sarbadhikary, and said I wanted to demonstrate a type of googly that he himself might use. "It's like a special kind of wrong 'un, old chap," I said, limbering up awkwardly. "I can't really bowl at all, now, y'know? But the thing is, it needs very strong fingers, which I had—still have—and I suppose that's what helped me as a military surgeon."

I bowled a few hopeless balls, wide of the stumps. Just when everyone was turning away politely, I got the ball to do what I wanted for once, rattling the stumps. "That's it!" I shouted. "Did you see that? The ball is squeezed between the thumb and fingers, so it spins backwards and skids low and fast with under-spin, after hitting the pitch. Bowled as a yorker, it is unplayable, but you don't get it often."

Both Ray and Sarbadhikary were now keyed up, and promised to practise for all hours until they had perfected the deliveries. Beresford, all admiration, carried us off to the Bengal Club, and toasted our genius several times until, tired from our exertions, and drowsy with food and drink, we decided to turn in.

The next day, I was surprised to receive a message from the Viceroy that he required my presence at a meeting, at eleven in the morning, in his offices in the southwestern wing. I presented myself, and found a large room full of officials, to whom the Viceroy introduced me as a military surgeon with several years' experience in some of the most inhospitable terrain to be found in India, and since I was fortunate to be his guest at present, he would value my advice. I was surprised at such cordiality, for although Lady Maud was all kindness, Lord Lansdowne had rarely even acknowledged our presence in his house.

Soon I realized why I had been asked to present myself: the Viceroy was presiding over a meeting of the Indian Hemp Drugs Commission, and was beginning to be irritated by the conflicting opinions of doctors; some of them would ban all hallucinatory drugs immediately as injurious to health, and, in extreme cases, causing death or insanity; while others refuted these statements as alarmist, pointing out the therapeutic uses of opium and similar drugs. Reports of the Royal Commission on Opium, Transactions of the Medical and Physical Society of Bengal, the work of Sir Reynolds and Dr Birch on the therapeutic uses and toxic effects of the drug, were all quoted to substantiate one position or the other. Surprisingly, the resolutions of the Finance and Commerce Department of the Government of India seemed to carry more weight than medical opinion.

"I am not for any interference in the normal course of trade," said Lord Lansdowne firmly. "It is against my personal principles, and against the policy of my Government. Over a hundred thousand chests of opium are exported to China alone every year. The trade, gentlemen, generates taxes for my Government equivalent to over half our total revenue, enough to cover the entire civil service and armed forces budgets. I am not about to forego this income to appease any missish objections of ill-advised people. The internal sale of ganja produces for the Bengal administration over one million sicca rupees in taxation. The profits generated for British trade, over and above this, require that we propose laws for changing the present system only with abundant caution, and after due consideration of all facts—especially the undoubted therapeutic use of these drugs."

Few had the courage to contradict the Viceroy, particularly when he had stated the benefits for all assembled in such plain terms. Only Mr Joseph Rowntree, a Quaker, refused to be cowed, and said the lunatic asylum of Calcutta was filled with ganja and hashish addicts. Mr Bingham, the banker, said that if opium were suppressed, ruining trade and several respectable business houses, people would turn to even more dangerous and potent drugs, since it was but human nature. Mr Stewart, a visiting Liberal MP for Bradford, asked whether the Viceroy in Council had considered the Report of the Society for the Suppression of the Opium Trade, and was it not that His Excellency was not prepared to suppress a very immoral trade just to protect the interests of a few Conservative supporters? There was an uproar, and the Viceroy insisted that the meeting would not proceed unless Mr Stewart withdrew his remarks, which he did reluctantly, although trying to clarify what he had said, to no avail.

Lord Lansdowne then turned to me, and asked about my experience as an army doctor, under the most trying of conditions, over several decades of service. Everyone fell silent and looked at me. While never having supported the use of drugs in any form, I had to admit that under the rough and ready conditions of the front, I had administered laudanum to relieve pain and prevent shock. The meeting then concluded that the Viceroy and Governor General were of the opinion that, while ganja might be among the most noxious of all intoxicants commonly used in India, even if absolute prohibition could be enforced, the result might be to induce the use of more noxious drugs, such as datura; apart from which it would be impossible to enforce a prohibition. It was: "Our duty to restrict consumption, but unnecessary to do more than persevere in the policy established in 1873."[44]

Lord Lansdowne positively beamed at me as I left the room, and asked if there was anything he could do to make my stay more comfortable. The positions taken during the meeting continued to distress me, and I shared some of my concerns with Lady Maud over lunch. She heard me out carefully, and agreed with my resolution to visit the lunatic asylum in Calcutta, talk to the doctors, and draw my own conclusions.

"Dear Dr Watson," she said gently. "You are such a good person to concern yourself with these worrisome questions, when most men would be relaxing at home, enjoying their retirement. You should meet some Indians, Sir. Let me see if I can manage an introduction."

My visits to the Calcutta lunatic asylum were horrifying experiences. A lack of every kind of human care, including simple sustenance, was combined with a harsh and punitive attitude towards the unfortunate inmates. They craved the drugs that had brought them to this state, and which were sadistically denied them by their keepers, who in reality were nothing more than their jailers. I was profoundly saddened by the experience, and wondered at the extent of despair in their previous lives that might have driven them to such depths of degradation.

I thought Lady Maud had forgotten our conversation, but some days later she asked me to accompany her to the Asiatic Society to attend a lecture. Dr Rajendra Lal Mitra, the very first Indian to be made President of the organization, was there, as well as Mr Beveridge, the then President, to hear some papers on stylistic differences between the various chapters of the *Mahabharata*. An Englishman's suggestion that perhaps the Vedic warriors were of the same blood as the ancient Achaeans, both deriving their origins from the steppes of the Farghana, was hotly disputed by Indian scholars.

After the meeting was over, Lady Maud introduced me to a tall, saintly-looking young man, with long hair parted in the middle and falling in curls to his shoulders. He moved among the others like the first among equals, a position of pre-eminence granted to him without his asking. Lady Maud had taken me by the hand, and led me to him.

"Dr Watson, I wish you to meet Mr Rabindranath Tagore, a poet whose verses, I am sure, will be heard in every corner of the civilized world before long. It would have known him by now but for his modesty. Is it that, or you care not for the world's adulation?"

Tagore smiled slowly at her praise, disowning all fame, without any pretension or artifice. He seemed simply unconcerned. "Dr Watson, his grandfather, the great Dwarakanath, was a leading light of this Society in his day; his father, the Maharishi, is respected throughout Bengal."

Bowing gracefully in response to Lady Maud's compliments, Tagore said he was delighted to meet me, and invited Holmes and myself to a soirée in his family garden the next Sunday. On our way back, Lady Maud assured me that Sunday would secure my entry into Bengali society, without which I could have no hope of understanding the Bengali mind in any real sense.

That Sunday, we were driven up the left bank of the Hooghly, through the crowded Shyam Bazaar, over the Circular Canal, and to the beautiful gardens set well outside the city. The rains had given the trees and plants a new lease of life after a hot summer. The gentle pitter-patter of water, dripping from the leaves, could be heard whenever talk subsided. Although the ground was still soft underfoot, a select group of poets, musicians, artists, and writers had gathered for learned discussions in those sylvan surroundings. The afternoon was passed listening to music and Bengali poetry. Of course, we did not understand the latter, although we could appreciate the sonorous music of the words. Fruit juices and rich vegetarian fare were served at regular intervals by the servants, who had set up a kitchen in one part of the gardens.[45]

At last, Rabindranath, as he preferred to be addressed, was cajoled to read some of his poems, his friends insisting that he read his own English translations for our sake. After some hesitation, he read the following lines, saying the poem remained unfinished:

Where the world has not been broken up into
fragments by narrow domestic walls;

Where words come out from the depth of truth;
Where tireless striving stretches its arms towards
perfection;
Where the clear stream of reason has not lost its way
into the dreary desert sand of dead habit;
Where the mind is led forward by thee into ever-
widening thought and action—
Into that heaven of freedom, my Father, let my
country awake.[46]

The political overtones of the poem were clear enough, and we fell to discussing it, the group of friends very kindly and spontaneously including Holmes and myself in the exchange of opinion. We discussed the meaning of freedom, each with his own interpretation, political, mystical, personal, or social. Holmes argued that in any culture, people must be able to hold their heads high, and that their minds must be without fear. I didn't find this a sufficient condition, and added that knowledge itself must be free, and shared by all, if people were to be free.

"Thank you, my friends," smiled Rabindranath. "You have helped me complete the poem—in fact, given me the first two lines:

Where the mind is without fear and the head is held
high;
Where knowledge is free.

All the friends applauded, we felt more than a little embarrassed at being given any credit at all, and took leave of our gracious friends with reluctance. After such an ennobling afternoon, I could hardly accept that people born on the soil of Bengal, whatever their circumstances, could be reduced to the shrieking invalids I had seen in the cells of the lunatic asylum. I was all the more determined to do what lay in my power, little as it was, to end the filthy trade in narcotics, irrespective of the financial consequences to the Treasury.

The Harris team arrived like conquerors; and while His Lordship held perfunctory discussions with the Viceroy about the narcotics trade, the rest went about town without the least show of seriousness. They even declined an offer of net practice that evening, although they did turn up at the college dinner held in their honour. For his post-prandial speech, Harris—after giving perfunctory thanks—launched into a message linking the glories of cricket with the triumph of Empire.

"The greatest game in the world is played wherever the Union Jack is unfurled, cementing the ties that bind together every part of Empire," said Harris. "On our cricket grounds is fostered the spirit of playing for your side and not for yourself. The future of the game and of Empire are inseparably connected." Mild, polite applause greeted these lofty sentiments. Then giving Eton and Oxford credit for what he himself had become, Harris went on: "England in her supreme confidence, in admiration of her own free institutions, has undertaken to educate Indians on British lines, to imbue them with British modes of thought, and to encourage them to admire and to strive towards British systems of government." An uneasy silence reigned in the hall. Harris, however, was not to be restrained. He continued to praise the British Army itself, and its role in India, as a moulder of character: "Outside of the English universities, no school of character exists to compare with the Frontier; and character is there moulded, not by arguments with fellow men in the arts or studies of peace, but in the furnace of responsibility, and on the anvil of self-reliance. The work, which an Englishman may be called upon to perform, may be that of the explorer, or the administrator, or the military commander, or all of them at the same time. Risk is the last thing of which he takes account. He feels that the honour of England is in his hands."

By then, we could see students leaving from the doors at the back, while those in front were fidgeting, a few more impetuous than the others being restrained by their fellows. It was an embarrassment for the Principal, who thanked Harris, before more damage could be done, for his noble advice. It was Hawke's turn to say something. He was far more perceptive of the prevailing mood, so he kept his speech as short as possible. However, he could not resist the urge to read a poem of his:

> A land that we've conquered and have to hold
> Though it cost us millions of lives and gold,
> Shall we call her the jewel of England's fame?
> Or throw our curse at her vampire name?
> But whether we bless her, or damn, or deride her,
> We are bound by our honour to stand fast beside her,
> The Empire's India!

We broke up in silence, the Principal wisely forgetting to ask for the national anthem to be sung.

The next day dawned bright and clear over the Eden Gardens cricket field. Half of Calcutta seemed to have turned up for the one-day match. It is difficult for me to describe the air of general festivity, overlaid with a sense of combat, as during a medieval joust. Gaily stripped shamianas and buntings fluttered in the breeze, shouts, laughter, and slogans in support of Calcutta and Bengal rent the air. Harris and his team were in immaculate flannels, and seemed not to notice the Bengali boys in simple white drill cloth. Looking back, I can say that the turning point of the match was achieved even before a ball was bowled, when Harris announced with sublime complacency that he would not have Jackson bowl that day, as "it would be unfair, fairness being everything in cricket". Beresford cheered up on seeing that Lady Evelyn herself had come to watch the match. He blushed when she pressed his hand and wished him the very best.

Beresford won the toss, and decided to bat. Harris's team, which had had a riotous time late into the previous night, after they had got back to the Bengal Club, were lethargic in the humid sun, dropped catches, and bowled indifferently to let the locals amass a respectable total of 137 runs. Harris displayed complete confidence at lunch, which seemed justified when his openers went past 50 without any trouble. A slow run cost one his wicket, and a careless shot saw the other opener back in the pavilion with only ten more runs added on the scoreboard. Harris had joined Hawke at the crease, and we settled down to watch them bat through the rest of the innings.

Harris had claimed several times in the pavilion that he would demonstrate the "Eton way of playing cricket", that no runs scored with a straight bat was better than a cross-bat "agricultural shot" to the ropes. He disdainfully let a few of Ray's off-breaks go past the leg stump, without moving a muscle. At the fourth ball, Sarbadhikary called out "doosra" to Ray, and Harris stood stunned as the ball broke back sharply, rattling his stumps. He wouldn't leave before threateningly asking the square-leg umpire if he had really been bowled, or the wicketkeeper had whipped off the bails. He then looked suspiciously at the pitch, tapped it a little, before walking back, to loud cries of "duck", and "quack, quack!" Hawke, a far sounder cricketer, lifted Sarbadhikary twice to the ropes. Confidently stepping forward to get a hat-trick of three consecutive sixes, he was astonished to have the back-spin shoot beneath his bat and dislodge a bail. Jackson's innings was a delight to watch, and even the partisan Calcutta crowd could not refrain from cheering his beautiful shots. He would have won the match for them, had there been a Bombay boxwallah who could stay at the other end against Sarbadhikary's back-spinners or Ray's doosras. With nine wickets lost, Jackson attempted a final six, which was caught at deep mid-off by a running Beresford, and the Calcuttans won by just one run. Jackson was the first to shake hands with Sarbadhikary and the other Indians. I could not help noticing that Lady Evelyn, who had sat in the pavilion throughout the heat of the day, went up impulsively and gave Beresford a peck on his cheek, which I would say meant far more to him than the victory itself.

Although Harris's team turned up good-naturedly for a victory dinner at Firpo's, given by Beresford, Harris could not refrain from making the point that winning was nothing, but playing the game as it should be played was all.

"Come off it, George!" said Hawke sportingly. "We were beaten fair and square, and all congratulations to Beresford, and especially to Sarbadhikary and Ray. Magnificent bowling! You must teach us how you do it. If any of you care to, you will have a great future in County Cricket!"

Harris turned away pointedly.

The day was nearing when Government House would be thrown open to the admiring public to view the resplendent palace, turned into a house of "art and beauty", in Moresconi's words. Workmen toiled in the building through the days and nights. Although the workmen muffled their tools at night, so as not to disturb the Viceroy's family on the second floor of the southwest wing, Beresford complained that Moresconi— who occupied the large, but badly kept quarters in the northwest wing—kept making an intolerable noise, with pieces of plaster falling regularly, and covering his files with dust. Only the patronage of Lady Evelyn prevented the Italian from being rudely dismissed.

It was to be a splendid affair, presided over by Lady Maud, while the Viceroy would keep to his own chambers.

A meeting would be held in the Council Chamber in the northeast wing for the elite of Calcutta, and for princes and nobility from the region, as well as all journalists. After a few speakers, chosen by Lady Maud herself, had expressed their happiness at the advances made by the Indian Empire under the leadership of His Lordship, and the equal advances made in the fields of the arts and culture, under the patronage of Her Ladyship, Signor Moresconi would take the gathering around on a visit of the paintings and artistic curios in the palace, pointing out to the press the significance of the captured jewels of Tipoo Sahib of Mysore, and the throne of the former King Thibaw of Burma.

The day before the event, Signor Moresconi cornered Holmes and myself in great excitement, as we left the southeast semicircular verandah after tea. "Ah! Moresconi is lucky man today, for long I have searched for the great Mr Om-mez and the Doctore, and I have not found them until now; but it is not too late! There is time still to see the ancient Bengalee miniatures, and advise me if they are worthy to be shown tomorrow! Signors, come, we must hurry!"

He had arranged for his carriage to be at the gate— he had always insisted with artistic eccentricity that he would travel only in the carriage he had rented in town; he wanted to feel Bengal in his bones, and the good natives took him everywhere, no matter that he understood not a word of their complex language. We got into a large, rather ramshackle vehicle, and Moresconi drew down the blinds against the sun—he did not want the Signors to fall sick just before the great day—and we were off as fast as the horses could take us to his discovery. He explained that his research among the natives had led him to some old mansions, now left deserted. It was the same, in Italy or Bengal—the young wanted to move to fashionable new houses, not respecting the invaluable old treasures they left behind.

Soon we had left the city, and were rattling down a dirt road between fields, with the river glimpsed through the trees to the left. It was hot and tiring, but Moresconi had provided us with an ample supply of sweet, spiced sherbet to keep us cool. At last, at sundown we reached a small town or large village on the banks of the river. We stopped at a dilapidated old house, almost certainly deserted, which Moresconi assured us housed "unbelievable" treasures of art. I really wanted to lie down by then, at least for a few minutes, and Moresconi, thoughtfully sensing my condition, led us down the steps to a cool room, a cellar really, with comfortable divans. Holmes had been strangely quiet during the journey, but he was also visibly tired by now, and we lay down together on a large divan, and closed our eyes for a moment.

I awoke with a splitting headache. It was already morning, for I could hear the chirping of birds outside. I tried to rise, but found I could not, and then realized that I was securely bound to a heavy chair. I turned my head, stiffly and painfully, and saw Holmes bound in similar fashion, looking at me. Perhaps it was something he had said that woke me.

"We have fallen into a trap, Watson," said Holmes

unnecessarily. "At least I walked into it with my eyes open. I have known for long that Moresconi was a fake, and was waiting for him to reveal his hand. I waited too long, it seems," he added drily.

I could make nothing of this. Holmes explained patiently that he had known the man was an impostor from the day Moresconi had shown no knowledge of Tintoretta, who had been named after her famous father, and was well known for her paintings to anyone living in Florence. He had also noticed that while Moresconi was a great showman, all of the restoration work was actually quietly being carried out by his Indian assistants. He had gone to visit some native ateliers, led by Balraj the rickshaw-wallah, and learned that the assistants were all established and well-known local artists, whom Moresconi had hired at unbelievably high rates. But none of his leads could give Holmes a clue as to what Moresconi's game was, and he had waited, as he said, too long. We had been drugged; it was the sherbet, but Holmes had drunk only out of the flask used by Moresconi…

"Ah! Ha! My English pigeons," said a strange voice. It was Moresconi, coming down the steps, but his Italian accent was gone. "So, the great Sherlock Holmes is caught in a trap, as well as the egregious Watson. And you still do not know who I am? And you still don't know why I am not drugged? Holmes, Holmes, it is tragic to see a once sharp mind dulled and stupid. My dear fellow, I had an antidote to the ganja; surely you should have known with your esoteric knowledge of drugs and toxins?"

"Who the devil are you?" I asked thickly.

Moresconi turned his back to us, tore off his huge beard, cap, and hair, and straightening, laughed in our faces.

"My God! It's Moriarty!" I cried in bewilderment. Holmes nodded.

"I should have shared my doubts, Watson," he said. "Just as I survived our duel over the Reichenbach Falls, I had a feeling Moriarty himself might have escaped."

The criminal genius, who could have been a great educator and used his wealth of talent in the service of mankind, stood and laughed long and loud.

"You are right, Holmes, for once. You did succeed in pushing me off, and even as you managed to find a hand-hold in that dreadful place, so did I. The root of a tree growing at an impossible angle from the face of the cliff saved me. I hung on there, God knows for how many hours, and then long after you had left, my men found me and rescued me with the help of a long rope. I had to decide what to do next. I was too well known in Europe, thanks to your meddling, so I planned to resume my career in the heart of Empire. It was easy to fool that stupid little Evelyn—these English misses are so confident that the world only waits to serve them. I did think of seducing the daughter of the Viceroy—it would have been an easy conquest, I can tell you, but I thought of a better way of punishing the English. And when I saw you in Calcutta, I knew my revenge would be classic! Perfect!"

We both pretended to be bored of his ranting, but he saw through our posturing in a moment.

"You don't fool me, Holmes," he said. "You are

blaming yourself for your incredible stupidity. But console yourself. You have met your match. Tonight, when that stupid, frumpy Vicereine leads her fawning crowd to see the treasures of her palace, they will find the place stripped bare! Everything will be gone! I have made all arrangements. How the Indian papers will laugh at this comical Viceroy, who cannot even protect his own house, let alone an Empire! Now, thanks to Ripon and the Ilbert Bill, they have the license to write what they will. And the princes in that palace turned back into a barn—they will draw their own conclusions; they will find the British Empire blustering but weak. The frontiers will be ablaze with revolt in a week! And all because of Moriarty! Think of that, Holmes! You should never have thought of crossing swords with me! And oh! Try to make your way alive out of an India in revolt!" With that he was gone.

We struggled with our ropes, but to no avail. We had been secured by a master, and we could not escape. We grew thirstier and hungrier as the day wore on. Through the blinds of ventilators set high in the walls of our prison cellar, we could occasionally see the shadows of people as they walked past. There was never any answer to our cries, and we concluded that the men must be guards posted by Moriarty to prevent any escape until the day was over. When all hope had died away, around five or so in the evening, we saw a ventilator being pushed open softly. A moment later, the face of the loyal Balraj peered down at us.

"Sahibs, are you all right?" he hissed anxiously.

I answered that we were all right for the time being, and that he should release us immediately. He said he was going for help, and would be back shortly, but we should be silent. Time seemed to drag on even more slowly, until around six, we heard several men coming down the stairs. A dignified young man, in ochre robes and a turban, led the anxious Balraj and several ruffians.

"Your ordeal, my friends, is over. I have ordered these men to release you immediately," said the Swami in excellent English, for so he was addressed with great respect, even by the wickedest looking cutthroat in the group.

Our ropes were swiftly removed. The Swami told us to remain seated, and had our erstwhile captors massage us to restore our circulation. As we waited for life to return to our limbs, he told us briefly that the village was called Baranagar, it was the site of a great saint's samadhi, and that he and his flock kept vigil over the grave. None would dare disobey him, not even the most vile of criminals, because of the supernatural power of the samadhi.

"I wish to be able to tell the Viceroy about our deliverer," said Holmes as we were leaving, after thanking him for our rescue. "That will not be necessary," he said evenly. "You can call me Narendra, if you wish. But do meditate on Shri Ramakrishna Paramahansa, whose samadhi is here. He is the source of all Enlightenment!"[47]

Balraj led us down to the river, and the Swami's helpers hailed a boat for us. As we sailed down the fast-flowing river, with the monsoon winds whipping us on, Balraj said he had come to the gate of Government House the previous afternoon with his rickshaw, to see if the Sahibs wanted to go anywhere; he had seen the carriage and had been concerned, knowing something about the coachman, an unsavoury character. When the coach had returned without us, he had grown anxious, and loosened the coachman's tongue in a den as they smoked ganja together. We thanked him as a friend and an equal, and promised, if at all possible, to retrieve his lands before we left for home. He embarrassed us by bowing to press his forehead against our palms, and calling us "annadatta", with tears streaming from his eyes.

When we reached the gates of Government House, we could see that the function was already in full swing, with all the lights lit in the great building, and the line of carriages lengthening on the street outside and along the garden's driveway. We had no difficulty slipping into the garden, since the guards knew us well by sight, but Holmes would not take the risk of running into an unknown member of Moriarity's gang. We raced round the corner in the dark, and silently effecting an entrance, went up the private curved wrought-iron staircase to the Viceroy's chambers, installed by Lord Ripon. Holmes said he would go directly to the quarters of the Military Secretary, instructing me to fetch my service revolver from my room, and to stand guard in the Throne Room.

I concealed myself behind the heavy tapestry that separates the room from the long hall, and waited in semi-darkness. None of the objets d'art appeared to have been touched, and I hoped Holmes and Beresford would be able to act in time. After a half hour spent gingerly waiting for action, I heard footsteps approaching rapidly. Drawing my pistol, I prepared to defend the Throne Room, but soon realized it was Holmes leading a force of the Viceroy's Guard. Stationing them around the room, he told me in a hurried whisper that we had been in time, the rascals had been apprehended, and that Beresford himself had taken charge of the false Moresconi, and requested our presence in the Council Chamber.

The reader may imagine my surprise on entering the packed Council Chamber, and finding a disguised Moriarty ensconced in the front row, but with Beresford's firm arm entwined in his. After all the adulatory speeches were over, Beresford rose and said he had an important announcement to make:

"Ladies and Gentlemen, it may come as no surprise for those of you who know Signor Moresconi that he is so enraptured with Bengal that he has decided to spend the rest of his days here. In fact, he has decided to embrace the life of a sanyasi, renouncing the world, and seeking salvation at the well-known samadhi of Shri Ramakrishna Paramahamsa, as so many other Europeans are doing. He wishes to shave off all his hair and undertake the necessary austerities on the path to inner peace. Being so near to him, we will be able to witness his daily penance and noble transformation. At least I will." Congratulations were offered on all sides to Signor Moresconi, which he accepted with a surly expression.

As the crowd surged forward to view the wonders of

the palace, Holmes sidled up to his old enemy. "Cheer up, old chap!" he said in a jolly voice. "I can assure you the young Swami is a genuine saint. And, who knows, he may yet reform you so that you use your mind— crooked though it is—in the service of mankind in your declining years!"

A few days later, when we were ready to take leave of our gracious hostess, and board *The Coromandel Star* for home, she suggested that we should go up to Lady Evelyn's rooms and say goodbye to her there, since she had made no public appearance after that eventful night. Accompanied by Beresford, we tapped on her door. A quavering voice said we could come in, and upon entering, she raised a tear-stained face from her pillow.

"God! Evelyn, did that fellow mean so much to you?" burst out Beresford.

"No, no! I have almost forgotten he existed," she said, sitting up, and drying her eyes. "Only I wish I hadn't been such a goose, and been taken in by a rascal."

Beresford went forward tenderly. "Then what is the matter, my dear...why the tears, I don't understand, when everything is going along spiffingly..."

"Dear William, don't you understand?" she cried out. "Men never do, do they? It's no use, I have tried to tell you, but you don't seem to understand. I can't bear to break your heart, William, but mine is already given... in England. We have known each other forever. It's Cavendish," she added simply.[48]

Holmes and I were embarrassed to be present, and

withdrew with some delicacy, leaving them to part ways
gently. We had not expected to see Beresford again, but
he was good enough to come and see us off on deck. We
waited in silence for the announcement that all visitors
should get off the ship. "I suppose I can't compete with
the future Duke of Devonshire," he said glumly at last,
then added quickly, "That was petty. Her heart is given,
and there's no more to be said."

We pressed his hand in silence, knowing, as older
men, that the heart is the one organ in young men that
heals the fastest.

"Oh, Holmes! I almost forgot. Silly of me, but with
all the other things going on, y'know? But I found this
piece of paper in my pocket. Do you think it's a prank,
or should we take it seriously?"

He produced a torn sheet from a notebook. On it was
written a curt message:

> The Viceroy's Private Papers on the Narcotics Question
> are now on their way to a European capital. They will
> be disclosed to the Press at a moment and in a way to
> ensure the fall of the British Government. A Person
> who has been close to Professor Moriarty.

Holmes looked up gravely. "Are the papers missing in
reality?" he asked. Beresford nodded glumly.

"In that case, if I were you, I would give it the most
serious consideration. You know that those remarks of
the Viceroy's can be grossly misinterpreted, especially by
a certain section of the Press. The Government would be
endangered. If I may, I think the Viceroy must change

policy, as soon as possible, before vindictive action is taken. And he must prohibit open sales of narcotics."

Beresford agreed after some thought, and said that in the circumstances the Viceroy would be forced to act as Holmes suggested.

We were on deck a dark blustery morning, a few days' sail from Calcutta, when I brought up a thought that had been bothering me. "Who do you think is this mysterious person, who has been close to Moriarty?" I asked.

Holmes laughed happily. "Why, myself, of course," he said gaily. "I have pursued that scoundrel for the better part of twenty years, and have come close to nabbing him a dozen times. I can truthfully say I am a person who has been close to him! Here are the papers I purloined that night when we went up Lord Ripon's staircase. I had better cast them into the waters, lest they fall into the wrong hands." With that he flung a large, thick manila envelope far out to sea. "It's a despicable trade, Watson, and the sooner it is ended, the better. I'm afraid we, as a nation, have much to answer for in this part of the globe, and Providence might yet exact condign punishment."

For some time, a curtain of rain from a huge, black cumulonimbus cloud had been approaching the ship. It now lashed the deck, sending us scurrying inside.

The Indian Summer of Sherlock Holmes

Iremember quite well now; it was on a cold late autumn afternoon, September 22, 1913, to be exact, that I shuffled across to answer the doorbell, and found Holmes on the landing of my flat, bundled up in a large motoring coat, and dangling his cap and goggles.

"Good Heavens, Holmes, what a surprise! What a welcome surprise!" I cried, ushering him in. "My dear fellow, what brings you to London? I had given up all hope of seeing you in the city, and meant to visit you at your cottage on the Sussex Downs, but you know how it is, something or the other always turns up just as I decide to catch the train...Do sit down Holmes, and take off that large coat...Let me make you a cup of tea."

Holmes cut short my rambling welcome a trifle abruptly, I thought. "I have come to town at the express wish of Sir Edward Grey, the Foreign Secretary," he said, unbuttoning his coat. "He writes to me that it is a matter of some importance. Nothing but the gravity of his letter, and the state of the world, would have induced me to leave the country. Watson, you must come with me to Whitehall. Whatever the matter, I will not get involved without you."

I sat down in astonishment at this. It was years since Holmes had retired to the depths of Sussex to raise bees. On the death of Mrs Hudson, that faithful old soul, I myself had bought a small first-floor flat overlooking Russell Square in Bloomsbury. When the sun was out, I could trot across to sit in the little garden in the middle of the square, and feed the pigeons. As they clustered round my feet, memories of old times would return, and sometimes I would drift off, until the thoughtful gardener woke me with a "Time to get back in, Guv'nor, we don't want to catch a chill, do we?" Life had been good to me, and I was in tolerable health, except for a touch of arthritis in my left knee, where I had received a bullet during the Second Afghan War, so many years ago. I admit I would have liked a family, at least at Christmas time, to have someone to visit, but one can't have everything, can one? I had done my bit for God, king, and country, and except for the occasional visit to Holmes's place, I had not a great deal to look forward to. So, this sudden call to action came as a bit of a shock.

Before I quite knew what was happening, I was seated in Holmes's twenty-four horsepower Austin Phaeton, with a large rug drawn round me, and we were making our way through the traffic to Whitehall, with Holmes leaning on the horn more than was necessary or seemly. Before I could remonstrate, we had drawn up at our destination, the car was handed over to the care of a sergeant in attendance, and Holmes was helping me up the narrow steps to the office of Sir Edward Grey. His secretary ushered us in, and withdrew discreetly.

That evening, Grey looked very much like his pencil and charcoal portrait, sketched by Sir John Sargent, which you might see in the National Portrait Gallery. Every aristocratic line of his lean, handsome face was etched with care and worry. A doyen among European ambassadors, he had prevented war on a dozen occasions. Single-handedly, with quiet diplomacy, learning, and gentle finesse, he had resolved the Agadir crisis two years ago, when everyone in England was convinced that war was imminent, following the intrusion of the German warship in Moroccan waters. Although I was not privy to high political circles, the newspapers kept the common man abreast of how Grey had swung France and Russia round to our side.

Handing us glasses of a dry tawny sherry, Grey opened his mind a little to the both of us. "Gentlemen, it is indeed very gracious of you to come and visit me. I should have waited upon you, but I dare not leave this office for even a minute these days. God knows, there is little I can do to bring sanity into the highest circles in Europe, but war I am determined to avoid, or, if I can't, delay it as long as possible. We are woefully unprepared, and the consequences…" his words trailed off, and left us staring out at the darkening window.

"Gentlemen, my request to you—the nation's request to you—is that you prepare yourselves to help where the Empire is the most vulnerable—in India. His

Majesty's Government has not forgotten your considerable services there."

"Performed, Sir Edward, almost twenty-five years ago," reminded Holmes drily. "We would not shirk our duty—I am speaking for Dr Watson as well, whose services merit greater recognition than mine—but what can men in their seventies achieve, of any significance, and that too so far away?"

"Mr Sherlock Holmes, brawn is not what we need at this hour, but sage advice from you—I have here with me an important letter from Lord Charles Hardinge, Viceroy of India—I may not show you the whole of it, I am sure you understand, but mark his words..." he hunted for the right paragraph, "...yes, here it is—'the tranquillity of India hangs by a thread; those our government fears most might turn out to be our staunchest allies, while those from whom we should expect loyal service could prove treacherous and bring the Empire down. No official intervention from London can have the slightest salutary effect, but I request the discreet advice of someone knowledgeable in the ways of crooked men...' and more to the same effect. Yes, here—'can Mr Sherlock Holmes be induced to come out to help me, as well as the excellent Dr Watson; we need the acuteness of the one, and the sturdy common sense of the other.' There, gentlemen, is the reason I sent for you. I know Hardinge, he and his family have served long in India, and know that country better than they know England. Hardinge has the coolest nerve of any

Governor of the British Empire, and I am determined
to help him. Will you?"⁴⁹

It is hardly possible for English gentlemen to demur
when asked to serve their sovereign, and so it was settled
we would leave by the next boat. Sir Edward assured us
repeatedly that in consideration of our "seniority", as he
put it, we would be very well looked after by the Indian
Government at all times, and should we want to return
to England at any time, for any reason, we could do so as
expeditiously and as comfortably as possible.

The shades of evening had fallen fast, and we were
sitting in the gloaming. "The lights are going out all over
Europe, gentlemen," he said grimly. "We won't see them
lit again in our time."

We rose and silently shook hands with him. "Oh, by the
way," he said as we turned to the door, "I am in touch with
a Hugh Whistler, a young police officer in the Punjab. Get
in touch with him, he may be of great personal service to
you, if needed. He is also an enthusiastic ornithologist, as
I am, and I believe he has managed to collect some bones
of the dodo. Do bring me back a set for my collection, if
you can. How terrible that our sailors killed off all those
poor, defenceless birds," he added bitterly, seeming more
worried at that moment about the fate of the extinct
species than of his own countrymen.

Our journey was accomplished uneventfully. I must
admit I did not travel as well as I did in earlier times, and
kept to my cabin most of the time. Whenever I went on
deck to take the air, I seemed to see the ominous grey

silhouettes of warships far out at sea. Holmes, as was his custom, sat indomitably in a deck chair, swathed in blankets, and reading from a pile of books.

Upon landing in Bombay, we were taken to the Taj Mahal Hotel, which was within a few yards of the P & O Landing Place. I certainly needed to recuperate for a few days before venturing further inland, and secured a sea-facing room. Three days later, we boarded a train for Delhi at the Victoria Terminus, and spent a couple of very comfortable days in a first-class cabin, with attendants waiting on our every wish. Looking out at the Indian countryside I loved dearly, I must say some warmth and vigour returned to my old bones, and I began to look upon our expedition with some excitement.

At our request, we had been provided rooms at the Officer's Gymkhana. Holmes was of the opinion, and I agreed, that the company of young officers would be invaluable to us on our mission, for we would pick up many tidbits of news and gossip, in the bar or in the pavilion, which could lead us to a truer assessment of the situation than tiresome briefings from officials.

The day after our arrival in Delhi, we were driven to the Viceregal Lodge, and received in Lord Hardinge's study. Carefully shutting the door behind us, Hardinge led us to a set of deep sofas. He was a handsome man, with a high, balding forehead and a trim dark moustache, who gave a general impression of quiet authority. With his back to large French windows, he sat studying us for some time. What he saw before him were not the most famous detectives in England, but two old gentlemen, rather bewildered at having been dragged out of retirement. He waited until the servants had withdrawn after serving us tea.

"Gentlemen, accept my grateful thanks, for so nobly rising to the occasion," he said. "We all know that we are heading towards war. We will win, that is certain, but at what cost? It is my sacred duty to keep India serene behind the bulwark of the British Empire. The Indian nationalists are divided equally in terms of influence between 'the moderates' and 'the extremists'. My aide-de-camp, Captain William Castlereagh, will give you all details about all of their leaders, their families, their education, their religious sects, their weaknesses. Gentlemen, you should get to know them."

After a short silence, and a thoughtful sip of tea, he continued. "Strangely, despite their avowal of extremism, I don't think the extreme faction is any threat to Empire. I find their political goals acceptable, attainable with negotiation."

"And yet, they made an attempt on Your Excellency's life at Chandni Chowk, as you entered Delhi," broke in Holmes seriously. "Very true," admitted Hardinge. "The criminal mind that thought up the dastardly attack remains at large. The misguided hotheads who committed the deed have paid with their lives for someone else's mischief, several innocent bystanders were injured, and that poor elephant, Sultan, another dumb witness to this madness, had to be put down. But to resume: The moderates could pose a greater danger, for they are constantly trying to reform their own societies; and the

Hindoo, and for that matter the Indian Mussalman, may dig his toes in when pushed to change his ways, to follow angrezi ways. There is a fierce desire in some quarters to change the status of women, and that is a dangerous thing to attempt in any society. My opinions on the suffragettes are too well known to need further elaboration. But the point is, gentlemen, I fear a threat from another quarter, a shadowy group that does not dare to show its face in the open, but that plots in its own interests. Gentlemen! The Indian Empire must be kept calm, at least during the coming war. I am determined to send all our forces to the aid of the King's Armies. We will be practically without soldiers in India! I want no incident of any kind occurring here. You must help me prevent it!"

The complexity of our mission dawned upon us. I gasped. The Viceroy continued, "I have complete confidence in the intelligence and capacities of Captain Castlereagh. He will be the confidential link between you and me. You can depend upon him to come to your aid at a moment's notice, if necessary. Keep him informed of anything you find suspicious, and I will know how to act upon it. I will call him in now."

Castlereagh seemed to be expecting the call, for he came in a moment later. I was immediately impressed by the young handsome Irishman, with pleasant, easy ways. He took us to his mess for a sumptuous lunch, and regaled us with funny stories about all the Indian nationalist leaders, their whims, their misadventures, and their ingenuous hypocrisies. I felt much more confident, at the end of lunch, that this parcel of woolly-headed men could be handled by the local British officers without any trouble. Our task might be no more than an enjoyable picnic in the evening of our lives, performed with the assistance of likeable young men such as Castlereagh.

Amused by the humorous descriptions of our young captain, I had forgotten to be cautious about spicy Indian food. I needed to rest in my room for a while, and so Holmes and Castlereagh dropped me off at the Club, and went on to meet other senior officials. The briefings we received that week seemed thorough in every way. By the end of it, we—or at least Holmes—had as true a picture of the Indian nationalists and their strategies as an Englishman could possibly have in such a short span of time. Knowing my interests, our young captain had arranged for me to be shown around Delhi by his equally charming colleagues, while Holmes plunged seriously into political study. I was amazed at the changes that time had wrought. Deserted, ancient Ferozabad to the south was going to be developed as the new capital of India. Shahjanabad itself had changed beyond all recognition, and modern houses, built in the temporary capital to the north, had spilled into what had once been Wazir Khan's and Narain Dass's gardens. The Rajpur barracks, where I had stayed, had been torn down long years ago, to be replaced by smart new cavalry lines.

A week or so later, Castlereagh arranged a top official briefing for Holmes and me. The gravity of the situation was emphasized by the fact that it was conducted by Sir

William Hailey himself, Chief Commissioner of Delhi, who held the additional charge of Inspector General of the Indian Imperial Police.[50] His kindly eyes, the humorous twist to his mouth as he spoke, and the casual manner of dress and speech belied the imperial burden resting on that pair of shoulders. "Mr Sherlock Holmes, Dr Watson, your fame as detectives has spread even to this quarter of the Empire," he drawled. "I know I am speaking to specialists, so I will come directly to the point. Although we lack the resources of Scotland Yard, or your own proverbial acuteness of intellect, we have a fair idea who poses what danger to the civil tranquillity of India. Let me map out for you the different groups, but in no particular order of importance, since any one of them could set the Empire in flames, depending on chance, and the right opportunity.

"First, the so-called bunch of 'moderates', such as the Servants of India Society and its mastermind, Gopal Krishna Gokhale, a mischievous lawyer, like several of them, a misguided educator, like many more, an indefatigable critic alike of Hindoo society and the British Government, and a member of the openly disloyal Indian National Congress. A few years ago, during a presidential address, he pronounced that 'the dignity of a consciousness of national existence has spread over the whole land'. This is a lie, but he has done his best to make it so, and is dangerous in a perfectly legal way, damn it! There are several more of his ilk and you shall meet them, especially in the south, where Madrasis profess reform. And we do not know when and how they will strike.

"The extremists are out in the open, we know how to deal with this lot, and they are very dangerous. Their leading spirit is Bal Gangadhar Tilak, a lawyer, and a publisher of seditious newspapers, who has openly demanded 'Swaraj', or independence for India, and hurt British interests deeply by threatening people to boycott our goods. He has diabolically used religious credulity to convert an animist festival for elephants into a political rallying point. Let me quote his words to the Congress: 'We shall not assist them in fighting beyond the frontiers or outside India with Indian blood and money. We shall not assist them in carrying on the administration of justice.' If this is not dangerous sedition, what is? His influence was so great, we had to put him away under arrest in the salubrious climate of Mandalay. He is back, old and ill, but a lion is dangerous even in extremities.

"Another sort of extremist is the pamphleteer, who seduces a semi-literate people with a clever mix of fact and fiction, apparent good sense that no one could object to with fiery idealism. Such is the Bengali Bipin Chandra Pal, with his weeklies *New India* and *Bande Mataram*. Nowadays he professes an interest in the Brahmo Samaj and the Vaishnavite sects, all a cover for his treasonable activities. He was hand in glove with that arch revolutionary and religious humbug, Aurobindo, but we could not prove it in court. Another of his ilk, the Punjabi Lala Lajpat Rai, is away in England spreading his poison among our simple-minded workers. The demented Madame Cama is a tool of Berlin. We try and prevent their magazines from entering India and confusing the simpler sort, but there is a whole teeming underground at their disposal.

"Hardcore terrorists are found mostly in Bengal, and thanks to Lord Hardinge's pacifism, Lord Curzon's partition of Bengal has been undone, and these groups are working closely together. The parent body is the Yugantar group, from which the Jatin gang have broken away, with headquarters hidden in Calcutta itself, and the Dacca-based Anushilan Samiti. They are very dangerous men, and we kill them at sight. Fortunately, several decent Bengalis are brave enough to inform the police of any suspicion of their hideouts. Look at this photograph—it is Jatin Mukerjee. Don't be fooled by those dreamy eyes: he is a killer, you can tell by the set of his jaw. He is the mastermind behind the Alipore and Howrah–Shibpur conspiracy cases. We are sure he is in touch with the Germans. For quite some time, we thought he was also behind the attempt on the Viceroy's life, but now we know it is another very dangerous shadowy gang, perhaps of Punjabis. We must find them soon, gentlemen, and I hope your presence here will help us to do so.

"Savarkar is now securely in the Andamans' jail. We will never let him out. We are more or less certain that a group of desperate men will try to help him escape. We think they are posing as religious mystics in Aurobindo's Ashram in the French colony of Pondicherry. You see, gentlemen, how all these groups link and support each other? It's a rabbit's warren of sedition! Aurobindo could have had a brilliant career in government service, or in academic life. He perversely chose to edit Bipin Chandra Pal's treasonable magazine *Bande Mataram*, which Mr Radcliff of *The Statesman* calls 'the most effective voice of nationalist extremism'. We are sure that he was behind the attempt on Kingsford's life, but again, how was proof to be had? Coming out of jail, he has cunningly pretended to turn mystic, and put himself under French protection. But look at his hypocrisy: he writes, 'I look upon my country as the mother. What would a son do when a demon sitting on the breast of his mother is drinking her blood?' We must penetrate his Ashram at any cost.

"That Russian woman Blavatsky's Theosophical Society in Madras is another cover for sedition, and leading it is a woman Fenian, Annie Besant. She has all the madness of Irish blood in her veins; back home she has been among the most shameless of suffragettes, she has instigated the working class, and now she comes here in support of 'Home Rule' for India, if you please. Of course, the Indians take her to their collective bosom, and very quickly she has become a leader of the Indian National Congress. As is to be expected, she has her own magazine, but also, mark my words, publishes in Bipin Chandra Pal's *New India*. A dangerous anarchist, demented to boot, and to be watched carefully every moment. Of course, she is not the only white person to meddle in India. Credulous victims like that unfortunate Miss Noble, who, true to type, most probably had only a miserable platonic attachment to that Swami Vivek whatever, and charlatans like Hume, and Sir Henry Cotton, another President of the Congress—how their

presence gives credence to treasonable aspirations!
Cotton also wrote a book titled *New India*—strange, is it
not, how they all talk about a 'new' country as if it can be
manufactured out of thin air? He said no one wanted the
partition of Bengal but only the Government, can you
believe that? And then, listen to this, 'You have become
a power in the land, and your voice peals like a trumpet
note from one end of India to the other.'

"And what about all the German missionaries in every
tribal heartland? Men of God they might be, but Germans
nonetheless, with a God-like hold over millions, who
can be inflamed to cut every rail link in India.

"Our list of worries does not end here. A brilliant
Indian civil servant, R.C. Dutt, used his scholarly powers
to attack the hand that fed him. And can we trust
Satyendra Prasanna, the first Indian Advocate General
of Bengal, and the first Indian in the Governor General's
Executive Council, when he speaks in measured tones
of 'autonomy within the Empire'? How loyal is he? And
what about the Muslim League, which pretends overt
loyalty, but should war come, and the Turks are able to
cut the Suez link, how loyal would the Nizam and the
Nawabs be? We must not forget that we displaced them
from imperial power—they certainly have not forgotten!
A brilliant young Bombay lawyer, Mohammed Ali
Jinnah, a member of the Viceroy's Executive Council
to boot, but a devoted Congressman, is trying to build
nationalist bridges between Hindoos and Muslims, and
he is to be watched as well. Single-handedly, he can undo
the statesmanship of my lords, Curzon and Minto. Lord

Hardinge himself, God bless him, adds to our problems. He is determined to strip India of all fighting men and send them to the front. Of course, that is right and proper. But to acquire peace and stability here, at least during the interregnum of the war, he wishes to negotiate with the Indians. He treats Indians as if they were Englishmen, with our values of fair play and justice, and that could be the most dangerous, misguided belief of all!"

We were silent when Sir William finished his long but terse briefing. What could two old men do in such parlous times, I wondered. Lord Hardinge and Sir William were in a desperate corner, it seemed. What was to be done? I must have unconsciously voiced the question, for Sir William replied.

"Before God, I don't know, Dr Watson," he said simply. "But if you gentlemen are willing, I would request you to go about India as if you had returned from a sense of nostalgia, and actively seek out these groups. They will suspect nothing. What have they to fear from two old men, if I may be pardoned for saying so. They will boast, they do so all the time—they are cocksure and self-righteous. You would hear far more than we can. If you hear anything of importance, let us know immediately. I cannot ask for more. This itself, I'm afraid, is too great an imposition."

Captain Castlereagh was smiling at us in his clean, frank way. "We have to cut the Gordian Knot somewhere, soon," he murmured. "You can help us do so." I remembered that smile of his for a long time, and for some reason I found it disturbing.

Before leaving, Sherlock Holmes turned to Sir William and asked, "Sir William, I should like to start by meeting an Indian in whom you have implicit trust. Is there such a man?"

Sir William thought a while. "Yes, I trust Sir Rahim Bhaksh, President of the Council of Regency of the Nawab of Bahawalpur. I shall send word to him to expect you both. He is a gracious host. Go down there and talk to him."[51]

In Indian fashion, a railway saloon was to be arranged for our comfort, but we turned it down, for we were to appear as simple tourists on a nostalgic trip. We left the following Sunday, skirting round to the north of the great Thar Desert, by way of Ambala, Amritsar, Lahore, and Multan, to reach our destination on the Sutlej, a journey as long as the one that had brought us north from Bombay. Desert sand kept blowing in from the windows of our first-class compartment, and we showered frequently. A luxurious landau drove us past rich, well-managed cotton and rice fields, along the tree-lined banks of the river to the palace of the Nawab, a gracious double-storeyed sandstone structure built like an English college, with an inner garden between the two wings that flanked the central durbar hall. While the zenana occupied the floors above and to the rear, our guest rooms were right at the front on the ground floor, to the left. When a servant indicated that dinner was about to be served, we went to an ornate dining hall, where His Highness graciously received us, enquiring politely if the journey had been too tedious. A dignified, portly man in his middle years, he had cultivated European manners, and these overlaid the native hospitality of a Muslim prince. Our delight was doubled to find among his guests, the ageing Nawab Viqar-ul-Mulk of Hyderabad,[52] who had no difficulty in remembering me. He came forward, a little stooped with age, but with the same bright and piercing eyes as before.

"Dr Watson, what a pleasure. I never thought to see the man, who so loved my palace, in these parts. The Falaknama is now the seat of the Nizam—it was too grand for a humble courtier, and it was a mark of great favour that my prince accepted the gift." I have never known the delicacy of expression favoured by Muslim princes to be matched in any other civilization.

We were next introduced to one of the handsomest of young men, in the latest Savile Row suit, the brilliant Mohammed Ali Jinnah. "Mr Holmes, Dr Watson, what a pleasure to meet two such eminent Englishmen," he said, taking each one of us by the arm. "Your deductive powers would have greatly enhanced the prestige of my profession, had you turned to the Bar. Sir Rahim has been diligent to gather as many Muslim princes as he can at his house parties, which really turn out to be 'informal' conferences on how we should support the government in its hour of need. I have come up to add my voice to our loyal coalition."

The dinner was a prolonged affair, with several dishes that I had to refuse regretfully in consideration of my weakened condition. I ate no more than a little river fish, some kebabs I could not resist, canard l'orange as delicious as the best French cook can make it, followed by mutton dhansak spiced with saffron. Over port and cigars, a few of us withdrew to a comfortable study to discuss the politics of the day, while the rest of the guests retired to their own chambers.

Jinnah took immediate charge of the discussion. "Loyal we are, Sir Rahim, there can be no question about that," he said, drawing deeply on a large Monte Cristo cigar. "But the Government needs to respond graciously to this wave of loyalty. You have been tireless in rallying our princes, and I have done my best to bring Hindoos and Muslims together to build a modern India that will take its place in the comity of nations. That should neither surprise nor shock anyone. Canada and Australia are Dominions under the Crown, but equal in every other respect with Britain herself. With our rich heritage, we are in no respect inferior to outwoodsmen."

Nawab Viqar held up a dignified hand. "We accept the need for change, Mr Jinnah, and all of us are glad that you are a close advisor to His Excellency, the Viceroy. But Muslim interests must be protected. We cannot tolerate Bengali babus dictating terms to our people. Sir Syed warned all Muslims of the consequences of neglecting science and education, and I have tried to follow his lead, but our people are still no match for these wily Hindoos. We discovered their true nature only when they agitated against the partition of Bengal. They wanted to keep the Mussalman farmer under their heel. That was what opened the eyes of Nawab Salimullah of Dacca, who demanded our own Muslim League; and that is also why I agreed to chair our founding session."

"Nawab Sahib, we have nothing to fear but fear itself," said Jinnah patiently. "A modern democratic nation must be based on the one-man-one-vote principle. No nation can advance by granting special privileges to any section. If Muslims cannot produce worthy candidates, why, they will simply have to accept better Hindoo men. In our history, Indians have never discriminated on the basis of religion, but men and armies have followed the better leader."

"Exactly!" broke in our host, somewhat anxiously. "Our leader today is the King Emperor himself! My ancestors, and all of yours, have been men true to their salt—we have sacrificed our lives rather than our honour. Now is not the time to talk politics, but for each man to draw his sword, and stand shoulder to shoulder in the front rank of war!"

A murmur of assent went round the room, a toast was raised to loyalty, and we stood and drank it with great solemnity. Jinnah continued: "I agreed to serve on the Viceroy's Executive Council, for I am a staunch believer in a liberal, secular, democratic government. The British connection assures our advance as a modern civilization. I am equally a staunch Congressman for the same reason and principles. Men like Gopal Krishna Gokhale, Srinivas Iyengar, and Motilal Nehru would be ornaments in the most brilliant courts of the world. True, Lokmanya Tilak has used Hindoo religious symbols in his political struggles, but who can doubt the sincerity of a man who courted arrest and exile by demanding his, and our, birthright? At this hour, the Muslim League needs to join hands with the Indian National Congress, and form a united front, to win political equality within the Commonwealth."[53]

The discussion raged in circles, and meandered into anecdotes of little consequence, under the soothing influence of the rich wine. At long last, we retired to our rooms. One of my last thoughts, before I drifted off, was that Sir William had been accurate in his assessment that the young Mr Jinnah posed the greatest danger to the integrity of Empire.

The next morning, I rose early to take a walk along the banks of the Sutlej. A gentle breeze blew in from the river, and the cotton balls in the green fields glinted in the morning sun. Hearing a horse behind me, I turned to see Jinnah approaching me at a fast trot. He leapt off his Arab, flinging the reins to a syce, who rode another animal in close attendance.

"Dr Watson, I am well aware of your mission," he said without preamble. "I could not but be, as a confidante of the Viceroy. You and Mr Holmes would do well to get a measure of Hindoo feeling. You will find, as Lord Hardinge does, that the Indian nationalist is not to be feared, but is to be respected even as we would a sturdy, honest Englishman. Around Durga Puja, there is always a meeting of nationalists at Jhansi, to honour the memory of their warrior queen, even as you commemorate the memory of Boedicea."

We then fell to admiring the beauty of the morning, and the neatness of the well-tended fields on the edge of the great desert. Jinnah's advice had made a deep impression, and I mentioned it to Holmes at the first opportunity. We agreed that we should heed his advice, and in a few days' time, took leave of our host and his noble guests, declining to join a duck shoot up the river.

Our journey back was uneventful, and having changed into fresh clothes at the Club in Delhi, we set off for Jhansi. We reached the town by nightfall, and decided to stay at the railway station itself, rather than trust ourselves to any hostelry the town might provide. The stationmaster was delighted to accommodate "Your Honours", and got an army of porters to clean out a large, well-aired waiting room, requisitioned solely for our use. A couple of Indian families, who were travelling with many trunks, jars, and other baggage of all shapes and sizes, were hustled away. We were dismayed, but assured on enquiry that they would also be provided for.

The dining room was surprisingly clean, with neatly laid out tables. Wire mesh double doors kept the place free of flies and insects. We warned the khansamah not to serve greasy omelettes; and, honoured at our visit, he so outdid himself that we scarcely touched the bottle of tomato ketchup. The caramel pudding that followed was excellent. A young sanyasi, with a rippling black beard and dressed in traditional ochre robes, entered as we were at dinner and came over unhesitatingly to our table, extending a small plate with a few flowers, a piece of turmeric, and a small pile of mixed grams.

"May Heaven's blessings descend on our honoured, elderly visitors," he intoned in singsong English. "Please accept Durga Mai's prasad." We dutifully popped a piece of dry coconut into our mouths. Rapid Sanskrit slokas followed, while the sanyasi held up his hands in benediction. The khansamah had come out of the kitchen in haste, but after some hesitation, he went back with a shrug. Holmes politely offered the sanyasi a chair, and the latter promptly fell into an easy conversation with us. It seemed the good fathers of St Joseph's had educated him until his matriculation, but the attraction of Vedanta had been greater. In his former life, before he had renounced the world, he had answered to the name of Gopal Das, and he invited us to address him thus.

"Mr Gopal Das, we hope we call you so without giving offence," I said, speaking slowly and clearly. "We are re-visiting places of our service in India, of which we have such good memories. We have never been in Jhansi, but being near, wanted to visit the famous fort from which the great Ranee of heroic memory held up the honour of her race."

Das had closed his eyes, and was mumbling a prayer as he counted his rosary beads. "Poor misguided soul," he said at last. "The maya of this world had her in its grip. Of what consequence are honour, power, wars, and pain—these are veils that stand between us and It, for It is where It always Is, and we struggle and search all our lives, and some find It in us and us in It. Others like the Ranee must be born again to suffer."

"We have heard that there is some service at this time in her honour," I mumbled. "Perhaps we can witness it...So many years have passed, the English were cruel to the Ranee. I say so, although we are English, and we would like to pay homage…"

Das opened his eyes wide and looked at me. "You are blessed that you see the truth. You will not be born again." I did not know how to take that. "Men of the world confuse what we should offer only to Durga Mai with their devotion to a figment of the world—the Ranee. Tomorrow evening, there will be a meeting in the Ghanshyam Das Gokul Das Reading Room at about five in the evening. Anyone will show you the place. God's blessings, I must return to the temple." And with that, he was gone, as swiftly as he had entered.

The clangs of a shunting goods train roused me from a troubled sleep in the dead of night. Lying awake, I listened to two express trains pass, their search lights sweeping broad swathes of light round the room. I must have dropped off long afterward, for suddenly I woke to the sound of low voices murmuring. A name, "Rash Behari", or something like that, was uttered, and then hushed by another, both speaking rapidly in Hindoostani. I lifted my head to see the sanyasi and another figure disappear into the darkness. Well, even those who renounce the world are dragged back into some business or other, whatever the time of day or night I thought, as I fell asleep once again.

The next day we hired a single-horse tonga, and went about town. Mustapha, the tonga's owner, was most uncommunicative. When we bought him tea and samosas, he lightened up, and spoke of what his grandfather had told him about the times of the Mutiny.

The Company Sahib Bahadur had dealt severely with the townspeople, many had been killed, and all had lost their wealth. It had been Allah's will, but the people, Hindoo and Muslim, could not afford to lose their izzat by deserting their queen. Yes, he knew where the meeting was to be held. Yes, he knew all the places of interest, and many more besides.

Holmes decided to visit the district kutcherry and meet the English Collector to search for some records. I had myself driven to the old fort, where an Empire had almost been lost more than six decades ago. The stone ramparts had been torn down in places, and the whole place looked unkempt and deserted. Leaving the tonga under a tree, to rest man and beast, I wandered around, past anthills and bushes, imagining the desperate scenes of long ago. It was around four in the afternoon, and I sat on a low stone wall, watching a group of boys play hockey in that deserted place. I had played the game myself at school, and nothing gave me greater pleasure than to watch youngsters learn to play as a team, for it is all pure teamwork as in no other game. Soon, I noticed a young slim boy, of no more than eight or nine years, who clearly outshone the others, all of whom were older and at least a head taller. I watched him fascinated as he dribbled the ball, and wove in and out among longer and stronger legs. He was thinking as he played, almost like a chess player, and his team, I fancied, formed the pieces, and the field his chessboard. A reckless shot from a tall fat boy brought the ball bouncing off my wall. The young boy ran up to pick it up.

"Hello! You play very good hockey," I said in Hindoostani. "Do you go to school? What's your name?"

"I am Dhyan Chand, Sir. We are all from the High School here," he answered breathlessly, in passable English. "We are practising hard for the inter-school tournament." From his clothes and his battered old hockey stick, I could see he came from a very ordinary local family. Once again, I complimented him on his dribbling, and he said ruefully he was not yet strong enough to shoot long and hard.

"Hockey, my dear boy, requires strength of mind, and not strength of muscle. Use your mind at all times, and your wrists, and one day, who knows, you may even play for India," I said, and then let him go, seeing he was eager to get back to the game.[54]

It was time for me to go as well, but I took the long way round the battlements to the tonga. Coming round a corner of a courtyard, with bushes sprouting between broken flagstones, I was surprised to encounter the sanyasi from last night huddled among half a dozen young men, the tails of their saffron turbans drawn across their faces. They sprang up agilely, but the moment of tension was dissipated swiftly by Gopal Das, who came across and took my arm in the friendliest fashion.

"Dr Watson, Sir, how kind you are to visit our old tumbledown fort, which has nothing but memories! My novitiate sanyasis are under strict oath neither to show their faces, nor to speak during the term of their vigil. The Ego must be curbed, made faceless, voiceless, so that It may speak to us."

He went on in that obscure vein, while seeing me to
my tonga, and then curtly ordered Mustapha to take me
to the meeting hall right away, and without wasting time
on chitchat. Mustapha, who had been understandably
startled at his sudden appearance, seemed to take his
commands literally, for I could not get a word out of
him on our way back to the town.

Holmes was waiting for me at the Ghanshyam Das
Gokul Das Reading Room, which was a rather dingy
affair, with cobwebs hanging from the low ceiling, and
walls lined with dusty bookshelves. The panels of some
bookcases had come off their hinges. The books were in
several languages, but mostly in Hindi and Urdu, with
a few in English by Indian authors, and a long line of
District Gazetteers. A table had been arranged at the
head of two columns of chairs, and at it sat three solemn
men. The one on the left, a short old man wearing a
flat black cap and thick glasses, was clearly the person
who owned or managed the reading room. On the right
was a nervous young man, who gave a rapid impassioned
speech about the great Ranee, and how it was everyone's
duty to die for one's country. He concluded by glaring
at me and Holmes. The man in the centre, who had sat
silently through the diatribe, now rose to speak. He was
introduced only as "Raja Sahib", for everyone but us
seemed to know who he was.

He spoke easily in Hindi and English, alternating
between both paragraph by paragraph, as if deliberately
including us within the audience. His exposition of
British rule in India was clear and pitiless, every political

ploy and economic measure being scrutinized realistically and presented to the audience for it to arrive at its own conclusions. He spoke of the fortunes of other countries, of Mazzini, of Garibaldi, of the French Revolution and the sweeping away of its decadent aristocracy, the Russian massacres of 1905, at which he stopped pointedly, as if to ask for comparisons with British action in India. He asked us to do nothing in haste, but to take whatever action was necessary to secure honour and welfare, for ourselves and for humanity.

Enthusiastic clapping greeted his speech, and the small but vocal audience rose to its feet and rushed to surround him with questions and congratulations. Awed as I was by his masterly speech, I had some doubts about the facts he had quoted, and wished to go up to the dais, but my way and Holmes's was blocked by our good friend, the sanyasi, who asked us many solicitous questions about our stay at Jhansi. By the time we had answered him politely, all had left the hall; we went out ourselves and walked down a couple of streets, but could see no one. Our sanyasi, by this time, had disappeared as well, so, more than a little tired, we made our way back to the railway station's waiting rooms.

After dinner, I was feeling into my pocket for some coins to tip the khansamah, when my hand came away with a piece of paper torn from a notebook. It said in a hasty scrawl:

> It was a pleasure to match wits with you, Holmes & Watson. Hope you will try harder next time, old chaps.

Shall we meet in Bengal for another séance? Yours, as
ever, Jatin the Sanyasi.[55]

Rather breathlessly, we rushed to the stationmaster's
office and sent a telegram to Castlereagh. In minutes
we received a reply that Mr Pierce, the Deputy
Superintendent of Police at Jhansi, would be with us
within the hour. I do not know what we found more
shocking: the cool audacity of the rascal, or his warped
sense of humour at a moment of great personal danger
to himself.

Mr Pierce also appeared to be a cool man under stress.
After we had given him a summary of the events, he said
he would alert the Allahabad Police to search the train
the criminal had undoubtedly taken to escape to Bengal.
It was common for such fellows to brag, and pose as
some kind of Robin Hood. Jatin, the head of a dreaded
gang, would be caught this time; he had put his own
head in a noose. We would pursue the villain. A single
compartment was attached to an engine, and we set off
at breakneck speed, all other trains on the track having
been ordered into sidings. We reached Allahabad by
midnight, and joined in a thorough search of the express
coming from the west. Later, we combed several other
trains, and this continued late into the next day, but no
one remotely resembling our sanyasi was found. Pierce
remained unruffled. The rascal would be caught, his days
were numbered. For Pierce, it was a routine job, without
any histrionics.

As we made our tired way back to Delhi, Holmes broke

his silence at long last. "That sanyasi was just a decoy, Watson," said Holmes, "to distract us from the speaker. What a daring rascal! That man was undoubtedly Rash Behari, the head of that shadowy gang that tried to kill the Viceroy! And the men you saw in the old fort were almost certainly the members of his group, planning another atrocity!"[56]

Castlereagh came round to the Club next morning, and smiled knowingly as we told him how we had been sadly deceived by Jatin Mukerjee. He told us that the Madras Police had information that a gang would try and rent, or steal, a fishing boat in an attempt to free Savarkar from the Cellular Jail in the Andamans. The trail needed to be picked up there; he had arranged for tickets on the Great Indian Peninsular Railway.

The three-day journey was tiring, despite the ministrations of Castlereagh's own batman, kindly lent to us for the journey. When it ended, we were glad to retire to the cool comfort of Connemara Hotel. I had had the pleasure of meeting Sir Robert Bourke—later Baron Connemara—who was Governor of Madras during my last visit, and I was glad that the hotel did justice to the name it carried.[57] On the second day after our arrival, we received a visit from Mr Nigel Young, Commissioner of Police, a large fat man with a short bristling moustache, and very different in every way from the dapper Colonel Pickering of twenty-five years ago.

"We are shadowing the miscreants, Mr Holmes," he said, sinking into a cane armchair, and gratefully accepting a brandy and soda. "Indeed there is no need for experts like you to be sent here on this trifling business. We are giving them a long rope, so that they may incriminate themselves. These Indians are dim-witted, and put their own heads into the noose. This damned climate!" he added, pulling his sweat-stained shirt away from his belly. "You need to bathe three times a day."

We learnt, as Sir William Hailey had predicted, that a gang disguised as mystics were headed towards the Aurobindo Ashram in Pondicherry. Young had spoken with his French counterpart, the Prefect de Police, and all arrangements had been made for our reception. We piled into a large Dodge tourer, and set off with two other police cars in attendance. It was slow going over the sandy road twisting south between casuarina groves. Occasionally, when the heat got to us, we would stop at a village, and men in short white dhotis would rush forward with fresh coconuts, which were sliced open before us. Coconut water seems particularly delicious when drunk under these circumstances.

That evening, we were lodged in a large old-fashioned colonial hotel overlooking the sea, and royally entertained by M Albert Boucher, Prefect de Police for Pondicherry. A few good bottles of burgundy were opened, and Boucher assured us the men had arrived, and even now were involved in some religious ritual. As far as the French were concerned, Hinduism and Buddhism were all the same. The French, although profoundly Catholic, were tolerant of other religions. It was, how does one put it, a matter of personal choice, no? And the Republic was neutral—so long as no French law was broken.

That was the crux of the matter, we assured him. These men were here to break the law. Which law? asked Boucher politely. They were planning to release a dangerous criminal from imprisonment in the Andaman Islands, Young reminded him. Ah, Boucher understood, they were there then to cogitate, to ask help from their Gods for their desperate and doomed adventure, was it not so? What a pity—so young, so soon to be imprisoned along with their friend! How noble!

Young, perspiring even in the cool of the evening, tried to reason with his counterpart. The men must be restrained. Boucher was all concern. He would attend to it himself. One wrong move, a spit on the public road, fishing where they were forbidden, resorting to the company of women of a certain sort, you understand, although itself not a crime, and they would be secure in a French prison. We informed him that the men belonged to a dreaded gang in British India. Boucher shrugged elegantly—that was a matter beyond his jurisdiction, and about which he knew nothing. After further such pointless talk, Boucher left us with assurances of his highest regard. Frustrated, we went to bed, and I could hear Young swearing in his room.

Next morning, Holmes and I arrived at the Aurobindo Ashram. Young had told us firmly that he would go there only to make an arrest, if permitted by that son of a frog, Boucher. The Ashram was no more than a simple circle of small neat rooms around a shady courtyard with a fountain.

Aurobindo sat in a meditative pose at the head of

a circle of devotees, among whom were the recently
arrived gang members from Bengal. I was shocked to
see how young they were, no more than striplings in
their late teens. Was this really the dreaded group that
would mastermind the release of Savarkar? I began to
fear that the police had once again led us on a wild-
goose chase. Aurobindo, if he were indeed the head of
a secret terrorist outfit, seemed supremely unaware of
it.[58] Perhaps in his fortieth year, he looked like a young
man of twenty, with long black hair, neatly parted in
the centre, large, deep-set, mesmerizing eyes, and a fine,
imperial beard. His clothes were a spotless white, and
he held a pink lotus in his hand as he meditated. An
hour of silence passed. Then those lustrous eyes opened
again, and he said, after some talk about the Atman and
the Soul Force of the Supreme Consciousness: "Some
of you come from India to hear words on how we are
to conduct ourselves under the British reign. Our actual
enemy is not any force exterior to ourselves, but our
own crying weaknesses, our cowardice, our selfishness,
our hypocrisy, our purblind sentimentalism." After
expressing other such sentiments, he added, "I say of the
Congress, then, this: that its aims are mistaken, that the
spirit in which it proceeds towards their accomplishment
is not a spirit of sincerity and wholeheartedness, and that
the methods it has chosen are not the right methods, and
the leaders in whom it trusts, not the right sort of men to
be leaders. In brief, that we are at present the blind led, if
not by the blind, at any rate by the one-eyed." There was
much more again in similar vein. The ashramites then

went out to beg ceremoniously for their daily food, from the houses of sympathizers.

Holmes and I wondered that evening if the show had been put on for our benefit, and determined to visit the Ashram again the next day. The next day, and the day after that, the routine did not seem to vary, and we were wondering what to do next, when Young received a coded telegram from his headquarters, which left him blaspheming vilely. It seemed a group of Mahratta terrorists had come south, but to Madras, not Pondicherry, and had the previous night slipped out in a boat. We made our way back to Madras in silence and a bad temper.

Of course, the authorities in the Andaman Islands were alerted, and they spent several weeks of tense night watches, with the Superintendent himself spending every night outside Savarkar's cell, but no surprise attack came, and they were eventually asked to stand down, after weeks of tension. We were to find out much later that the boat of desperate men had been driven off course, and that they had landed on the beaches of Aceh province in northernmost Sumatra. The Dutch refused to take any action against them, and they ultimately settled there, married, and led, by all accounts, peaceful and prosperous lives.

To salve his pride, Nigel Young organized a raid on the Customs House in Madras to seize any treasonable literature that might have been smuggled into the country. We all spent a hot day at the docks opening packages, with the policeman strewing the contents on the oil-stained yards in frustration. Finally, he let out a cry of triumph. Clutched in his hands were some foolscap-sized notebooks.

"I have caught the rascals at last, Mr Holmes," he shouted. "They will confess to everything after a good caning, I promise you!"

The pages were covered with symbols in a strange green ink. A shy young Indian came forward, stammering. "I am a clerk here, Sir. Ramanujan is my name, and they are my mathematical notebooks. I shouldn't have left them around."

Nigel Young glared at him suspiciously. "You shouldn't have, should you, you sly rascal?" he shouted angrily. "You are one of them, and I shall deal with you as mercilessly as with the rest of your gang!"

By now, the British Collector of Customs had come forward to attest that indeed the young fellow was in the employ of the Customs House, and that he spent any free time he had doing "mathematics". Young was not satisfied.

"I have no doubt that all this is a secret code for communicating with Germany. Secrets about the docks, military secrets, all disguised as mathematics! There isn't anything here I can recognize, no addition, no multiplication, no division. This is not mathematics, I tell you, it's code, damnable code!"

After further discussion, during which Ramanujan stood unhappily by, it was decided that Sherlock Holmes should take away the notebooks to see if they indeed contained codes. Ramanujan begged Holmes to be very careful, since the notebooks contained, as he said, several months of very hard work. That evening, Holmes retired to his rooms rather early, clutching the notebooks, and he would say nothing to me either.

The next morning, a meeting was held in the office of the Collector of Customs, with Young sprawled in an armchair, and Ramanujan standing anxiously in attendance. "I have gone through your notebooks," said Sherlock Holmes. "In fact, I spent most of the night doing so. What you have done is brilliant. What seems simple on the surface has many hidden factors."

Both Ramanujan and Young looked up sharply at Holmes, although for different reasons. "What do you call these sets of patterns you have discovered?" asked Holmes.

"Parti—partitions, Sir," stammered Ramanujan.

"Hmm, how very interesting, and you have found that all whole numbers can be broken into sums of smaller numbers, called—partitions—eh? The number 4, for example, contains five partitions, so we have five different ways of adding up to 4. I noticed the same curious feature when I was reading mathematics, but you have discovered that there are congruences, that all partition numbers can be divided by 5, 7, or 11. How curious!"

Ramanujan looked delighted, the Collector looked relieved, and Young looked baffled.

"You mean, Holmes, the notebooks don't contain seditious material?" he boomed.

"On the contrary, Mr Young, they contain what might one day be considered a glory of British Indian learning. Here you are, Mr Ramanujan—you were quite right to warn me to be careful with the notebooks, they are priceless!"

As Ramanujan was mumbling his incoherent thanks, Holmes interjected with, "Oh, by the way, just a thought, Mr Ramanujan. Try to construct an equation to analyse any prime. I have a feeling all primes will be found with congruences."[59]

We left Young muttering to himself that he was glad he never had anything to do with damnable men of genius. Before leaving Madras, we decided to pay a visit to Madame Blavatsky's Theosophical Society on the banks of the Adyar, where we had spent a delightful half hour so many years ago. We sent word that we would visit, and had ourselves driven by the old, familiar route, but now dotted on every side with houses and other signs of urban growth.

Miss Annie Besant, the dreaded Fenian, was there in person to welcome us.[60] A large lady, who must have been very handsome in her prime, she still retained a mop of red-gold hair and two very merry blue eyes.

"Ah, the Viceregal sleuths! You are very welcome, gentlemen," she said, smiling pleasantly and shaking each of us vigorously by the hand. "Yes, the police are right for once. I am determined to give India her independence, and want all the British out of here, including the Irish, God bless them! Lord Hardinge had better look sharp now, and do something. He has tried soft soap, but we know all about British tricks, don't we now? You have split the Irish between Orangemen and Fenians, let loose the horrible Royal Irish Constabulary on defenceless biddies, you have destroyed Parnell with a canard, you have used religion in the most ungodly manner to serve imperial interest, and all for nothing, wouldn't you say? Do have some tea. I pride myself on the excellence of my tea. I brewed it especially for you."

She spoke in such a disarmingly candid manner that no offence could be taken, and beneath the hard political exterior, one soon caught a glimpse of genuine human kindness. "Well now, Mr Sherlock Holmes, and the redoubtable Dr Watson, tell me, what have you discovered about Indian nationalist terrorist plots, for that's what you came here to discover, didn't you? We are just asking for our human rights like anyone else in the world."

"And yet, Miss Besant, attempts have been made on the life of the Viceroy himself," reminded Holmes gravely. "Oh, Jesus, Joseph, and Mary!" exclaimed Miss Besant. "What do you expect if your police keep killing and torturing people who simply want the freedom to read and speak their mind? Not everyone is going to sit on their hands in meditation. Did you discover the bomb factory in Aurobindo's Ashram?"

She rose suddenly, strode to her large table, and brought back a sheaf of papers, which she dumped in my lap. "That is the speech I shall be giving in the Punjab on Baisaki day. I am calling for unity, of Hindoo and Muslim, for Home Rule today, and independence tomorrow. Poor Mr Sherlock Holmes, poor Dr Watson, poor Lord Hardinge, your Emperor is in deep trouble,

isn't he? We all know war will come any day now. And
when these emperors have bled their countries white of
men and money, what do you think will happen? All
peasants will be free, Ireland will be free, India will
be free!"

Soon afterwards, we took cordial leave of Miss Besant.
She insisted, however, on coming down the steps to our
car. "Have I shocked you, poor Dr Watson, poor Mr
Holmes?" she asked with genuine solicitude. "You are
such dears to come out all this way to do what you think
is right. God bless you! There!" and she kissed us both on
the cheek with affection.

The train journey back to Delhi was accomplished
mostly in silence, each of us reflecting that we were no
wiser than when we set out that afternoon to meet Sir
Edward Grey. The news from home worsened by the
day, and by the hour. None could doubt that war was
at hand, but while brash young men in barracks toasted
the coming day, others like myself, who had witnessed
much pointless suffering in the far corners of the earth,
lay tossing and turning, fearing for all that we held dear.
After making our report to young Castlereagh, who
heard us out with the same equanimous smile, we found
ourselves sitting in the Club, feeling rather hopeless and
bitter.

"How stupid of me to have forgotten," cried Holmes
in sudden animation. "Do you remember, Watson, that
Sir Edward recommended we go to the Punjab and meet
this young policeman, Hugh Whistler, was it not? The
ornithologist? This Rash Behari, who gave us the slip

in Jhansi, and by all accounts tried to kill the Viceroy, once worked at the Forest Research Institute in Dehra Dun and also at a government press in Simla. I am quite certain that's where he hides, and young Whistler may be able to run him to ground. Once we have done that, this tangled web could unravel!"

At the last minute, we decided against revealing our plans to Castlereagh, for in helping us with our travel he would undoubtedly have to disclose the details to several of his staff, and by now we were not sure how deeply the nationalists had penetrated the lower echelons of government. We left a hasty note that we were very tired after our journeys, and planned to relax for a few days at a quiet hotel in Mussoorie. And then we took the train for Simla. We could explain later, without giving offence, that we had changed our minds at the last minute, hearing there was some snow higher up.

Fearing to draw attention, we declined to stay in any of the better known hotels—Hotel Cecil, Hotel Metropole, or the Imperial Hotel on the ridge—and decided to enquire at the station whether any cheaper cottages might be available for a few days. We were told that Rose Villa was available for weekend leases, as the owners were away on a long period of home leave. A trusted servant, who could take care of all our needs, was on duty on the premises. The agent at the terminus, who undertook to make all the necessary arrangements, tried to interest us in more expensive residences at more fashionable locations. But we insisted that the price was just right, and we would have no other.

My joy was complete on finding that the trusty servitor in the cottage was none other than Ganga Din, my old Regimental bhistee. He enquired kindly after Memsahib, and I had to tell him that she had passed away very many years ago. He had no family either, and the news of our mutual loneliness drew us old men together for a moment. I informed Holmes with confidence that all our creature comforts would be taken care of without even our asking, and that at a pinch Ganga Din was handy with his fists or a gun, as the need arose.

Late that cold night, as we sat by a roaring fire Ganga Din had kindled, sipping excellent cups of coffee, a slight tap on the door announced the man we were expecting. Hugh Whistler was a young man of quiet determination, slow but firm in his ways, as most men are who spend the better part of their lives out in the open jungle. Unlike others, who hunted the animals they loved, he merely observed birds in their natural habitats, noting everything down in minute detail for posterity. Neither with undue modesty nor with forward pride, he acknowledged that he regularly corresponded with the great Sir Edward Grey on the subject of ornithology, which bound them together in a knowing but distant fellowship.[61] That evening, he told us a little about his police work, and said he was aware of the shadowy presence of Rash Behari Bose in his beat, particularly after the man had recently disappeared once again. The hills, however, were not yet terrorist spots. We sat in silence for a long time as the embers burned down, and then with a quiet good night, he left.

I have always loved the hills of India, and although my left knee gave more trouble in colder climes, I braced myself to take long walks along the ridges, up the hills high over Simla, and down the valleys to where the waterfalls fell gossamer white against the dark green of the trees. The powdery snow and pristine air, and the absence of any treacherous slush underfoot made my walks an utter delight.. Holmes and Whistler had struck up an immediate friendship, and spent most of the day in the Secretariat, poring over old records.

I was high on Prospect Hill one day, enjoying the view through my binoculars, when idly swinging down towards the Infantry lines in Jutogh I spied two familiar figures, that of Holmes and Whistler, deep in conversation with some sepoys. What could they want with the sepoys, I wondered. There had been a rumour that Rash Behari was trying to foment another mutiny, and it was possible they had tracked the villain down at last. I hurried to Rose Villa in excitement, and over tea, after Holmes had come in dusting the snow off his coat, asked him if he had succeeded in tracking down the conspiracy.

"What do you know about that, Watson?" he asked, taken aback. "Oh, you mean the rumour that Rash Behari is stoking another mutiny. Romance never dies in some minds, especially after a heavy dose of Garibaldi!" With that, he dismissed the whole affair, and in turn asked me about what I had discovered on my walks.

Three evenings later, on my return after a long walk past the Observatory and down the Glen, I was dumbfounded to find two liveries of bearers neatly laid

out on our beds, with pugrees complete. When I asked
Ganga Din what the devil he was playing at, he replied
expressionlessly that the Bara Sahib and SP Sahib were
preparing for a fancy dress party. I was going to exclaim
on this foolishness when both gentlemen appeared.
"Excellent, you are back in time, Watson," said Holmes
with barely suppressed excitement. "Come, let's get ready
for the party. Here is some blacking, and walnut juice.
Be careful to paint the back of your ears as well. And
your feet. As bearers, we may have to go barefoot."

It seemed wise not to argue before Ganga Din, and I
got ready, tired as I was. When we were well clear of the
house, and on our way through the darkening streets, I
asked Holmes what it was all about. "We are going to
witness a conspiracy, Watson," he whispered. "A devilishly
cunning conspiracy. Whistler has had wind of something
like this for some time, but it was too preposterous for
him to give it credence, until he and I put things together.
He won't be with us, but hiding in the trees outside, and
should we get into trouble, he will fire to break the lights,
and we must dodge out the best we can."

With this, we made our way up to the Town Hall,
and then turned right. Soon the lights of the United
Services Club shone through the trees. Asking me to
hide behind a thick hedge, Holmes went forward alone.
He was back in a few minutes to whisper that all was
well. Whistler was waiting at the servants' entrance to
the Club. A gigantic Sikh loomed out of the darkness.
"This is Jagjit Singh Grewal, head bearer at the Club,"
whispered Whistler. "A trusted friend, we have worked

together for several years. He will take you to the map room. Good luck!" And with that, he was gone into the night.

I was tense, hoping that I could play my part, wondering and fearing whether any officer would discover my disguise. Holmes's proximity steadied my nerves; but for his presence I would have cut and run. But I need not have worried. None of the three officers who came in ever looked in our direction, except to order dishes, drinks, and cigars. They were clearly there to plan for the next day when important personages were to be expected, and even more important decisions take. With a shock, I heard that Sir Michael O'Dwyer, Lieutenant Governor of the Punjab, and General Sir Reginald Dyer were both expected to come and depart in secrecy. If some military secrets were to be shared, it was very wrong of Holmes to make us privy to them without the express consent of the authorities. Only his restraining hand on my arm stopped me from chucking the stupid charade then and there. As the last of the junior officers left that night, they shared a chuckle and an obscure joke about the foxy Orangeman from Delhi, but I could make nothing of it.

Holmes was too grim-faced the next day for me to summon the courage to remonstrate with him. When I did bring up my doubts in a roundabout way, Holmes looked straight at me, and said with quiet sincerity: "We have been together all these years, Watson, and seen each other through many scrapes. I assure you the service you are about to render King and country will far outshine

any of your other past exploits." I had to be content
with that.

I was as nervous as a cat that evening. All pretence
that it was a fancy dress party was laid aside. Ganga Din
knew me of old, and knew that this was in dead earnest.
The honest fellow offered to follow me at a distance with
his pistol, but I assured him that the evening demanded
finesse, and God willing, we would all come through
unscathed. There was a bustle about the Club that evening,
as there is when servants sense that great men will be
coming. The khitmatgars were busily polishing the silver,
the swords, and shields that hung on the walls, arranging
the tables and flower vases, and brushing out the durries
and carpets. The lights were brilliant, the glasses shone,
and all was ready. The junior officers, who had been there
the previous day, took their places. The sudden sound of
cars drawing up disturbed the whispered silences of the
United Services Club, and a moment later in strode Sir
Michael O'Dwyer and Sir Reginald Dyer.[62] Lighthearted
conversation ensued with the drinks. I had occasion to
study both men at close quarters, as I poured out their
drinks. I had known them before only by reputation. Dyer
was everything I had heard him to be, haughty, insolent,
and brave, as only a man born in India to an officer can
be, knowing only the unquestioning obedience of men of
lower rank. O'Dwyer was an older, more complex man,
with a cruel streak about his set lips sunk between his
florid cheeks. He was descended from several generations
of Anglo-Irish landlords, with an unenviable history of
ruthless exploitation of tenants.

Suddenly, the doors burst open, and I almost dropped my salver on seeing Castlereagh stride confidently into the room, with that pale, fixed smile of his. "Sir Michael, Sir Reginald, my apologies for being late," he said carelessly. "All arrangements have been made. The men are ready. Every one of them is an Orangeman, hand-picked by me, sworn to secrecy, and keen. They have been rehearsed. They know what the stakes are. They will be dressed as Indians, their faces, hands, and feet darkened, as dark as these chaps here." At that, my heart missed a beat, but he did not even give me a passing glance. "We know where Miss Besant will be holding her Baisaki meeting of Unity in Amritsar, not far from the Golden Temple. It couldn't be a better spot. Halfway through her speech, there will be a fracas, deliberately started, and my men will fire on the police standing in protection. They will shoot to kill—it is distasteful, but for verisimilitude, they will gun down Whistler, raising shouts of 'Inquilab Zindabad!' They have heard it often enough, they will do it to perfection. An infantry brigade commanded by one of our group will happen to be passing. They will rush in and return fire. Everyone on the dais will be killed, including, unfortunately, Miss Besant. Our men will retreat behind the soldiers, and quietly withdraw in good order. Even the most nationalistic of newspapers will have to report that Miss Besant lost her own life in a futile attempt. The Viceroy will have to yield to wiser counsel, and agree for draconian laws to be promulgated. We will sweep this land clear of Fenians, busybodies, nationalists, and woolly-headed idealists."

"By God, I see that you want that woman dead!" said Sir Reginald Dyer forcefully. "But first, is it necessary, and second, will the plan work?"

"Sir, the fate of Empire is at stake. My spies inform me that the Kaiser has sent word to that woman! It's our duty as Englishmen," said Castlereagh.

A murmur of assent went round the room. All turned towards Sir Michael O'Dwyer. After a measured silence, he nodded his head ever so imperceptibly. The officers broke into talk, and more was said about the plan, refinements suggested, and noted. As they left, with strict instructions to Castlereagh to keep O'Dwyer and Dyer informed of all changes, Sir Michael laid a hand on his shoulder, and said softly, "You will go far, Castlereagh, I will see to that. I am so glad I have some stout Orangemen at hand during this crisis."

Whistler, Holmes, and I held a council of war at midnight in Rose Villa, while Ganga Din served up coffee, toast, and brandy. I wanted to inform the Viceroy straightaway, or wire Sir Edward, or warn Miss Besant. Holmes shook his head sadly. "Who will believe us, Watson?" he asked. "We would be made to look like fools, or worse, like a parcel of mad knaves. The word of Sir Michael alone would outweigh a jury room of witnesses. And they will hatch some other murderous plan. If we warned Miss Besant, do you honestly think she will be deterred? She would march proudly to the meeting, and half the idiots of the Indian National Congress will join her to die for India. We cannot take any action, Watson!

Not directly, at any rate. We have to see to it that the meeting does not happen!"

The very next day we left Simla unnoticed, and made our way to Delhi. Without even going to the Club, we changed trains, and were headed for Bombay. The day after we reached the Taj Mahal Hotel, Holmes had made an appointment to meet Jinnah alone. He was insistent that I was not to come; so slightly put out, I decided to look up an old army acquaintance who had got religion, and was looking after the Scottish Orphanage out on Mahim Bay. He was happy to see me, and I spent the next few days taking the boys out for long walks through the two-mile stretch of open empty beaches and woods that separated Mahim Fort from Worli Fort. One day, I took them to St Michael's Church on Dharavi Road for a sermon from the padre I had met on my walks. And another day, I took them to watch Baloo Palwankar and his brothers, Shivram, Vithal, and Ganpat, play in the Quadrangular Tournament. The untouchable brothers had overcome caste prejudice to dominate a side mostly composed of Brahmins, and people now called the Hindoo side the Baloo brothers' side.[63] The boys watched the great left-arm spinner in action, and I hoped they would be inspired to see how he had overcome all odds. But best of all, they seemed to like my stories of the wars their fathers had fought in, and I asked for nothing more than an appreciative audience of youngsters.

Four days later, I returned home to find that the strain

and anxiety had left Holmes's face, and he was quite pleasant over dinner, discussing the merits of the various Indian dishes laid out before us. I gathered, without a word being said, that whatever our mission with Jinnah might have been, it had been successfully accomplished. Without any explanation, Holmes bought us two tickets for Delhi, and we journeyed north once again. We kept to our rooms at the Club until word was received that the Viceroy desired our presence. We were welcomed at the Viceregal Lodge by Castlereagh with the same smile, which now looked to me pasty and thoroughly false, but Lord Hardinge was all cordiality. "I don't know how you did it, gentlemen," he said as soon as the door closed on the servants who had brought in tea and sandwiches. "But it was a brilliant stroke. The threat of nationalist Hindoo–Muslim unity that was looming over the horizon has been dissipated, I believe, in no small measure due to your efforts. Mr Holmes, I shall recommend to His Majesty that it would be a fitting acknowledgement of your services to elevate you as a Grand Commander of the Star of India!"

I gasped with confusion and joy that at long last my dear friend should receive a just token of appreciation from his sovereign. I could not believe my ears when I heard Holmes gently decline the offer. Lord Hardinge tried a few times to make him change his mind, but Holmes was as adamant as I have known him to be in the past. Taking leave of the Viceroy, Holmes informed him that we both might take a holiday in the south at Hyderabad and Madras for a few months, to rest and observe the situation, and if nothing untoward happened, we would then like to ship back home.

Mir Osman Ali Khan, the little patient I had saved from malaria twenty-five years ago, had become the Nizam on his father's untimely death, and he had cordially invited us to spend a few weeks in Hyderabad. We accepted the offer, and were housed in the same palace rooms we had occupied long ago, with greybeards in attendance who told magical stories about our previous visit, the cures I had wrought, and the evil demons Sherlock Holmes had slain.

Holmes carefully scanned all the newspapers every day, and after several days, satisfied that his stratagem had worked, told me in detail what had happened.

"When we learned of the diabolical plot that our friend Castlereagh had hatched with the consent of Sir Michael O'Dwyer and Sir Reginald Dyer, I saw at once that the only way to avoid a tragedy would be to prevent that meeting of Hindoo–Muslim Unity from ever happening. How was that to be done? To talk about the plot would be useless, and would open us up to derision, if not worse, and I wouldn't have put it past Castlereagh to try and shut our mouths forever. To warn Annie Besant to cancel the meeting was equally useless. So the only solution was to destroy the unity among Hindoos and Muslims that Miss Besant aimed for. One man alone was capable of bringing these two communities together, and he alone could keep them apart. I had to present Jinnah with convincing evidence that the time was not yet, that the Hindoos he trusted so implicitly were playing a double game. Without the help of the police, I could not have done it, Watson, truly. They collect all pieces of news, as you know, but never know which one to use and when. I had made a point of meticulously going through their records, wherever we were, for at that time I did not know what piece of news would be valuable at what time. When I knew what had to be done, I knew I held the solution in my hand. I carefully sifted through all the newspaper interviews, and government reports written about the Hindoo Mahasabha; I put together an artistic collection of all the purloined letters its leaders had written to their other friends in the Congress. Jinnah was most reluctant to look at the evidence, but when I thrust it all under his nose, he did promise to go through the lot. I was very relieved to find him worried one morning, when he agreed that he would not consent to the meeting until certain issues had been resolved between the Indian National Congress and the Muslim League. I put in the idea that only a federal form of government would serve such a vast country, with separate electorates, and weightage for minorities to protect their interests. You may remember how strongly he had opposed the same ideas when we met him first at Bahawalpur. Now he saw that indeed there was no other way, if natural justice was to be secured."

I was stunned by the risky brilliance of the game Holmes had played. I asked him then why he had refused the knighthood the Viceroy offered. "It would be wholly improper," said Holmes mildly. "Don't you see, Watson, I did it to stymie that murderous conspiratorial gang within the highest echelons of power in India. They forced my hand; the ultimate result of my actions is still not very clear to me. It might turn out to be the worst trick that has been played on Indians, but I hope not. With true goodwill on all sides, a truer understanding might yet bind Hindoos and Muslims together, rather than the present shallow hope. At least, let me hope so, for the sake of my conscience." I said amen to that silently.

Early hopes of unity among nationalists petered out in India, while war clouds thickened over Europe. August brought war. It was time to go home. We would take an early steamer to England, but knowing this would be our last visit to India, we lingered over our goodbyes, and it was not until late September that we sailed from Madras. It was the 22nd, exactly a year since we had set out to meet Sir Edward, and even as we stood on deck discussing the curious coincidence, the Second Officer David Craddock, who was standing nearby, let out his breath sharply and held out his glasses to us. We saw the lean grey shape of a warship glide across the horizon, with three funnels furiously belching smoke. "No doubt at all, Sir," said Craddock. "That is a German Light Cruiser, *The Emden*, if I am not mistaken. She must have slipped out of her berth at Tsingtao before my uncle, Admiral Craddock, could catch her. She seems to be making her way back to Germany the long way round, but what is she doing in Madras waters, I wonder?"[64]

The distant thunder of her guns answered the question a few minutes later. We knew then for sure that we were at war.

Notes

1. As far as we know, there was never a religious centre called the Kumbakokam Mutt at that time, or later. The Kamakoti Mutt, as it is known today, was moved from Kumbakokam to Kancheepuram many years after the incidents related by Dr Watson.

2. Surely Dr Watson is mistaken here, since the school, later named the School of Oriental and African Studies, opened its doors only in 1916. Or, perhaps, Mr Ayer may have referred to some other research institute with a similar name interested in Eastern matters? Nor can the gentleman in question be Mr G. Subramania Aiyer, regarded as the greatest journalist of his time in India. Similar names often lead to a confusion of identities in India.

3. Lord Randolph Churchill held the post of Lord Chancellor in that period, although he once confessed that he never understood what decimal points meant. His son, Winston, would have been at Harrow at the time of the story, but it is doubtful he would have made that famous remark of his about democracy at such an early age. He was a fag of Stanley Jackson's, who appears later in the story entitled "Art, Crime, and Enlightenment". Several years later Lloyd George is said to have shaken

Jackson's hand, saying he was glad to meet the man who
had once given Winston Churchill a hiding.

4.   George Frederick Samuel Robinson (1827–1909), KG,
       PC, GCSI, FRS, First Marquess of Ripon, Earl de Grey,
       Earl of Ripon, Viscount Goderich, Baron Grantham,
       and baronet, was born at 10 Downing Street, when his
       father Earl Ripon was Prime Minister for a brief period.
       Coming from a great Whig family, he entered the
       House of Commons as member for Hull in 1852, and
       later succeeded his father as Earl of Ripon and Viscount
       Goderich in 1859. He was a member of every Liberal
       administration for the next half century. The offices he
       held included those of Under Secretary of State for India
       (1861–3) and Secretary of State for War (1863–6), under
       Lord Palmerston; and later that of Secretary of State for
       India (1866) under Earl Russell. In Mr Gladstone's first
       administration he was Lord President of the Council
       (1868–73). In 1874, he entered the Catholic Church.
       When Gladstone returned to power in 1880, he was
       appointed Viceroy of India, where he made himself
       beloved to the Indian subjects of the Crown as none of
       his predecessors had been. He held this office until 1884.
       In 1886 he was First Lord of the Admiralty, and from
       1892 to 1895 he was Secretary of State for the Colonies.
       When the Liberals again returned to power, he became
       Lord Privy Seal, resigning the office in 1908. A fervent
       Catholic, Lord Ripon played a great role in educational
       and charitable works.

5.   Holmes might have been mistaken in thinking that
       "white elephants" were worshipped in Ceylon. The
       practice, as far as is known, was restricted to Southeast
       Asia in those times.

6. Even the most careful scrutiny of records does not reveal a Colonel Pickering, an expert in oriental languages, employed in Madras at that time. However, a reference to such a person is made by George Bernard Shaw in *Pygmalion*. I should be grateful if any descendant could throw more light on this illustrious officer.

7. Sir Alexander J. Arbuthnot established the Madras Cricket Club (MCC) in 1846. In its early years, it hosted friendly matches against army teams, visiting ship's crews, the Bangalore Gymkhana, and the Kolar Gold Fields Club. The first "Test" match was held in 1864 against the visiting Calcutta Cricket Club. The MCC operated from the Island and Assembly Grounds until 1865, when it shifted to the Chepauk ground.

8. Undoubtedly he refers to Mr Eardley Norton, a descendant of three generations of legal luminaries, and known for his wit and wisdom. He was a staunch supporter of the Indian Congress, and was regarded by the British as a seditionist.

9. Holmes could have mistaken the ritual. Sanyasis do not perform the sandhyavandanam.

10. The Rev. Dr William Miller, was the Principal of Madras Christian College from 1862 to 1909. Under his tutelage, the college burgeoned from a modest institution into one with 800 students and 12 professors. A bachelor, Miller's dedication to his students was absolute. Several students, like my grandfather, grew up under his care. It was mostly due to his enthusiasm and initiative that the college later moved to the present, sprawling 400-acre site in Tambaram.

11. Helena Petrovna Blavatsky (1831–91) was born of Russian nobility. Her mother, Helena Andreyevna,

wrote novels concerning secluded Russian women and
was called the George Sand of Russia. Helena's first love
affair, at age sixteen, had been with Prince Alexander
Galistin, cousin to the Viceroy of the Caucasus. At
seventeen, she married General Nicephore Blavatsky.
After an unhappy honeymoon, she escaped to Tibet
where she studied with a Lama for several years. After
several affairs, occult experiences, worldwide travel, and
another failed marriage, she formed a firm friendship
with Colonel Olcott. In July 1878, Blavatsky became the
first Russian woman to acquire United States citizenship.
She may have done so to prevent the English in India
from thinking she was a Russian spy. She and Olcott
came to India at the end of that year, and gained support
from Allen O. Hume, the first President of the Indian
National Congress. In 1882, the headquarters of the
Theosophical Society was moved to Adyar, in Madras.
By then the French-born Swedish countess, Constance
Wachrmeister, was helping her with *The Secret Doctrine*
(1888), which is her best-known work. During 1889 she
finished two more books: *The Key to Theosophy* and *The
Voice of the Silence*, a mystical and poetic work. The work
of the Theosophical Society was continued by Ms Annie
Wood Besant, who appears in "The Indian Summer of
Sherlock Holmes". Besant brought another generation
of liberal intellectuals into the society, and became
President following Olcott's death in 1907.

12. "Smartas" or Iyers, are Shaivites. The mistake was not
Dr Watson's. He faithfully transcribed Madame
Blavatsky's original error.

13. Bangalore Nagaratnamma, a famous devadasi danseuse,
musician, and scholar, became even more famous

for rebuilding the samadhi, or tomb, of the greatest composer of Carnatic music, Thyagaraja, at Tiruvaiyar. The Kumbabishekam, or inaugural ceremony, took place with great fanfare in 1925. From 1940 onwards, the annual musical festival held there, called the Sri Thyagaraja Aradhana Mahotsava Sabha, has included women as well. She is also known to have researched and published poems by her celebrated predecessor, the devadasi Muddupalani, of the Nayaka king of Tanjore, Pratapsimha (1739–63). However, it is doubtful whether she was old enough to participate in the events related by Dr Watson.

14. The great traveller, Count von Keyserling, is known to have visited India in 1911. Watson's account clearly relates to an unknown earlier visit. The Right Livelihood Awards were established many decades later by the grandson of the Count's friend.

15. Perhaps, it was the unusual offer of gold mohurs as fees that induced Dr Watson to mention "money matters", normally never referred to by gentlemen of his times, and never mentioned again in these papers. It seems very likely that Colonel Pickering would later have suggested to the Ranee that a cheque drawn on the Imperial Bank of India would suffice.

16. It is a pity that Dr Watson could not get along with Dr Lawrie. The *British Medical Journal* of 1895 noted: "In the Nizam's dominion, medical treatment and medical education reached a high standard of excellence. Here was held the famous chloroform commission which was due to the liberality and scientific interest of the Nizam and the energy and enthusiasm of Dr Lawrie, the Presidency surgeon." However, it is interesting to

note that Dr Watson's steps in identifying the anopheles mosquito as a carrier of the malaria parasite closely parallel those undertaken much later by Dr Ross, who also had an assistant named Husein Khan, undoubtedly a younger relative of Watson's compounder.

17. Dr Ronald Ross (1857–1932) was born in Almora to General Sir C.C.G. Ross. He studied medicine at St Bartholomew's Hospital in London in 1875, and entered the Indian Medical Service in 1881. Ross married Rosa Bessie Bloxam in 1889, when he was Acting Garrison Surgeon at Bangalore. He is not known to have commenced the study of malaria until 1892. In 1899, he joined the Liverpool School of Tropical Medicine under the direction of Sir Alfred Jones. He was immediately sent to West Africa to continue his investigations. Ross's research was confirmed by many distinguished authorities, notably Koch, Daniels, Bignami, Celli, Christophers, Stephens, Annett, Austen, Ruge, and Ziemann. In 1901, Ross was elected a Fellow of the Royal College of Surgeons, and also made a Fellow of the Royal Society. In 1902, he received the Nobel Prize. In 1911, he was elevated to the rank of Knight Commander of the Order of Bath. In Belgium, he was made an Officer in the Order of Leopold II. He made many contributions to the epidemiology of malaria. His papers related to "pathometry" are best known and, decades later, constitute the basis of much of the epidemiological understanding of insect-borne diseases. It must have been a matter of some satisfaction to Dr Watson that he was instrumental in getting this great scientific career started.

18. The child poetess Dr Watson met in Melkote's house is

most certainly the future Sarojini Naidu, whom Mahatma Gandhi called the "Nightingale of India".

19. It is curious to note that Devan Sahib Melkote Shankar Narayan Rao's love for theatre was inherited by his equally illustrious grandson.

20. It is interesting to note that the Prince's life was saved by Subedar Ambadvekar, the scholar–soldier father of Dr B.R. Ambedkar, who was to write the Constitution of independent India.

21. Rumours have persisted down to present times linking the unfortunate Duke of Clarence with the "Jack the Ripper" murders, but this account of Dr Watson's removes any suspicion for all time.

22. It is more than likely that Dr Watson is mistaken again, and that they met at the Garrison Club, later renamed the Secunderabad Club.

23. There can be little doubt that Holmes is referring to Carl Jung himself. It is indeed astonishing how early in life genius often manifests itself.

24. Unfortunately, too many of the common sort in those days alluded in such disrespectful terms to the Prince of Wales, and the children begotten by him out of wedlock.

25. The archives of *The Pioneer* have no records of Rudyard Kipling visiting Hyderabad on the occasion of the Duke's visit, but that would not be unusual, considering the secrecy of his mission.

26. This story records the valuable services of several civilians, including those of Sir Alexander Mackenzie, who was Chief Commissioner of the Central Provinces from 1887 to 1889, and those of Sir Andrew Fraser, who became Chief Commissioner a decade later.

27. History records the services of the Chitnavis family to the governance of these unsettled provinces at that time.

28. Mr A. Bloomfield's *Notes on the Baiga of Central India* (first published in 1885) formed the basis of much later anthropological work by such eminent men as Dr Verrier Elwin.

29. The Colonel Montgomerie of the narrative is undoubtedly the nephew of the famous geographer of the same name. It was a common feature of colonial history that several members of the same family, following in the footsteps of a famous ancestor, rendered valuable service.

30. It is intriguing to find a relationship here with the well-known Canadian author of *Anne of Green Gables*, who must have been quite precocious to have corresponded with an "uncle" at such a tender age.

31. Indeed, Rajah Gokuldas left a great name behind him, for his power, his wealth, and his munificence, but it is difficult to verify his role in ameliorating the conditions of the particular famine mentioned in the story.

32. We cannot find a historical record of a Dr France. But, perhaps, Dr Watson, writing the story years later, might have meant to refer to a Dr French, who lived in the Provinces in those times. If other references have not been kind to Dr French, this story at least explains the difficult circumstances under which he worked.

33. Mr Percival was another colonial officer with an exemplary reputation behind him.

34. In the interests of authenticity, it must be mentioned that there is no historical trace of any Major Reston, although a Major Repton served in that region, and was known for his hot temper. Perhaps Dr Watson deliberately changed the name.

35. Of course, there is no official record of the brief appearance of the Naga Baiga of Moogli Hills, but such an intriguing episode may indeed have inspired Kipling to create his immortal character.

36. The Rev. Henry Budden, assisted by his daughter Mary, established a highly respected mission in Almora, and service is still conducted in the Budden Memorial Church there. On January 1, 1926, the American Methodist Episcopal Church took over the Almora mission, the schools, and the leper asylum.

37. This story presents an improbable account of several Indians—who became national leaders later—meeting together in Naini Tal. But often, fact is stranger than fiction. Motilal Nehru, a great nationalist of his times, was already the best paid lawyer in India by the time of the story, although the other national leaders, Pandit Madan Mohan Malaviya, who founded the Benares Hindoo University, and Lala Lajpat Rai, the "Sher-e-Punjab", were still relatively unknown. But we do know that Sir Auckland Colvin was Governor of the United Provinces at the purported time of the story, and we can be quite certain that, at the time, Captain Francis Younghusband was back in India from Central Asia.

38. It is doubtful that the new Lee-Enfield rifle could have been introduced in India that early, although the cartridge head markings mentioned on the cache from Cossipore seem accurate enough.

39. There is no record whatsoever of a visit paid by an American, calling himself Clark Gable, to Naini Tal at that time, or later, although the name of a Rhett Butler is mentioned in a fictional account of life in Atlanta during the American Civil War, written much later by Mary

Mitchell. The great O'Hara clan spread all over the world after the Irish famine of the 1840s, and genealogical research can perhaps verify the details of the story.

40. I was surprised to read of Holmes and Watson's encounter with Balraj, the peasant who had lost two bighas of land to moneylenders. By a curious coincidence, the great Indian film director, Bimal Roy, based his 1950s film, *Do Bigha Zamin*, on a similar theme, and Balraj Sahni was the actor.

41. Sherlock Holmes and Dr Watson stayed at Government House in Calcutta, as guests of the then Viceroy, Lord Lansdowne, a man of great wealth, and large Irish properties, who had previously been Governor General in Canada. Lord Lansdowne, while not as punctilious as Lord Amherst in preserving his importance as Viceroy, was not as informal as Lord Lawrence, another predecessor. He was known to be a great supporter of free trade, and in consequence loath to disrupt the lucrative narcotics trade.

42. Large-scale renovation of Government House started in the time of Lord Lansdowne, most probably supervised by Lady Maud, the Vicereine. The descriptions of the renovations accord with the history of the building, although the spiral staircase set up by Lord Ripon has since been pulled down.

43. Lord George Harris, Governor of Bombay, was a keen cricketer, after whom the Harris Shield has been named, as was Lord Hawke, captain of Yorkshire, who brought a team to India in 1892. His earlier visit, mentioned in the story, is not recorded. But their opinions are substantially the same as recorded in history. Nagendra Prasad Sarbadhikary (1869–1940) was paid a great compliment

by Lord Hawke: "European sports in India have a brief lineage, more so for a costly sport like cricket which has barely begun here; but your phenomenal talent has ensured that your name is not unknown in distant England." S. Ray & Co, 62, Bowbazar Street, Calcutta, patronized by the Calcutta Cricket Club, is known to have been generous in their support of Indians playing the game. Stanley Jackson (later Sir Francis), better known as "Jacker", was one of the greatest all-rounders of the time, almost gaining a victory single-handed for Harrow against Eton in 1888. Later, as captain of Cambridge, he gave Ranjitsinghji his blue. Although never captain of Yorkshire, he captained England in 1905 to win the Ashes, scoring a total of 492 runs, with an average of 70, and took 13 wickets at 15.46 runs each—an unrivalled performance. In 1927, when Governor of Bengal, he was shot at by a female student. Fortunately, she missed him.

44. The proceedings of the Indian Hemp Drugs Commission seem to be reported with great accuracy by Dr Watson.

45. In the 1880s and 1890s, a large garden was situated to the northeast of Calcutta, and named after Rabindranath's grandfather, Dwarkanath.

46. Rabindranath Tagore (1861–1941) is said to have first read from the *Gitanjali* two decades later, to a select audience in London that included W.B. Yeats. Yeats recorded his impressions thus: "I have carried the manuscript of these translations about with me for days, reading it in railway trains, or on top of the omnibuses and in restaurants, and I have often had to close it lest some stranger would see how much it moved me. These lyrics which are in the original, my Indian friends tell me, full of subtlety and rhythm, of untranslatable delicacies

of colour, of metrical invention—display in their thought a world I have dreamed of all my life long. The work of a supreme culture, they appear as much the growth of the common soil as the grass and the rushes." However, it is always possible that Tagore wrote the poem quoted by Dr Watson much earlier.

47. Narendra was, of course, the given name of Swami Vivekananda, who first established a Mutt around the samadhi of Ramakrishna Paramahimsa in Baranagar by the Hooghly, soon after the passing away of his guru.

48. Lansdowne's daughter, Lady Evelyn, who later married the future ninth Duke of Devonshire, is not known to have felt sentiments warmer than those of ordinary friendship for the bachelor Military Secretary, Lord William de la Poer Beresford (1847–1900), who had received a Victoria Cross for gallantry on July 3, 1879, at Ulundi, during the Zulu Wars.

49. In the last story, Holmes and Watson are recalled to India in 1913, at the behest of Sir Edward Grey, the Foreign Secretary, and the one person who held together the Entente Cordiale, linking Russia and France to British interests against those of the central European powers. Lord Hardinge (1858–1944), the Viceroy, had been attacked by revolutionaries, during his ceremonial entry into Delhi, at Ajmeri Gate in 1912. The grandson of a previous Governor General, he remained calm and never initiated any vengeful action. Instead, his tenure of office witnessed a significant improvement in relations between the government and the nationalist leaders.

50. Sir William Hailey, GCSI, KCSI, CSI, GCMG, CIE, D.Litt., D.Laws, DCL, ICS, epitomized the best qualities of British civil servants during his tenure of office. However,

there is no record of a Captain Castlereagh on his staff, although that well-known Anglo-Irish landowning family has left a long record of distinguished, albeit reactionary, service in British annals, from the days of the Congress of Vienna of 1815.

51. The British Government had many supporters, notable among them being Sir Rahim Baksh (1857–1935), KCIE, President of the Council of Regency of the Nawab of Bahawalpur from 1907 until 1924. He signed several treaties with the Government and neighbouring Rajputana states, for the development of railroads, canals, and irrigation projects. While working with Dunlop Smith, Bakhsh became known to Lord Minto, the Viceroy of India from 1905 to 1910. He was considered one of the most honourable nobles from the Princely States, and was chosen by the Viceroy to be part of the Reform Committee in 1919. He received the honour of Khan Bahadur in 1909, and was knighted in 1913.

52. The Nawab Viqar-ul-Mulk (1841–1917) took a neutral political position. He started his career under Sir Syed Ahmad Khan as a worker of the Aligarh Movement. In 1870, he was awarded the second prize in an essay competition arranged by the Society for the Promotion of Education among Muslims. In 1875, he was invited to serve in the state of Hyderabad, where, after seventeen years of service, he was elevated to the position of Nawab Mushtaq Hussain Viqar-ul-Mulk. As a member of the Simla Deputation in 1906, he wanted Muslims to organize themselves politically, and to safeguard their political rights. He played an active role in the establishment of the Muslim League as its first President.

53. Mohammed Ali Jinnah (1876–1948), was strongly

opposed to British rule. Lawyer and statesman, Jinnah probably earned more than any other lawyer in Bombay. Jinnah's first active move towards politics took place during the 1906 session of the Indian National Congress in Calcutta. Dadabhai Naoroji's and Bal Gangadhar Tilak's slogan, "Swaraj", was now writ on the new banner of the Congress, behind which Jinnah marched. Jinnah became one of the elected members of the Imperial Legislative Council from Bombay. His association with the Muslim League began with the annulment of the partition of Bengal in 1911. At their next session in December 1912, which Jinnah attended, the League proposed to amend its constitution, so that it could ally itself with the Congress in a common demand for "Swaraj". In December 1915, the Congress was to hold its annual session in Bombay. Jinnah, with the approval of leading local Muslims, sent a letter inviting the All India Muslim League to hold its annual session in the same place and at the same time. He had, however, to face strong opposition from extremists in both the Congress and the League. In the autumn of 1916, he was elected once again to the Imperial Legislative Council. In December 1916, he succeeded in prevailing upon both the Congress and the Muslim League to hold their annual sessions in the same place, Lucknow, and at the same time. Jinnah presided over the League session. The sessions warmly assented to the "irreducible minimum" of reforms worked out by their joint committee and passed it to the Government of India. The main domestic problem of separate electorates was overcome with the Congress agreeing to Jinnah's plea to allow weightage of seats in the legislative councils of certain provinces where the Muslims were in the minority. This became known as the historic Lucknow Pact, and it made Jinnah a leader of Indian Muslims. After the Rowlatt Act was passed in March 1919 to give the Government of India summary powers to curb seditious activities, Jinnah resigned from the Imperial Legislative Council in protest, and Mahatma Gandhi launched a movement of non-violent civil disobedience. The expectations raised by the Lucknow Pact in 1916 were never met, and the rift between the two communities continued to widen. Jinnah's links with aristocratic Muslim leadership turned bitter, because the latter group was inclined to abandon its traditional loyalty to the Raj.

54. Dr Watson had a providential meeting with the young Dhyan Chand while in Jhansi. Dhyan Chand (1905–79), the wizard of the Indian hockey team for over twenty years, won three Olympic gold medals for India between 1928 and 1936. At Amsterdam, he scored two out of India's three winning goals. At Los Angeles, India beat the USA by 24 goals to one, setting an all-time record. In 1932, India scored 338 goals in 37 matches, 133 being his contribution. In Berlin in 1936, under Dhyan Chand's captaincy, India beat Germany eight to one. He exhibited such wizardry with his hockey stick that Germans thought there was a magnet embedded in it to attract the ball. His hockey stick was ordered to be changed, but his play continued to hold the spectators and his opponents spellbound. In 1947, he accompanied a young team to East Africa when he was 42, and was the second highest scorer with 61 goals in 22 games. According to Keshav Dutt, another Olympic gold medallist, "His real talent lay above his shoulders. His

was easily the hockey brain of the century. He could see a field the way a chess player sees the board. He knew where his teammates were, and more importantly where his opponents were without looking. It was almost psychic."

55. Jatindranath Mukerjee (1879–1915) was known as Bagha Jatin, after killing a tiger single-handed and without arms. In 1908, he was implicated in the Alipore conspiracy case, and later in the Howrah–Shibpur conspiracy case. He was involved with Rash Behari in trying to rouse Indian soldiers to take revolutionary action in the years leading up to the Great War, but was betrayed. Jatin was made the Commander-in-Chief of the entire revolutionary forces. The police, however, discovered his hideout in a paddy field in Buribalam, and on September 9, 1915, killed him after a heavy exchange of gunfire.

56. The Indian revolutionary, Rash Behari (1886–1945) was influenced by the ideas of the French Revolution, while studying at Dupleix College in Chandernagore, and also by the ideas of Surendranath Banerjea and Swami Vivekananda. He worked for a time at the Pasteur Institute in Kasauli as a guardian tutor in the house of Pramantha Nath Tagore, and at the Dehra Dun Forest Research Institute. He was responsible for the attempt on Lord Hardinge's life. His colleagues, Master Amir Chand, Avadh Behari, and Bal Mukund were arrested and hanged in Delhi Jail. The Maulana Azad Medical College is located at the site of the old jail. The section where the hanging took place has been preserved, and every year people gather to pay homage to the martyrs. Basanta Viswas, who threw the bomb disguised as a

lady, was hanged in Ambala Jail. Rash Behari avoided arrest using clever ruse. He remained on the run from Punjab to Uttar Pradesh to Bengal in different disguises. A police officer noted that Rash Behari could have been a "great stage actor" instead of a revolutionary if he so desired. He escaped to Japan, as Raja P.N.T. Tagore in 1915, possibly with the help of Rabindranath. He settled down in Japan, marrying Tosiko, a daughter of the Soma family who were sympathetic towards Rash Behari's efforts. He learned Japanese, and became a journalist and writer. Rash Behari organized conferences in 1942 in Tokyo and Bangkok, where he hoisted the Indian tricolour and inaugurated the Indian Independence League. With the help of Captain Mohan Singh and Sardar Pritam Singh, he formed the Indian National Army (INA) on September 1, 1942. Rash Behari was elected President, and later gave Supreme Command of the INA to Subhash Chandra Bose in 1943.

57. Dr Watson is clearly too much of a gentleman to mention the scandal that was caused by one of his lordship's affairs, leading Lady Connemara to take up residence in the hotel, which later came to be named after her rather than her erring husband.

58. As Principal of the Bengal National College, Sri Aurobindo (1872–1950) started to write articles in 1907 for Bipin Chandra Pal's *Bande Mataram*, and soon became its chief editor. He was arrested for sedition that year, released, and arrested again later in connection with the attempt on Kingsford's life. Released from Alipore Jail after a year, he first went to Chandannagore, and then settled in Pondicherry in 1910. Mirra Richard (born Alfassa), the Mother, arrived in 1914. When the

Second World War broke out, Sri Aurobindo and the Mother came out openly on the side of the Allies because Hitler represented the forces of darkness. He who had fought the British earlier now put his full support and spiritual help behind them for their victory. Although Sri Aurobindo had retired from the political scene, when the Cripps Mission came, he broke his silence and sent an emissary to ask the Indian leaders to accept the proposals.

59. Sherlock Holmes was able to establish the innocence of Srinivasa Ramanujan in the eyes of the Madras Police. Ramanujan (1887–1920) became India's pre-eminent mathematician after he was "discovered" by G.H. Hardy, when, as a clerk in the Madras Port Trust, Ramanujan sent him some of his papers. Among his many mathematical discoveries, which still offer fertile ground for research, are the concepts of "partitions" and "congruences". It was only in the late 1990s that mathematicians in Wisconsin University stumbled across an equation in one of Ramanujan's notebooks that led them to discover that any prime number—not just 5, 7, and 11—had congruences. Mathematicians also note that partitions can be used to understand advances in particle physics and the various ways particles can arrange themselves.

60. Dr Annie Besant (1847–1933) started the first trade unions in London, and joined the Fabian Society, becoming a close associate of Sidney Webb, George Bernard Shaw, George Lansbury, and Ramsay MacDonald. In 1866, she was influenced by the writings of Blavatsky and joined her in 1889. She was President of the Theosophical Society until her death on September

21, 1933. She first came to India on November 16, 1893. In October 1913, she spoke at a great public meeting in Madras, recommending that there should be a Standing Committee of the House of Commons for Indian affairs, which would address how India might attain freedom. She founded a weekly newspaper, *Commonweal*, in January 1914 for her political work. In June 1914, she purchased the *Madras Standard* and renamed it *New India*, which thereafter became her chosen organ for her tempestuous propaganda for India's freedom. She called for "Home Rule" for India. In 1914, she was a delegate to the Indian National Congress. In June 1917, with G.S. Arundale and B.P. Wadia, two of her principal workers, she was interned at Ootacamund. Because of wide protests all over India and abroad, the internment order was withdrawn, and in August 1917, she was made the President of the Calcutta Session of the Indian National Congress. As a result of her campaign, the Montague–Chelmsford proposals were enacted by the British Parliament. In 1917, she started the Women's Indian Association to which she gave her powerful support. By 1924 the Association had 51 branches. In 1927, the first All India Women's Conference was held in Poona, and it became a permanent and powerful body.

61. Hugh Whistler (1889–1943), the greatest ornithologist of his time, helped Holmes uncover the conspiracy being hatched in Simla. He entered the Indian Imperial Police in 1913, and served in the Punjab. He is known to have collected a complete set of bones of the extinct dodo. His best-known work, *The Popular Handbook of Indian Birds*, continues to be widely consulted even today, and the great Indian ornithologist, Salim Ali, acknowledged

the support he received from Whistler in his early days. If he corresponded with Sir Edward Grey, yet another ardent ornithologist, the letters have since been lost.

62. General Sir Reginald Dyer (1864–1927) was born at Muree, campaigned in Burma in 1886–7, in Waziristan in 1901–2, and in Persia during the Great War. No record, official or unofficial, exists in papers available to the public of his role in any conspiracy, prior to the infamous massacre at Jallianwalabagh in Amritsar on April 13, 1919, when over 1,600 unarmed people were shot down in cold blood on his orders. He carried out this brutal deed, in his own words, to produce a "moral and widespread effect". Similarly, no records connect Sir Michael O'Dwyer, who was Lieutenant Governor of the Punjab, with any incident related in the story. However, typical of his Anglo-Irish mentality was a statement he made in court many years later when questioned about his tenure in office: "Floggings in India are not inflicted with cat-o'-nine-tails but always with bamboo, sometimes with a cane. They are mild compared with the cat." He even went so far as to state that Indians were flogged for failure to salaam British officers. But he tried to explain this away by asserting: "At that time there were rumours circulating that the British Raj in India was going and there was rebellion about. This order [requiring the salaam] was one of the means by which it was sought to bring home to the Indian people that this was not so." He was assassinated by a Sikh in 1940.

63. Palwankar Baloo (born in Dharwad in 1875), a left-arm spinner and a Chamar, was India's first great cricketer, taking over 100 wickets in first-class cricket during the tour of England in 1911. No other Indian bowler matched

his record for decades. His brother, Vithal, became captain of the Hindoo team in the Bombay Pentangular tournament of 1923. The Palwankar brothers were so well regarded that the Hindoo team was commonly referred to in those days as the Baloo Brothers plus seven. A hero for Dr B.R. Ambedkar, Baloo Palwankar was instrumental in negotiating the Poona Pact of 1932 between Mahatma Gandhi and Ambedkar.

64. Finally, it must be noted that Dr Watson's papers are accurate in stating that *The Emden*, a German Light Battle Cruiser, shelled Madras on September 22, 1914. Admiral Spee's German Asiatic squadron left Tsingtao for the South Pacific once Japan entered the war as an ally of Great Britain's. *The Emden* was detached from that squadron, and tried to make her way home through the Indian Ocean. After shelling Madras, she tried to evade action, but was sunk off the Cocos Islands on November 9, 1914. Admiral Craddock's elderly squadron, on watch in the South Pacific, was destroyed by Spee in the Battle of Coronel, off the coast of Chile, on November 1, 1914. Spee's squadron itself was destroyed by Admiral Sturdee's in the Battle of Falkland Islands on December 8, 1914. Several members of the Craddock family served in India, or on the India route.

Acknowledgements

I would like to thank my family and friends, without whose encouragement this book would never have been written; especially my wife, K. Lalita; good friends, Deepa Dhanraj and Navroze Contractor; Shankar Melkote, the Director of the Little Theatre of Hyderabad; and untiring friends at Thinksoft Consultants, who helped prepare the manuscript. I have a special word of thanks for my daughter, Diia Rajan, for her support. I also thank Anirban Sarma of Random House India for making the path to publication as smooth as possible, and Moonis Ijlal for a most attractive jacket illustration. Above all, I should like to express my heartfelt gratitude to Professor P. Lal, the doyen of English writing in India, who encouraged my creative writing by first publishing my work under the Writers Workshop imprint.

A Note on the Author

Vithal Rajan has served as a mediator in Northern Ireland, and was a founder and faculty member of the School of Peace Studies, Bradford University, UK. He has worked with numerous civil society organizations and NGOs in India, and has held various positions across Europe such as Director, World-Wide Fund for Nature International, and Executive Director for the Alternative Nobel Prize (Sweden). In 2006, he was made an Officer of the Order of Canada—the country's highest national honour—for a lifetime of achievement. He has written extensively on academic and development-related issues. His other fictional works include *The Legend of Ramulamma*, *Sharmaji Padmasree*, *"Not So" Stories for Older Children*, and *The Anarkali Diary*.